"If I'm to help find you a wife, I must know your most important attributes for a bride," *Olivia said.*

Edward couldn't tell her the first thought that came into his mind—one who was of respectable enough breeding to please his father, but not so aristocratic that she would spend the rest of her life looking down on her husband for being a bastard.

He didn't think such a woman existed anyway.

"The type of woman I desire," he said, "should be intelligent and interested in a variety of things so we have conversational topics to discuss in the evenings."

She looked at him blankly.

And spoke after a moment. "Is that all you want, Mr. Wolcott?"

Oh, he wanted much, much more.

But he would let her find out what else for herself . . .

By Megan Frampton

MEGAN FRAMPTON

The DUKE'S DAUGHTERS

LADY BE RECKLESS

DISCARD

AVONBOOKS

An Imprint of HarperCollinsPublishers

Excerpt from *Lady Be Bad* copyright © 2017 by Megan Frampton.

THE DUKE'S DAUGHTERS: LADY BE RECKLESS. Copyright © 2018 by Megan Frampton. All rights reserved. Printed in the United States of America. No part of this book may be used or reproduced in any manner whatsoever without written permission except in the case of brief quotations embodied in critical articles and reviews. For information, address HarperCollins Publishers, 195 Broadway, New York, NY 10007.

First Avon Books mass market printing: March 2018

Print Edition ISBN: 978-0-06-266664-2
Digital Edition ISBN: 978-0-06-266665-9

Cover illustration by Gregg Gulbronson

Avon, Avon & logo, and Avon Books & logo are registered trademarks of HarperCollins Publishers in the United States of America and other countries.

HarperCollins is a registered trademark of HarperCollins Publishers in the United States of America and other countries.

FIRST EDITION

18 19 20 21 22   QGM   10 9 8 7 6 5 4 3 2 1

A12007 057976

To Myretta, because I can't imagine being where I am without you.

Author's Note

Illegitimacy in Victorian England was a great stigma for both mother and child. An illegitimate child would have no claim on its father, and the Bastardy Clause of the 1834 Poor Law set law that said children would be the sole responsibility of the mother.

Of course, there are examples where a father would take care of his children; perhaps the most famous example just prior to this era is the Duke of Clarence, whose mistress, the actress Dorothea Jordan, bore at least ten of his children. The duke ensured his illegitimate children did well in the world, either through marriage for the daughters or occupations for the sons.

Chapter 1

It is not proper for a young lady to propose to a gentleman. Unless, of course, the gentleman has a deep and abiding (and silent) love for the lady, and he is not aware she reciprocates.

LADY OLIVIA'S PARTICULAR GUIDE TO DECORUM

1847, London
A Polite Drawing Room Currently Being Used for Sewing of a Dubious Quality

*O*livia!" The duchess's call could probably be heard from two floors away. And Olivia was seated in the same room, in full view of her mother.

"Yes, Mother?" she replied in an aggrieved tone. She had promised to deliver no fewer than ten shifts within a month's time to the Society for Poor and Orphaned Children, and she was only on the second one, since her needle skills were not as good as her skills in promising things she might not be able to deliver, apparently.

Not for the first time, she wished that things were as she wanted them to be, so she wouldn't have to constantly be trying to improve things. Her needle-pricked fingers would no doubt wish that also.

"I cannot deal with Cook today. You will have to," her mother announced, not paying attention to what Olivia was already occupied with. As was usual.

Olivia merely nodded. Her mother had often said the same thing, or a variation thereof, in the year or so since Olivia's eldest sister, Eleanor, had married Lord Alexander Raybourn. The Duchess of Marymount hadn't always been so helpless; but once Olivia's sister Della had run off with the dancing master and Eleanor had refused to marry the gentleman their parents had chosen for her, the duchess seemed to have given up all the duties she'd previously handled, leaving her remaining three daughters to handle everything. And since Olivia's twin, Pearl, was shy and preferred to be outdoors, and their sister Ida was too busy reading and looking down her nose at everyone else, it was all left up to Olivia.

Olivia did not flinch from doing what was necessary to make things right. Hence the shift making.

"Olivia, are you listening to me?"

"Of course I am," Olivia replied, frowning at the knot in her sewing. She had to admit to being a terrible seamstress. "You want me to speak with Cook, and you probably also want me to review the guest list for next week's dinner party to be certain all the invitations went out properly. And to remind Cook that the Marquis of Wheatley does not like green beans."

"*Hmph.* Well, yes," her mother replied in a grudging tone.

The guest list for the dinner party included Lord Carson, who was the marquis's son and the gentleman Eleanor had refused to marry.

Leaving him free to marry Olivia, something she had wanted since the first moment she saw him. Her parents had wanted the same thing since Eleanor had married the man she'd fallen in love with instead of Lord Carson.

Lord Carson. She sighed as she thought about him. He was handsome and kind and very, very busy. Olivia wanted to help him, and she could tell, from how he spoke to her, that he wanted her to help him also. It would be a perfect match. Even though her parents thought the same thing, and she seldom agreed with the elder Howletts.

Not to mention it would mean she would be able to run more things as she wished to. Including Lord Carson.

But it wouldn't be a match at all if the dinner party wasn't absolutely perfect, which meant she should go straightaway and speak to Cook.

Olivia dropped the fabric and thread onto the table beside her as she prepared to take care of things. Again.

The door to the sitting room was flung open and her twin, Pearl, launched herself inside, her eyes wide. "Olivia, you have to come quickly!" Pearl said in an urgent tone.

"What is it?" she asked as she rose to her feet.

"The gardener next door, he's—" And then Pearl stopped, shaking her head.

Olivia marched out of the sitting room, Cook and sewing forgotten, shoulders squared, as she went to right whatever was wrong that was making her twin so upset.

"He found some kittens in the shed and now he says he's going to—oh, Livy, you have to save them!" Pearl said, her voice wavering with emotion.

"Indeed I will," Olivia declared, brushing past a few startled servants to the back of the house.

She felt herself start to burn with the righteous fury that had become her constant companion over the past few years, since she'd realized that the world was not entirely just and that there were, indeed, terrible people who existed in it.

She hadn't been able to eradicate all the terrible people in the world, but she could acknowledge to herself—privately, not wishing to draw attention to her deeds—that she had made the world a slightly better place in the time since she'd come to her senses.

Only a few years ago she'd been equally consumed with parties and balls and pretty dresses. And Bennett, Lord Carson, whom she had to admit to still being consumed with.

She continued to enjoy those things, of course, but they couldn't derail her from her purpose in life—to help people.

And, apparently, kittens.

It had happened gradually, making it feel as though she had awoken from a long, slow sleep. She'd started noticing things, things that were not immediately in her world, and she'd started questioning.

Why were people so cruel? And what could she do to help?

It was that urge that drove her more than anything now.

"Sir!" she said as she stepped outside into the garden. She glanced around, Pearl on her heels, until she spotted the man in the Robinsons' garden, who was holding a small, wriggling thing in his hand.

"Sir!" she said again, louder, so that he turned and looked at her across the fence that separated their properties.

The two families had been neighbors for as long as Olivia could remember; the children had grown up together, but now the only Robinson left in the house was Lady Robinson, the matriarch of the family, a terrifyingly proper woman who always looked at Olivia as though she knew she was thinking of parties and balls and dresses when she should be thinking of better things.

I'm thinking of better things now, Olivia thought as she stomped toward the fence, swinging her arms furiously. *Namely saving small, helpless animals from your ogre gardener.* "What are you doing?" she asked. Then she shook her head as she planted her fists on her hips. "Never mind, I know what you are doing. Although I can't fathom why you would want to harm such precious little creatures," she continued, her voice softening as she saw the tumble of kittens at the man's feet.

There were three more down on the ground, all looking small enough to fit in her hand, all bumbling in and around each other in an adorably confused way. Their mother was nowhere in sight, which likely meant these kittens would be dead if they weren't taken care of soon.

That furious anger heated.

"These precious creatures are living in the shed, making a mess everywhere," the man said, shaking the kitten in his hand for emphasis.

The kitten in question was a grey tabby with, it seemed, one bent ear and whiskers that were nearly as long as the kitten itself was wide.

Olivia unlatched the gate separating the properties and launched herself through until she was able to remove the kitten from his hand.

The kitten promptly clawed her, but it was all part of the ongoing battle. *Every war had its wounds*, she'd told Pearl often enough. Usually when Pearl was complaining of a hand cramp after Olivia had wrangled her into helping with her latest charity project. Pearl was a much better seamstress than Olivia, after all. Something Pearl pointed out more often than Olivia liked, though Olivia might have mentioned a few times that she was taller than her twin. Most people assumed Olivia was the older sister, since the two of them were not identical.

"I will inform Lady Robinson of your behavior today, and I will be removing these animals myself," she declared, holding the struggling kitten up to her chest.

The man shrugged. "The lady don't care. And as long as they aren't living in my shed, I don't care either."

Olivia opened her mouth to tell him just what

she thought of his behavior, but decided it wasn't worth it to waste her breath. Not when she could be speaking out about injustice or helping poor families find a better way in the world or sharing her most fervent desire with Lord Carson. *Bennett.*

She would act instead. Solving the immediate problem was more important than stating her opinion, correct though it was.

"Pearl," she said instead, turning her head back to address her twin. Pearl had already anticipated what she was going to say and had retrieved a basket their own gardener used for roses, its handle slung over her arm.

"Good, take this one," Olivia said, putting the kitten into the basket and then bending down to gather up the remainder in her arms. They were so tiny they all fit, their tiny claws shredding the fabric of her gown, not strong enough to draw blood, but stinging. The three looked similar enough to the first one to be siblings, and Olivia felt a swell in her heart as she thought about what would happen if she and her sisters were just as lost as these little mites, one of whom had just begun to bite her wrist.

"If you find any other helpless creatures," she said as she marched back over to their property, four kittens mewing in the basket, "please send word so I can rescue them from your evil clutches."

The hero in *The Notorious Noose*, the latest penny dreadful she and Pearl had read, had used those same words. Olivia found it useful—not to mention entertaining—to read those books for language she could borrow to make her points. She had found people responded better to hyperbole than plain facts.

Besides which, wrongs were always righted, and then were suitably punished, which left her with a satisfied feeling after reading them. Not like in real life, where rights were often left unright, and people kept suffering.

But at least, she thought as she glanced into the basket, these four kittens wouldn't suffer any longer. Not if she had anything to say about it.

Which she did. And she always would. It was what drove her now, even more than wanting to find her own happiness. She needed everyone to have happiness.

"Did you pay no attention at all?" Bennett asked as he glared at Edward. They stood in the enormous ballroom of the house Edward's father had rented in London, a soft rain falling outside, the inside silent save for Bennett's practically vibrating outrage.

Edward couldn't help but smirk at his friend. Bennett was as vehement about this as he was on the Parliamentary floor, and this was about—

"You're asking if I paid attention during *dancing lessons*," Edward said, emphasizing the last two words to show his disdain.

Bennett flung his hands up, hands that had been trying to put Edward into the correct position for the waltz just a few moments ago.

"Yes. You do know that polite society deems it important to dance, don't you?"

"Ah, and that's the problem." Edward bent into a deep bow, spreading his arms wide. "Have you been introduced to Mr. Edward Wolcott, the most notable bastard of your acquaintance?"

Bennett rolled his eyes. "You don't have to constantly be rubbing the fact into everyone's faces all the time, you know."

Oh, but I do, Edward thought. *Because if I don't make reference to it, remove the sting of its mention from anyone who might say something, they will think they've hurt me when they mention my dubious parentage.* Most people assumed being illegitimate indicated a lack of character, as though being born on the wrong side of the blanket made someone simply *wrong*.

But he didn't tell his friend any of that. Bennett knew precisely why Edward did what he did, he just didn't understand how much it did hurt.

The sidelong glances that had supplanted the outright fights his schoolmates had baited him into. Fights that Edward took pride in winning, even though winning meant he was called to the headmaster's office after each fracas. *Mr. Wolcott*, the headmaster would say pointedly. Making it clear he knew just why Edward didn't share his father's last name.

School was where he had met Bennett, and Bennett had stuck with Edward ever since, no matter how many times Edward pointed out that the son of a marquis should not be friends with the bastard son of a financier. Even though— remarkably—the financier had claimed his son, something very few gentlemen did. Most natural-born children were never acknowledged by their fathers, for fear of ruining their reputations.

But Edward's father had done what few men would, and now Edward could ruin his own reputation when he appeared on the dance floor.

"Why can't I just speak with people about horses and hunting and the things I actually like to do, rather than dance or make irritatingly banal conversation?"

Bennett did not deign to reply, instead holding his arms out. "Let's try this again. I cannot believe that someone so athletic can be so terrible a dancer."

"It's not the same thing," Edward grumbled.

Mostly because he'd concentrated on athletics as a way to circumvent the cruel talk; he figured if he was stronger than any of his potential tormentors, he could keep their comments at bay with the very real possibility of physical violence. And his strategy had worked; very few men dared to mention anything now, not after appraising Edward's physique.

"I do know," Bennett said as he adjusted Edward's hands, nudging his feet into the right place and heaving several exasperated sighs, "that you loathe dancing. I am well aware, nearly as much as you, of how much you hate all this rigmarole. But I also know you have to do it. You told me what your father said."

Edward felt his chest tighten at the mention of his father. *Mr. Beechcroft.* The man who, inexplicably, had loved and raised him as well as if he had been legitimately born. The man who wanted nothing more than to see his son take a position in Society, a position that he himself could never take, thanks to his merchant upbringing. Edward wished it were enough that he had learned the business and enjoyed doing it. But his father wanted more.

"Fine," he replied in a grouchy tone.

"And if you cannot bear it for another moment, there is usually an unused library or another type of room you can go to escape for a bit."

Edward made a harrumphing noise, indicating his thoughts on that idea.

Running away from a problem was not his way; he usually did the opposite, running headlong toward it without considering the consequences.

Bennett, who was accustomed to Edward's grumpiness, ignored his friend, instead instructing him on how to count out the rhythm of the waltz.

If only Bennett could teach him how not to see mockery in everyone's faces when he attended his first Society function, introduced with his mother's name though everyone knew who his father was.

But that would be even more difficult than his mastering the waltz. And he was currently smashing all ten of Bennett's toes.

"STOP!"

Edward paused as he heard the woman's voice, even though she wasn't speaking to him.

He had left the town house about half an hour after Bennett, knowing he just had to walk somewhere, anywhere, that wasn't inside.

It had started to drizzle, and people were scurrying about, most dressed moderately well. He'd wandered toward his father's London office, which was situated just a few streets over from where London's most fashionable people shopped and mingled.

The woman who'd spoken was clearly one of those most fashionable people—dressed in a long coat that appeared to be as warm as it was exquisitely detailed.

A maid stood nearby holding an umbrella over her mistress's head, but the lady herself paid no heed to the rain, stepping out from the cover to stretch her hand forward to a merchant who had hold of a small, struggling child.

The child looked to be about ten, perhaps older, since he or she was rail thin.

He stepped forward to intervene, but by now the lady had extricated the child from the merchant's hold and was holding her hand out to her maid, who was dropping a few coins into the lady's gloved palm.

"Here," she said in an imperious voice to the merchant, "this should pay you sufficiently for what you think you've suffered." She allowed the coins to slip from her hand into the merchant's raised hand, punctuating her words with a dismissive sniff.

The merchant glowered but took the money and stepped back inside his shop, while the lady knelt down in front of the child.

Edward couldn't hear what she said now—she was speaking too quietly—but he saw the child's face break into a smile and saw her tuck a few more coins into the child's pocket, then frown and unwrap her scarf from her neck, placing it around the child's instead.

He had never seen an aristocrat do something so directly to help—yes, many of the people with whom his father did business gave money to various causes, making certain to mention it in polite company—but he hadn't seen anyone do something so small, and yet so important, as this. It made him more hopeful about the Society event that evening. Perhaps, if there were people like her in attendance, he wouldn't be made to feel out of place.

The child ran off, a grin on his face, and the lady rose, looking weary for a moment before straightening her shoulders and raising her chin, returning to looking every inch a proud, uncaring lady.

She glanced over in his direction, a cool, haughty expression on her face, and he felt himself start to smile. He knew her secret—she wasn't what she appeared to be; she was someone who cared, and cared deeply.

She was young, he could see, and quite lovely, at least as far as he could tell from across the street.

He felt an urge to meet her, to discover what it was that made her different from others of her kind, but before he could, she'd swept off, her maid trailing behind, valiantly trying to shield her mistress from the rain.

Edward shrugged, knowing it was likely just as well he couldn't meet her. What if she wasn't truly as good as she appeared to be from this one instance?

But still. It made him wonder who she was, and why she was so caring.

Perhaps he would meet her, and then if he were lucky, he would ask her to dance. And then he would step on her feet, and she would discover who he was, and his warm feeling toward her would be gone.

But for now it was enough to feel the warmth surrounding his heart.

Chapter 2

If you have to choose between being polite and doing good, always choose the latter.
LADY OLIVIA'S PARTICULAR GUIDE TO DECORUM

Oh, how delightful!"

Olivia spoke to herself since Pearl had disappeared in search of some refreshment, as usual, leaving Olivia to the side of the ballroom.

Their mother was fanning herself in the chaperones' corner, talking non-stop as was her habit. Olivia and her sisters had gotten to the point where they were able to communicate with one another through hand gestures so they knew what topic their mother was discussing without having to listen.

Olivia's dance partner, a slight gentleman who had stepped on her feet at least six times, had made his bows and departed as soon as the music had stopped.

Was it, she wondered, because she had taken

the opportunity to remind Lord Frederick of the essential steps of the dance they were engaged in? But surely he would welcome a gentle reminder of how he was supposed to move?

That settled, she glanced around the room, her gaze searching for Bennett.

The party was at the Estabrooks' house, and she knew—because of course she followed his career avidly—that Bennett was hoping that Lord Estabrook would lend his support to one of Bennett's ongoing projects. She'd heard that Queen Victoria had deigned to read one of his papers, which boded well for its success.

She hadn't followed closely enough to know just what he was hoping to accomplish, never mind what the queen actually thought of what he'd written. When she was his wife, she would of course be conversant with the issues that occupied his time. But until then, she had to admit that reading all the arguments for and against a concern made her eyes wander.

Besides which, she always knew that it was better to be *doing* than to be reading. It was something she would point out to him, when she was properly ensconced as his wife. Her sister Ida had not received Olivia's guidance well, but her true love would agree.

She wrinkled her nose as she spotted Bennett at the edge of the dance floor speaking with Lady

Cecilia, another debutante having her first Season this year.

Bennett looked bored, although her conscience forced her to acknowledge that it was difficult to see his expression from this far away. But he had to be bored speaking with Lady Cecilia—Lady Cecilia was fresh from the schoolroom, and Bennett was a *man*, accustomed to matters of great importance, not where a gown was coming from or how many invitations one had received.

That type of flighty girl had been Olivia not so long ago, even though it felt like a lifetime ago. It had taken a starving child begging outside her father's house to finally make her realize that not everyone was like her. Very few people were, actually. And not in character, but in opportunities.

That anger had started to burn inside until she was forced to do things about it, but few people in her world knew of her works.

It was no wonder Bennett had always regarded her as though he were mildly amused by her. It was time for him to see her as she truly was.

Tonight.

Thus decided, she began the slow walk to where Bennett stood, skirting the edge of the room and smiling politely at the guests who nodded at her.

It wasn't entirely proper for her to approach him, but she knew that once he heard what she had to say, he would forgive her. More than that, he would agree to what she asked him, and neither one of them would have to spend any more conversation with people who bored them. Who didn't share the same passionate interests in justice and change and righting wrongs that they did.

"Lord Carson?" she said as she joined Bennett and Lady Cecilia, the latter of whom raised her tiny, perfect nose at Olivia's intrusion. "Might I beg a private word with you?"

Bennett glanced from one lady to the other, his brow furrowed, but after a moment he nodded. "Of course, my lady," he said. He bowed to Lady Cecilia. "You'll forgive me? Lady Olivia is my sister-in-law's younger sister—nearly family."

Lady Cecilia shot a glare at Olivia, but her mouth curved into a sweet smile as she looked at Bennett. "Of course, my lord." A pause, then Lady Cecilia spoke again. "When you are finished with familial concerns, I would like to ask your opinion on a few things."

Olivia nearly emitted a noise that would have indicated what she thought, but that wouldn't be fitting for the adult young lady she was now.

So she just returned Lady Cecilia's smile and took Bennett's arm, allowing him to lead her into one of the rooms adjacent to the ballroom.

"MR . . . WOLCOTT?" THE older lady said, her pause between the *Mr.* and the *Wolcott* an indication she knew precisely who he was. Especially since one of Bennett's friends, a Lord Something-or-Other, had just introduced them.

He seldom bothered to remember people's names, since he usually only met them once, since after they discovered who he was—or more precisely, *what* he was—they took pains to never encounter him again.

Bennett had left unexpectedly, pulled away by one of the fluttering debutantes in attendance. It wouldn't normally matter to Edward, but Bennett was the only one who could ensure Edward wasn't treated as rudely as he might otherwise be. The most recent example being the lady's pause between words.

Bennett's friend glanced from Edward to the Pausing Lady, his look one of confusion. Edward appreciated that Bennett didn't gossip about him, but giving this friend of his some word about why not everyone would want to meet Edward would not go amiss.

But that was Bennett. Seeing the good in everybody, and not recognizing that some people reveled in ignorance. Only one of the reasons Edward was grateful he was the one born a bastard, and not Eternally Optimistic Bennett.

"Yes." Edward accompanied his reply with a bow. "I have just arrived in London, and my friend Lord Carson invited me to this function."

He might as well get the explanation over with, given that she was likely about to question him about just how he happened to be here with the likes of her.

"Ah," she replied, visibly softening. Bennett had that effect on people.

Edward did not.

"And how do *you* happen to be here?" Edward asked, making Bennett's friend's face turn white and the lady gasp in outrage.

Damn. And he'd been doing so well. For at least fifteen seconds or so.

"If you'll excuse me," he continued without waiting for her to speak, bowing again and turning on his heel in search of one of those vaunted private rooms Bennett had promised. Anything but being open and exposed out here, like a frightened fox being stampeded by vicious dogs.

He had to admit to having far more sympathy for the animals he hunted right now. And also understood why they turned around and snarled rather than succumbing to the attack.

But he couldn't snarl. He had to escape.

He walked quickly to a door at one corner of the room, slipping inside without having to make eye contact with anyone.

The room was empty, thank goodness, and he took a deep breath—his first of the evening—

glancing around at what seemed to be a small visiting room.

A few chairs were scattered about, as were a few tables, their tops cluttered with the type of bric-a-brac that seemed to accompany these people's homes.

He exhaled, stepping forward to the sofa that sat directly in front of a still-burning fire.

Leaping over the back, he plopped down on the soft cushions, twisting his long body so he was lying down staring into the fire. The flames were mesmerizing, and he let his mind drift.

Away from the party outside, the people who despised him, the constant bitter tang of his birth fell away.

"Is Lady Eleanor all right? I know that Alexander was worried she was doing so much, what with the—" And then Bennett hesitated.

"Baby coming?" Olivia allowed herself the luxury of rolling her eyes at him. "Honestly, it is not as though we all don't know what is happening."

Bennett uttered a sort of strangled noise in his throat, and then took a deep breath. "Yes, the baby."

"Everything is fine." She swept ahead of him and pushed a door open, one that was in one of the far corners of the ballroom. She glanced back to see that Lady Cecilia had already found some other gentleman to converse with. *So much for perseverance*, she thought, wanting to toss her head in triumph, then she gestured for him to precede her. "Go in, I want to speak to you."

Now that it was the moment she'd been dreaming about for so long, she had to admit to feeling nervous. Not that he wouldn't agree, because of course he would, it was the right thing to do, plus she knew how he felt about her, even if he didn't. Hadn't he paid particular attention to her during her come-out? He'd danced with her twice—twice!—at a party the prior year, and she'd caught him looking at her when he didn't know that she was looking.

But she was always looking.

The nervousness was merely because her whole life was about to change; she would be Lady Carson, she would finally be able to do all the things she wanted, no *needed*, to do.

And she would spend the rest of her life with him.

Just thinking about it made her calmer.

She closed the door behind them, leaning against it with her arms behind her back.

He raised an eyebrow at her action, but didn't say anything. Wise man. Already knowing she had all the answers.

"What is it, Olivia?" he spoke brusquely. "It is not proper for us to be privately together, even if we are considered family." Perhaps he was so swept away with his feelings, feelings he hadn't acknowledged before, that he couldn't speak properly?

She didn't reply at first, just walked toward him and put her finger to his lips. "Shh," she said, when he appeared to be about to open his mouth. "The thing is, I have something to say, and I want to say it without interruption."

He looked as though he wanted to argue, but instead he gave a brief nod. She withdrew her finger from his mouth and took a deep breath.

"You and I met when I was just—what?—fifteen years old?" She walked past him and put her hand on the back of one of the chairs in the room. She took a moment to look around at where they were—some sort of sitting room, it appeared, since there were small tables and chairs scattered about, with one sofa facing a fireplace, though the fire had died down. A good thing, since she already felt quite warm. Likely due to Bennett's presence and what was about to happen.

"And I know at the time you saw me as someone still in the schoolroom," she continued, continuing to pace around the room, forcing herself not to look at him because she was concerned she would forget everything she wanted to say because of all the love she had oozing through every pore. Which sounded far messier than she wanted.

"But I am, if you have not noticed, a woman now." And she returned to stand in front of him, forcing herself to breathe naturally, looking him in the eyes.

His gaze appeared startled, and she wanted to reassure him that it would all be fine, they would sort things out, and they could have their respective futures settled. Together.

But first she had to tell him how she felt. So he would be able to admit how he felt.

"When I was younger, I said and did many things I am embarrassed about now," she began. "I didn't realize there was more to life than wondering what party you'd be able to attend next. When I first met you, I couldn't even attend any parties because Eleanor wasn't married yet." She cringed to recall how selfish she had been. But she wouldn't say all that to him—she wanted him to maintain his good opinion of her, after all. "And now that I have had the opportunity to be out in the world, I know that there are things I wish to change."

And not just things like allowing ladies to waltz all the time, if they wanted to, although that would be lovely. She meant things like making sure all people had enough to eat and that children be given an education and that there should never be the possibility of an animal suffering because of human neglect or irresponsibility or particularly willful action.

"Those are excellent sentiments," Bennett said.

She beamed at him, glad they were in accord. "I know you feel the same way I do—I have followed your efforts in Parliament." Albeit not that closely, and then she paused, taking a deep breath before adding, ". . . Bennett."

His eyes widened at her use of his first name, and he blinked a few times. Overcome by his emotions, perhaps? She smiled reassuringly. "We feel the same way about so many things." She put her hand on his sleeve. His gaze went to where her hand lay, and she wished she was daring enough to run the fingers of her other hand through his hair. She wasn't, not yet. Perhaps later, after everything was settled.

"And since we are of much the same mind, I know that it only makes sense for us to get married. So we can finally be together." She exhaled. "There. I've finally said it." And she tilted her face up so he could kiss her.

And edged forward, since it seemed that he wasn't going to. Perhaps he was unsure if a kiss would be welcome? She should let him know it would be perfectly welcome.

"You may kiss me, if you like. Since we are now betrothed."

He still did not kiss her, and she felt a pang of regret. Instead, he closed his eyes and leaned his head back so that even if she wished to initiate a kiss, she couldn't. He was too tall, and now his mouth was too far away from hers.

A slow, uncomfortable feeling began to unravel inside her, and she felt her breath hitch.

"I am aware of the great honor you do me, Lady Olivia," he said, his eyes still closed. Then he opened them, and she wanted to leap back at what she saw in his gaze. Was it possible he did not love her? "But I do not regard you in that way, and I think it best if we forget this conversation ever happened."

Olivia froze for a moment as she absorbed the words. And then felt her face blaze as fiercely as any fire she'd ever encountered. "You do not regard me in that way?" she repeated, hearing the words fall out of her mouth even though she didn't think she could speak. "You're saying you are not in love with me?"

She snatched her hand off his sleeve and dropped it behind her back, her fingers wiggling in the air as though trying to find purchase. Because it felt as though she were falling off a very high cliff. "Not in love with me?" she said again, wishing he would step forward and take her in his arms and say it was all a mistake, he was testing her, but knowing he wouldn't.

"Oh," she said in a soft voice, looking anywhere but at him. "I've just thrown myself at you, and now it seems you don't feel the same way." Something caught her eye and she walked forward, past him, to snatch it up from the small table. It was a dome encasing a small yellow flower, one of those ornamental things everybody had as part of their everyday clutter.

This isn't you, a voice said in her head. *This isn't who you are, or who you want to be.*

But she couldn't keep herself from curling her fingers around it, feeling the cool glass on her palm. Knowing she could throw it if she wanted to. Which she very much did. *This,* at least, she could do. She could control her actions now, even if she couldn't control his. She'd just thrown herself at him? She could throw other things too.

She raised the dome over her head, all of her pent-up emotion channeling itself through her upraised arm, flinging it toward the opposite wall, not close enough to possibly hit him, but startling nonetheless.

The object shattered into pieces, the noise of the impact the only sound in the room. It wasn't loud enough to cause anyone to notice, not with the band continuing to play in the ballroom as though hearts weren't currently being broken.

"Olivia, you should consider," he began, but

she shook her head before he could get more words out.

"Get out." She spoke in a low tone, because if she raised her voice she would scream, and she couldn't cause that kind of scene, not as one of the duke's daughters, who already had a penchant for causing trouble. Not to mention it would be horribly embarrassing. *Yes, Lady Olivia was proposing to me, and I was rejecting her, and then she threw a decorative object at my head.* If he said anything about it at all, which she knew as a gentleman he would not.

"Get out," she repeated in a stronger voice this time.

Something in her expression must have told him not to press the issue, because he shook his head and walked past her and back out into the ballroom, closing the door behind him.

Leaving her alone with her thoughts and her humiliation.

She took a deep breath and withdrew her handkerchief from her pocket, preparing herself for an epic cry.

"Pardon me," a deep voice said from the depths of the sofa opposite, "but I think it is probably best that I make my departure as well."

Olivia's mouth opened in shock as a man—a tall, perfectly dressed, and remarkably handsome man—emerged from behind the sofa, his hair disheveled. He offered her a sly grin and she felt all of her ire direct itself onto this stranger who'd had the effrontery to listen to her make a fool of herself.

"And who are you?" she replied haughtily, taking refuge in her bred-to-the-bone aristocratic manner.

He spread his arms and made a low bow. "I am Mr. Edward Wolcott, at your service," he replied in an amused tone.

"Oh!" she said in recognition. "The bast—" she began, then put her hand to her open mouth.

His smile halted and the look in his eyes got fierce. "Yes, my lady. The bastard."

Chapter 3

Whatever anyone says, do not lose control.
LADY OLIVIA'S PARTICULAR GUIDE TO DECORUM

*E*dward's feelings of *Poor Bennett* were quickly supplanted by *Idiotic Bennett* when he finally saw the lady who'd thrown herself at his friend.

And a piece of bric-a-brac at the wall.

But given how she'd just exposed herself, he couldn't necessarily blame her, although he was wary, of course.

It was she. The lady he'd seen on the street just a day prior. His first impression had been correct; she was lovely.

Blonde with hazel eyes that sparkled as brightly as the diamonds in her ears. Her mouth, currently set in a sharp line, was lush, her lips a kissable rose color.

Although she was of average height, her whole presence seemed outsized, like a fierce flame contained within the usual package of Debutante

Dressed in Silk. It was as if her body couldn't contain her personality, as though the edges of her real self were outlined with passion and wit—and anger. He wanted to touch her, to see if that spark was as warm and exuberant as it appeared.

"What were you thinking by not announcing your presence, sir?" she said, her voice crackling with that very same anger. So definitely forget about touching her. Not that he was thinking of that in the first place.

Edward raised his brow. "At what point should I have announced myself? When you told Lord Carson how you knew he was in love with you?" He stepped forward, drawn by the light of her, even though he suspected she might very well slap him if he drew close enough. "Or when you plotted out the course of your lives together, with you being his wife for his just causes?" Yes, he knew he was being out of line, but damn it, so was she. "Or perhaps when you threw whatever it was you threw at Bennett. I guess it is a good thing you don't have accurate aim."

"I wasn't aiming for him!" she replied, the color along her cheekbones a deep red to match her passion.

"Ah, good to know," Edward replied, shrugging. "The thing is, Lady Olivia"—because he knew who she was, not just because Bennett had addressed her by name, but also because word of

the Duke's Daughters had reached even him—
"that there would have been no convenient time
to disclose my presence. Until it sounded as
though you were about to cry." It was dangerous,
of course, to be speaking so bluntly to someone
like her—a duke's daughter, one of the highest
members of the Society that didn't want him to
join—but he couldn't stay silent, not with her
having done what she just did. Not with him being friends with Bennett.

He owed it to both of them, even though he'd
just met her.

He shook his head slowly. "I don't think it's right
to be privy to anyone else's sadness, not if the person doesn't agree to it." He reached into his pocket
and withdrew his handkerchief. "You might need
this in addition to yours." She took it, her face now
drained of color, perhaps as the impact of what
had just happened seeped into her being. "Do just
one thing, Lady Olivia," he said, drawing closer
to her, so close he could see how she was blinking
more rapidly, perhaps to stem the coming storm.
"Never let anyone see your pain," he continued in
a low voice. "Keep it to yourself, because if they
see it, they will attack you."

And then he walked out of the room, closing
the door firmly behind him, but not before hearing a smothered sob.

"EDWARD!"

Edward turned as a visibly strained Bennett walked toward him, a wineglass in each hand. He must have left the room after Lady Olivia's outburst and headed straight for where he could find wine.

"Here, I thought you might need this," Bennett said, handing him the glass. "Given how unpleasant you find all of this." He drained his own glass in one swift gulp, depositing it on a passing footman's tray, all before Edward could even take a sip.

"I think you might need it more," Edward said, returning the glass to Bennett's hand.

Bennett stared at it as though not aware of what he was doing, then shook his head. "Maybe I do," he said, taking a big swallow, sputtering as he did.

"I was there," Edward said in a quiet tone. "In that room while Lady Olivia was speaking with you. To you."

Bennett's brows drew together in confusion. "You were? But how?"

"I ducked in there to give myself time away from the party, as you suggested, and I was lying down on the sofa when you came in. I would have made my presence known, but the lady had launched into her proposal by the time I could have spoken, and then it was just . . . awkward," he said with a smirk. He knew Bennett well enough to know that his friend was likely mortified by the situation; if he could get him to acknowledge the humor of it, he wouldn't carry the guilt around with him like a pack mule.

"*Awkward* is one word for it," Bennett replied, taking another long draught of the wine.

"Did you know how she felt about you?" Edward asked. *Weren't you tempted?* He wished he could ask. It would have been hard for Edward in that same situation to resist the lady, no matter how imperative her demands were. And he thought he might like to hear what it was she wanted as well.

But those were not thoughts he should be having about any young proper lady, especially one who might find a handy object to fling at him. He couldn't always count on her having bad aim.

And then he'd be a bastard with a busted head.

Bennett nodded his head, the expression on his face rueful. "I knew, but I never imagined she would be so bold as to share her feelings with me. I was hoping she would grow out of it. Or find someone else to admire."

Edward had to admire the lady's boldness— seeing what she wanted, then going after it without hesitation. That kind of fierce single-mindedness that he valued in himself when on the hunt.

It was a shame she considered herself in love with his friend, because otherwise he would have found the hunt of her intriguing. If she could look past his birth to know the man inside, which he knew full well she could not.

"Lord Carson." Both men turned at the voice, which belonged to an older gentleman with a full head of white hair and a genial smile, the latter of which froze when he saw Edward.

The hair remained on his head, however.

"My lord," Bennett replied, bowing. "Please allow me to introduce—" he began, only to be interrupted.

"I know who he is," the man replied, his eyes narrowing. He glanced past Edward's shoulder, clearly trying to quell the words that seemed to bubble on his lips. Edward glanced backward and saw—her.

"Lady Olivia, how delightful," the lord said, his tone oozing charm and politeness, the epitome of aristocratic hypocrisy.

Edward felt his fists clench.

"Lord Smithton," Lady Olivia replied, glancing from the lord to Bennett, looking as though she wished she were anywhere but here.

Her color was still high, but not flame red any

longer. Merely a delightful pink. Her eyes were bright, but unless you knew, it would be impossible to guess she had been crying only a few minutes earlier.

His estimation of her rose higher, even though she felt as this Lord Smithton did—that he was a bastard, unfit to be in their company.

"Lady Olivia," Bennett said stiffly, bowing.

"My lord," she replied. She spoke hastily, as though desperate to escape. He couldn't blame her. "I didn't mean to interrupt—I am actually trying to find my sister Lady Pearl. You haven't seen her, have you?" she continued, her words coming quickly out of her mouth, her eyes darting around the room. He saw the strain of her smile. He knew how she felt, how much she wanted to be anyplace but here at this moment.

And she wouldn't like what he was about to do, but it was better than forcing Bennett and her to stand together.

"My lady, we have not been formally introduced," he began. Even though he had technically introduced himself, he couldn't very well reference the circumstances under which they'd met. "I am Mr. Wolcott, and I would be pleased to help you find your sister." He held his arm out for her, waiting a heart-stopping moment before she took it, placing her fingers on his sleeve. "If you will excuse us, gentlemen?" he said, stepping away from Bennett and the hypocrite, feeling the swish of her skirts against his legs.

But not before he heard Lord Smithton. "You cannot allow Lady Olivia to make that man's acquaintance! I am appalled you . . ." And the rest of his words were lost as they walked out of earshot.

Her fingers tightened on his arm. "Thank you," she said in a high voice. As though there was so much emotion curled inside her she couldn't manage it. "For rescuing me even though I was so terrible." She paused and glanced up at him, her expression curious. "Is everyone so unpleasant when they find out—" And she blushed again.

"That I'm a bastard?" Edward finished. "Yes."

"I apologize, Mr. Wolcott," she said in a low tone. "I should not have used that word."

"But it's true," he replied, not knowing why he was arguing the point, but that somehow it took his mind off the sting of all the Lord Smithtons in the room, their disdainful sniffs and pointed looks a reminder that his heritage was not what theirs were. Even though his father was probably more of a real father to him than these legitimately born aristocrats who sent their children away as soon as was convenient. Even though he couldn't give his son the benefit of his last name.

"It's not right," she said, so fiercely he would have sworn she'd thumped his chest with her words. "It's not right, and I will not have it." She raised her chin and looked around the room, a challenge in her gaze. As though she was his own Boadicea determined to fight.

It was endearing, even if it was unwarranted and likely to be fruitless. The only possible way he could ever be fully accepted into Society would be if Queen Victoria kissed him open-mouthed in front of all the best families, and he didn't think that would be happening. Even without the threat of a punch from Prince Albert.

But it wasn't worth the bother of explaining it to her, the subtle ways people would indicate their displeasure at his presence, the insidious feelings of being less worthy than someone whose parents were married to one another.

"Thank you," he murmured. "Perhaps we should look for your sister?"

"Yes, but do not think I will forget, Mr. Wolcott," she said, now looking directly at him. He blinked at how . . . *intense* her expression was, full of that fire and spark he'd noticed before, but now her anger was not, thankfully, directed at him.

"I could not imagine how I would possibly think that, my lady," he said, beginning to walk her through the crowd again.

Oddly enough, he believed her, if only because of her burning fierceness. He had no doubt she would pick up his cause as she had that child's on the London street.

"Oh, there she is," Lady Olivia said in a grateful tone, walking more quickly now. She looked up at him, her face showing the strain of maintaining a cool façade. "I must go see her at once," she continued, dipping into a curtsey. "Thank you for your help," she murmured, before slipping away toward another young lady standing in the corner right near a large plant.

"You're welcome," Edward replied, but she was already out of earshot.

He shook his head, feeling as though he'd been blasted by some force of nature, and returned to where Bennett appeared to be under siege by older lords and desperate debutantes all at once.

"You DID WHAT?" Pearl asked, perched on the end of Olivia's bed, her mouth dropped open.

"Don't act so shocked. You've known me since I was born," Olivia said, wanting to shift in her embarrassment, but forcing herself to stay still so Pearl wouldn't know.

"I'm your twin—that makes sense," Pearl replied in a dry tone of voice. "Though right now I am grateful we are not identical."

Olivia waved her hand airily. "You know what I mean. Of course I was going to tell him how I felt. I thought he felt the same." And she had, truly, until that moment when he'd told her, categorically, that he did not. She'd assumed he just hadn't recognized his own feelings, but that when she showed hers to him he would reciprocate.

She was so terribly wrong. It hurt. It stung, even, a painful barb that felt lodged in her throat and her heart. She'd never felt so much agony before, but she wasn't surprised it hadn't flattened her entirely. That wasn't who she was. She was not going to give up. She would just have to try harder.

She felt a stab of something on her leg and looked down to see one of the kittens, the one she'd started calling Snapper, trying to gnaw on her shin. Hence his name.

It was a remarkable coincidence that she was suffering from both actual and emotional pain.

She removed him carefully, placing him on the coverlet between her and Pearl, petting his head with her index finger. Wishing she could solve her emotional pain as easily.

One of the other kittens was in Pearl's lap, while the two others were not visible, which probably meant they were under Olivia's bed chewing on her slippers.

"Did you really think he felt the same?" Pearl asked. "I mean, you might have wished he did, but did you see any indication?"

Her twin's tone was soft and gentle, which only made Olivia more irritated.

"I thought that he did," she said, looking down at hearing Snapper's squeak of protest. Apparently she'd become too vigorous in her petting. "He always asks after me when he visits Eleanor. He danced with me twice last year, and there was that one time he brought me flowers from his garden."

"He brought flowers to Eleanor too." Pearl's unsaid words—*and he's not pining after her either*—hung in the air. Olivia felt her face heat. Did he not care for her, not at all?

And then it hit her, and she practically bounced on the bed. Snapper escaped her enthusiasm, darting off the bed and onto the floor with remarkably fluffy speed. "He might not love me now, but if I can just prove to him . . ." She let her words dangle as she thought it out.

"And the only way to do that is to prove that I would be an excellent wife, one who can assist him with whatever he needs help with. Perhaps help him with one of his projects or"—and then she sat straight up as the idea hit her—"I can help ease his friend's way into Society." She turned her head and looked at Pearl, who was regarding her with an expression that mixed fascination with suspicion, the same expression she had on her face every time Olivia took up a new project.

The only time she had not had it was when Olivia rescued the kittens.

"What friend?" Pearl asked slowly.

"Mr. Wolcott, he—" And then she wanted to squirm again, reminded of what had dropped out of her mouth when he'd popped up from the sofa. "His father is Mr. Beechcroft, the man who handles Father's financial dealings. And I believe owns several factories and such up north. I saw how he was treated at the party. Lord Smithton practically ignored him." She felt herself heat at the memory. Of how she'd promised to help him.

Pearl's face looked confused, then cleared as she realized what Olivia had said. "He is not Mr. Beechcroft's—?" she began, then shook her head and bit her lip, still staring at Olivia.

"He is Mr. Beechcroft's natural son. And I believe his heir as well. His father is likely one of the richest men in London, if not England, and that is why his presence is tolerated. But just barely." Her words came out more rapidly as she considered it. "It is not his fault he was born as he was, and it is our duty—or more accurately *my* duty—to make certain that everyone accepts him as they should."

Pearl shook her head. "He's not just another one of your causes, solved by the donation of some garments or funds. He's a person. He might not want you to make him into a project."

"Oh, but don't you see?" Olivia edged forward on the bed to get closer to her twin. Although she knew from long experience that proximity wouldn't necessarily convince Pearl about anything; there had been one time Olivia had climbed on top of her sister and Pearl had still refused to agree to whatever it was that Olivia was saying.

But perhaps one day Olivia would be surprised.

"This project, as you call it so accurately, will not only help poor Mr. Wolcott, but will also prove to Bennett—Lord Carson, that is—that I am a forceful, forthright woman who can accomplish many things."

"I don't think he has ever doubted that," Pearl said in an odd tone. As though she were stifling a laugh. Even though Olivia hadn't told a joke for twelve years. There were more important things to do than tell jokes, after all.

"Perhaps not," she replied. "But after I prove this to him, he's going to have to realize he loves me after all." It had to be that Lord Carson just didn't know his own mind.

It was such a wonderful idea she wasn't going to wait for Pearl's approval. Even though she did want it.

"So . . . what do you think?" she asked, smiling brightly at her twin.

Pearl stared back at Olivia. "You don't want me to say what I think." She shook her head. "You never want me to say what I think. You only want me to say that I think what you think. And that's not what I think at all." Her words spilled out in a rush, their tone imbued with a frustration Olivia had never heard from her twin before.

"It's a good idea, though," she pressed.

Pearl rolled her eyes. Not the response Olivia wanted. "I won't say it is. I will say you should be careful. These are men you are dealing with, not unfed orphans or gentlewomen who just need a bit of embroidery to brighten their day." And then she definitely rolled her eyes even harder. "Or—or kittens," she finished, hoisting one of the four, probably Scamp, up from the floor.

"I will be fine. And when I am Lady Carson, you can come live with me and you'll be able to do whatever you like."

Pearl's lips drew into a thin line. "Are you saying you don't think I will get married? That I won't have my own life?"

Oh dear, how did she always say the wrong thing? "No, that's not what I mean at all." She didn't think, she just spoke. "It's just that I thought I would be the first one to get married out of the two of us, because you're not . . ." She paused, trying to think of the right word.

"Never mind," Pearl said in a weary tone. "Go ahead and do what you want to. It's not as though I can change your mind." She glanced at

Scamp, who was kneading her gown with two tiny paws. "As long as you also make it a project to find a home for these kittens." She pinned Olivia with a hard stare.

Olivia's heart hurt to think about it. "All of them? Surely not Scamp. Or Snapper. Or—or Mr. Whiskers," she added, even though they had only chosen two names since they knew naming all four would mean it would be harder to let them go.

Although perhaps she would present one of them to Bennett—he was certain to welcome it gladly, and he'd be reminded of her every time he saw it.

Another excellent idea.

"Mr. Whiskers?" Pearl shook her head, then glanced down at the kitten in her lap, her expression softening. "Fine, we can discuss that. Get Mr. Wolcott accepted by Society and then we can decide what to do with these little love bugs." She lowered her head to rub her nose in Scamp's fur.

"It's a plan," Olivia said. Now she just had to figure out how to get Mr. Wolcott accepted while at the same time ensuring Bennett recognized her efforts.

It would be just like any of her other projects. Starting with her goal, then working out the steps until she achieved what she wanted.

Chapter 4

If you believe something is right, you should do it. Even at the risk of being wrong. But you are never wrong.

LADY OLIVIA'S PARTICULAR GUIDE TO DECORUM

"You're home!"

Edward paused at hearing his father's voice, then continued to shrug his cloak off, handing it to the waiting butler.

It was close to two o'clock, and normally Mr. Beechcroft was long asleep—*the early bird catches the worm,* he'd say with a grin as he headed to his bedroom at some ungodly early hour. As though worms were desirable.

Apparently the current worm his father wished to catch was an account of Edward's evening.

Oh, it was wonderful. I was snubbed by no fewer than a half dozen of Society's best and was called a bastard by a lady who'd just unknowingly thrown an object at my head.

A beautiful young lady. Not that that mattered, given what she'd said.

His father rounded the corner, huffing as he did. That shortness of breath concerned Edward; it had only started recently, a few months before they had arrived in London. When he asked his father about it, he'd dismissed it as just the excitement and fast pace of being in the city after so long leading a predictable existence. But the way his father's expression looked as he spoke led Edward to believe there was more to it than that.

"Put those things away, Chambers, and bring a bottle of port and glasses to the library. Come, son," his father said, clasping Edward on the arm and drawing him down the hall.

The house they'd rented was enormous, far too big for two people. But Mr. Beechcroft enjoyed flaunting his wealth and, as he'd explained to Edward when the latter had expostulated about the cost of something, showing your financial power meant people paid attention a lot faster.

It was unfortunate, Edward mused, that he couldn't just walk into a Society ballroom with a sheaf of bills in his hand. It would certainly make things a lot simpler. His father's enormous wealth was one of the few reasons Edward was tolerated in Society as much as he was—money was usually able to solve many problems, including the problem of illegitimacy.

He and his father walked down to the library, Edward slowing his normal, long-legged pace to accommodate his father's shorter steps.

"In here," his father said, unnecessarily, as he drew Edward into the room.

Edward took his father's arm and assisted him into one of the comfortable chairs. The fire had burned low, so Edward knelt down and added a log to the flickering flames, waiting patiently until the wood began to burn.

"There," he said, leaning back on his heels and looking at his father. "Now why are you up so late?"

His father opened his mouth to speak, only to be interrupted by Chambers bearing a tray with port and two glasses.

"I'll pour, just leave it there," Edward said, getting to his feet. The butler nodded, placing the bottle and the glasses on the small table next to his father's chair.

Edward poured out a healthy amount for himself and a smaller amount for his father and handed him the glass, returning his father's look of dismay with an arched eyebrow—Dr. Bell had told Mr. Beechcroft he should not drink to excess, and it was up to Edward to enforce that, since his father could never say no to good food or drink.

"You are determined to ruin what days I have

left," Mr. Beechcroft said in a grumpy tone of voice as he took a sip from his glass.

The hastily spoken words—that there were only so many days left in his father's life—made Edward's chest squeeze tighter, and the casual words he'd normally reply with stuck in his throat.

"I want you to be here for many, many days, Father," Edward said instead, settling into his own chair opposite his father. Mr. Beechcroft paused as he was setting his glass down, his eyes suspiciously bright as they rested on his son.

"But you haven't answered my question. Why are you up so late?"

Mr. Beechcroft adjusted himself in his seat, accompanied by a few grunts and groans. His usual way of delaying speech when he had something difficult to report.

Edward's chest got even tighter.

"Dr. Bell came to the house this evening," he began. Edward resisted the urge to interrupt— *Are you all right? What happened?*—and merely nodded.

"I had a turn, you see, while I was working in my office. I was able to call for help, and Chambers called Dr. Bell, who came quite quickly. There's the benefit to always paying your bills on time, unlike some of his more aristocratic patients," he added with a chuckle.

Edward wanted to scream at his father to get

to the point rather than chortling over how his wealth continued to benefit him, but he knew his father would never be deterred from pointing out his situation versus his well-born business associates.

Some of Edward's earliest memories were of his father drawing comparisons between the local aristocracy and their own family, such as it was, since it was only Mr. Beechcroft and him. The acknowledged bastard child of the wealthiest man in the area.

"And Dr. Bell said he believes I have an illness that might take me off within three months or might allow me to last for as long as a year." His father picked up his glass and drained it. "So you see, you can fill up my glass again, since it won't matter anyway." He spoke in his normal light tone, as though he was just commenting on the weather or sharing his insight from one of his business meetings.

Not that he had just told his son he only had a few months, perhaps, to live.

Edward leapt to his feet to kneel on the rug in front of his father. He gripped the arms of his father's chair, focusing on how his fingers were gripping the wood. Not on how the news was making his heart clench.

"What else did he say? What kind of illness is it? When are we returning home?"

They would get a second, third, and hundredth opinion, Edward thought. What was the point of having so much money if you couldn't spend it on important things like this? The most important thing?

He couldn't imagine the world without his father in it. He didn't want to.

Mr. Beechcroft shook his head slowly, a small smile on his face. As though he knew something Edward did not.

"We're staying right here, son." He rested his palm on Edward's hand, patting it softly. "I had an idea that this would be the news for some time now. That is why I wanted to come to London in the first place."

Edward's mouth dropped open, speechless for a moment. And then he spoke. "You are saying you've known about this? How long? What are we doing here?" Why had his father kept something like this from him?

"The thing is, I wanted to come to London and confirm my suspicions, and I did." Mr. Beechcroft nodded his head in satisfaction. As though he'd concluded a successful business transaction, not been told he was going to die. "I have one unfulfilled wish left, son, before I go." He placed his other hand on Edward's remaining hand and looked his son directly in the eyes. "My wish is to see you settled and happy. I know it isn't possible to give you my name—that was lost when your mother died before we could marry—but I can give you everything else. London is the only place you would be able to find a bride suitable for your, uh, situation." He sighed as he spoke. Edward's birth bothered Edward's father more than it did Edward himself. Edward knew his father had loved his mother, but that his mother's father had forbidden the match. But he had not been able to forbid Edward's birth.

"I want to see you with a lady. Someone whose family name will give you the legitimacy I couldn't."

"You," Edward began, taking as deep a breath as he could, "you want me to marry? Marry someone from Society?" *The Society that turns its patrician nose up at me, that whispers behind my back, that will take my advice on what horses to buy and follow me when hunting, but doesn't want me to dance with its daughters?*

Oh, Father. You ask an impossible task.

But he didn't say any of that. He couldn't. This was his father's last wish, and Edward had spent his entire life showing his gratitude to the man—his father hadn't deserted him, he had given him every opportunity, he had loved him—and he wasn't going to let a few turned-up noses and some disdain stop him, not now when it was so important.

"I do," Mr. Beechcroft said, smiling broadly. "I would like to know that you are happy, son, and I believe you will be happy if you marry someone who shares your education and beliefs." He left aside the obvious distinction of Edward's birth. "I knew this day would come. Not so soon, obviously, but that is why I have insisted that you understand the business and can take over when I am gone. And why I wanted you to have every opportunity I never did—in education, in manners, in company."

Edward felt his throat choke with tears, tears he couldn't spill in front of his father. It would only upset him, and Edward never wanted to upset his father. His own birth had done enough of that.

Instead, he spoke. "Yes, I'll marry, if that is your wish."

Even though it was not what he wanted, not at all. And, he knew, it would be difficult to accomplish. But he would since it was what his father wanted, and he didn't know how much time he would have to get it done. At least, he'd need to find someone suitable who would also agree to marry him within three months.

This would be far harder than his usual type of hunt. But it was one where he needed to succeed.

He just needed to assemble his hounds—namely his charm, his looks, and most important, his bank balance—and chase his fox, a lady who would accept his proposal despite who he was.

"YOU LOOK TERRIBLE."

Well, at least Edward knew he wouldn't have to find a way to introduce the topic. It seemed it was written on his face.

"Thank you." Edward gave his cloak and hat to the Raybourns' butler, then followed Bennett down the hallway to the Marquis of Wheatley's study, the room where Bennett conducted most of his business.

"Is your father never home?" Edward inquired, momentarily putting aside his worry for his own father.

Bennett's lips twisted into a grimace. "Not often, no."

The way his friend clamped his mouth together told Edward he wouldn't get any more information than that. One of these days—on a day when he wasn't reeling from the news his father only had a few months to live—he would pry deeper into Bennett's relationship with the marquis.

"Sit down," Bennett said, gesturing to the small sofa that was placed in front of the fireplace. Edward sat, stretching his legs out in front of him. The warmth of the fire felt good. Bennett sat in a chair next to the sofa, his elbows on his thighs, his expression focused and intent.

"What happened?"

Edward shook his head slowly. "My father, he was waiting up for me last night."

Bennett nodded.

"And he told me he's ill. He says he only has a short amount of time left. Three months? A year?" Edward swallowed against the lump in his throat. "And he wants me to get married before he goes."

"I am so sorry, Edward," Bennett said. "For your father's news, not your marriage plans."

Edward couldn't help but laugh, grateful that his friend would know how to cheer him up. "Thank you."

The two of them sat silent, Edward's mind churning through all the possibilities—what if the doctor was wrong? Could he convince his father to leave London? He would be far more comfortable at home, Edward knew, but then Edward would have far fewer options for a bride. Which is to say none.

"How can I help?" Bennett asked after a few minutes.

Edward smiled. "Just being able to talk to you is helping. Thank you. And if you happen to know of any young ladies who might possibly wish to marry the illegitimate son of a merchant? Well, perhaps you could share their names." He paused, then raised an eyebrow at his friend. "If only I could find a lady like Lady Olivia to propose to me, I wouldn't have to do any of the hard work."

Bennett emitted a short laugh, even though he winced. "Lady Olivia is very certain about things."

"It must be so difficult being as irresistible as you are," Edward replied in a dry tone.

Bennett laughed, then his expression changed. It was one Edward had seen many times before, and usually it meant that Edward was about to get in trouble. And then Bennett would feel terrible. But not before a wrong was righted.

He hadn't seen it in years, however.

"I am thinking," Bennett began, "perhaps you could distract Lady Olivia?"

"With what, my birth?" Edward spoke more roughly than he'd intended; the lady's blurted-out insult still smarted.

"Ouch, no." Bennett paused, then shook his head. "No, it probably won't work."

"What won't?" Now he had to know precisely what his friend was thinking.

"Your getting to know Olivia. Perhaps being able to gently suggest she look elsewhere for a husband."

"You have no interest in her, then?" Edward

couldn't keep the skepticism from his tone; after all, he'd seen the lady, all the vibrating intensity of her. She was lovely, and she seemed eminently suitable to marry Bennett.

"I do not." Bennett spoke with a finality that emphasized his statement. "But I do not wish her to be hurt."

"Of course you don't," Edward interjected.

"And you're charming, when you want to be. You could get to know her."

"If she would allow it," Edward retorted.

"If presented the right way, she will take it as a challenge."

He already knew Bennett was right about that; her words at the ball were proof. The lady seemed to live for challenges, undeterred by anything that might stand in her way.

Which made him concerned for Bennett, but he knew his friend could take care of himself.

"Fine. I'll do it."

Distracting Lady Olivia would also be a good distraction from his worry for his father. And if he could help his friend as his friend had helped him for so many years?

By spending time with a woman who crackled with life, who made him want to touch her to see if she actually sparked?

He would gladly do it all.

EDWARD ALLOWED HIMSELF to think about her as he mounted his horse, one of his own that he'd brought with him from the country.

"Settle down, Chrysanthemum," he said as the mare sidestepped skittishly.

She liked London society less than he did, which was why he urged her into a trot, heading straight for the park.

It was early, far too early for anybody who might snub him to be out of doors. Which was why he continued to keep country hours—at least for waking—while in London.

He did like London, at least at this time of day. People were out doing work, not paying him any attention, which was just what he wanted.

Chrysanthemum settled into a regular pace, and he took a moment to appreciate the passing view—tall, thin houses gradually giving way to broader expanses of green as they approached the park. A pack of workers with shovels and spades headed into the park also, probably to beautify it before the right people appeared to tour its perimeter.

And when had he gotten so critical? He hadn't always felt the sting of his birth so keenly, but here, here where Society could—and did— punish him for something that happened before he was born made him even more aware of who he was.

Thank goodness for his father, who had been able to see past the prejudice and love Edward as his own.

He urged Chrysanthemum into a gallop, lowering himself over her mane, looking between her ears toward the vast expanse of green.

He gripped her sides with his thighs, urging her faster, and faster still, feeling all of his pent-up anger and energy dissipate with each passing step.

"Good girl," he murmured as she continued her fierce and furious pace.

Fierce and furious returned his thoughts to her. Of course.

Lady Olivia was just as determined to run as Chrysanthemum, only in her case it was to run toward injustice. To gallop hard against indifference and intolerance.

She used her clout to further others who couldn't do it on their own. No wonder she was so determined to assist him, though he knew he was strong enough to withstand whatever Society might throw his way.

But his father wasn't. Or, rather, his father would prefer to see his only son participating in the race, not observing from outside, or worse yet, forbidden to even watch.

He needed her help. He should admit that, if not to her, at least to himself. She was a duke's daughter, she could enter worlds and speak to people he could not. Would not, if he had his preference.

But he didn't. He owed it to his father, at least, to try. He was doubtful of his ability to succeed, but he had to try.

"Do you see him?" Olivia asked Pearl. They were at the Lindens' party that evening, a small affair with no dancing offered, which meant that there were only two hundred people or so in attendance.

Two hundred people, all of whom appeared to be taller than Olivia, so why she was asking her shorter sister was a good question. But not the one she'd asked.

"Which one? Lord Carson or the other one, Mr. Whatever-Is-His-Name?" Pearl snapped back. She was not in a good mood. She'd been forced to attend this evening, despite claiming a headache.

Olivia suspected it was because she actually wanted to stay at home and play with the kittens rather than go to yet another Society function where she'd attempt to sneak into the corner and Olivia would drag her back out.

It was unfortunate that Pearl was so shy, but Olivia knew it was her duty to ensure her twin was known to as many people as possible so that she could hopefully meet the man she would marry.

"You never met Mr. *Wolcott*," Olivia said, emphasizing his last name. She regretted even thinking of him as "the bastard." And that she had said it to his face! If she ever admitted she had done something wrong, she would definitely be admitting it now.

Thankfully, she did not.

"So you are asking me if I see Lord Carson? Be more specific, Olivia, for goodness' sake," Pearl grumbled. "Besides which, no. I have not. As you have frequently noted, you are taller than I am, and neither one of us can see past this wall of lordly height," she continued, still in the same tone of voice.

It was true that there were quite a few gentlemen standing in front of them, their broad, dark backs the only thing either she or Pearl could see. But that kind of impediment wouldn't stop Olivia from finding him. Surely he would want to know the kindness she was going to do for his friend.

"Ah, there he is!" she announced. "And Mr. Wolcott is there too." She began to walk forward, then remembered Pearl. "You don't mind . . . ?" she began, only to stop speaking as Pearl shook her head far more vehemently than the occasion warranted. And then, predictably, she escaped from the ballroom to go out onto the terrace.

"Fine, then," she muttered to herself. With her eagerness to avoid crowds and parties, Pearl might have to find her own husband.

Perhaps the gentleman was wandering through the maze beyond the terrace. And then Pearl would get lost, and he would help her, and Olivia wouldn't have to worry about her any longer.

But she couldn't lose herself in thoughts about her sister, not right now. She had other things to worry about.

Decided on her priorities, she stepped past one of the dark coats in front of her to where Bennett and his friend were standing.

As she walked toward them, she couldn't help but notice how attractive Mr. Wolcott was. And not in the traditionally handsome way Bennett was; Mr. Wolcott looked wild, and fierce. His dark hair, while brushed and in place, had a curly unruliness to it that made him look untamed. He was clean-shaven, but his cheeks were stubbled, making him look more dangerous. His eyes were dark as well, focused on the crowd with a wary intensity that made her very glad he was not looking at her.

And where Bennett's form was sleek and lean, Mr. Wolcott was both broad and angular, his shoulders wide, his legs long and lean and encased in his evening trousers.

Everything about him, not just his birth, seemed as though he had been made without attention to propriety. He was unsettling. And she had never been unsettled by anyone before.

She would have her work cut out for her, taking this dangerous-looking person and making him appear to be a respectable gentleman.

As much to herself as to her world.

Chapter 5

Never back away from a chance to do something right. No matter how much personal turmoil it might cause you.

LADY OLIVIA'S PARTICULAR GUIDE TO DECORUM

*G*ood evening, Lord Carson." It was her again, the lady who practically vibrated she was so alive. Edward felt his skin prickle as though she'd touched him.

"And good evening, Mr. Wolcott," she added with a bright smile directed squarely at him.

It was a hefty weapon, her smile. At least to him. He felt flattened by it, aware of what she thought of him but still unable to keep himself from feeling more intrigued and interested by her.

"Good evening, Lady Olivia," Bennett replied in his usual charming tone. As though the lady hadn't offered him a marriage proposal the previous evening, which he'd firmly rejected.

Edward had to admire his friend's aplomb.

"Good evening," he echoed, bowing.

"I am glad you are both here," Lady Olivia said, shifting her gaze from Edward to Bennett and back again. "I have something I wish to say to both of you." Edward's unease grew; what knowledge was this unexpected woman about to impart? Judging by the pleased expression on her face, it was something that brought her pleasure. But since the only time he'd heard her speak her mind it was to announce that she and Bennett shared mutual feelings for one another—well, he did not trust her to know what would bring happiness to anyone.

"What is it?" Bennett sounded as wary as Edward felt. His aplomb had deserted him, no doubt scurrying away to regroup after feeling the force of her personality.

"Well," she replied, beaming in satisfaction. "I have thought of something I can do to help your situation."

"What situation?" Edward blurted out. She gave him a reproving look.

"The situation of your acceptance into Society, Mr. Wolcott, since you asked," she replied. Sounding as though she were delivering a lecture, not speaking in conversation. "I know there are many who would snub you for the circumstances of your birth," she began, her cheeks coloring as she spoke. Because she had snubbed him herself? Even called him a bastard?

"And it is my duty to ensure you are fully accepted by everyone whom you might meet." She gave a firm nod as she finished speaking. As though what she had said would be done merely because she had said it.

"It doesn't work that way," Edward said. Bennett shot him a look, which he ignored. He needed to tell this insufferable, vibrantly blazing woman that it wasn't that easy, despite how simple she made it sound.

He also had to admit to not wanting to see her hopes crushed so soon after having them crushed by his best friend. If she knew how hard it would be, she would be better prepared for when she failed.

"You can't just bestow a few smiles and dances on me, introduce me to your friends and family, and expect that everyone will be absolutely fine with the circumstances of my birth. It doesn't work that way," he repeated, realizing that now *he* was vibrating, but with anger.

Not necessarily at her, but because of the entire situation. How was it possible that a piece of paper could stand in the way of his being accepted? Of making friends? Of finding a bride?

Of pleasing his father?

Lady Olivia lifted her chin, a fiery, determined look in her eye. The one he was coming to both dread and admire. "But, Mr. Wolcott, here is the thing. I am the Duke of Marymount's daughter. I have successfully helped a wide variety of people and causes—"

"Such as?" Edward interrupted.

Her color heightened, and she glared at him as much as a young lady at a polite Society party could. "I am on the committee for the Society for Poor and Orphaned Children, I am a strong supporter of mothers' rights, and I do not back down from something I see as wrong."

He'd want to laugh if she weren't absolutely serious. "You are saying that because you have shown up at some meetings and possibly spoken out—shocking some people, I'm sure—that you can force my acceptance into the most entrenched company?"

Her mouth opened as Bennett stepped between them, putting his hand on Edward's arm. Edward hadn't realized he was only a few inches away from her, close enough to see the golden lights in her hazel eyes, close enough to kiss.

Not that he wanted to do that. Not at all. He was furious with her—wasn't he?

"I might have a solution," Bennett said in his calm, arguing-a-bill-in-the-House-of-Commons voice.

Edward turned to regard Bennett with one brow raised. "What do you suggest?" he asked. Was this Bennett's distraction plan? The one that would keep the lady from proposing again and Edward from losing his temper? Even though he'd found himself nearly as amused as he was frustrated, which was different from usual. Normally he just growled inside his head, but at least now he wanted to laugh also.

She was still looking at him, her cheeks flushed red, her lush mouth set into a firm line. As though she had much more to say but was being polite.

"Well," Bennett began, gesturing between them. "Edward, you have a situation, one that requires you to be accepted by Society."

He was not going to—

"Which is that your father has made it clear he wishes you to marry someone deserving of you. Someone of gentle breeding and good stock."

He was. Now who was the bastard?

"You're not saying she—and I," Edward sputtered, gesturing between them.

She looked more startled than he felt, which was saying something.

"No," Bennett said hurriedly. "Not that. Just that if it were to be seen that Lady Olivia found favor with you, perhaps it would be easier for you to find a lady who would suit. And," he continued, turning to Lady Olivia, "I believe there is no better person who could assist my good friend in finding a wife."

Lady Olivia's expression changed from horror to relief. Edward wished that didn't bother him quite so much.

"Oh, what a splendid idea!" she said, smiling. Her whole face was lit, her eyes wide and excited. Her lips shaped into a perfect O of delight, making Edward lose his focus for a moment.

What would it be like to kiss that mouth? Those rosy lips that seemed to be so bitable?

Although he knew full well that was not at all in the lady's thoughts, given her reaction to even the possibility of marrying him.

She took his arm, nodding to Bennett at the same time. "If you do not mind, Lord Carson, I will whisk your friend away so we can discuss this further in private. Thank you so much for bringing us together."

Edward couldn't help but notice Bennett's look of smug satisfaction as Olivia steered him toward two chairs at the edge of the ballroom.

OLIVIA TRIED TO calm her breathing, but for once she was not in control. Not of her breath, her future, or of how she felt when she was in Mr. Wolcott's presence.

As he had been the first evening she had seen him, he was dressed impeccably, all of his clothing obviously tailored precisely to his admittedly attractive body.

She was surprised he didn't tip over because his shoulders were so wide and his waist and hips were so lean. If she had paid more attention to her governess when she was discussing maths and gravity and other things that made no sense to Olivia, perhaps she could have understood it better.

As it was, she just had admiration for the entire presentation of him.

And now he was one of her official projects, perhaps the most important project of her life: if she were to get him accepted into Society and find him a bride, Bennett would finally see she was the wife he was meant to have.

So it was terribly vital that she not get distracted by pondering the strength of Mr. Wolcott's arms. Or how his dark curls made him look like a rakish devil. Or how his legs were so long his tailor must have charged him more for his trousers.

But from what she knew, Mr. Wolcott could well afford it, given who his father was.

Olivia nodded to Mr. Wolcott to sit as she was sitting down on one of the chairs. "Please get comfortable, Mr. Wolcott. I will have several questions for you."

She regretted that her small evening purse couldn't accommodate a notebook and pencil so she could jot down what he said. She'd just have to try to remember.

"I appreciate your interest, my lady," he said, grimacing as he spoke. As though he did not appreciate her interest. "But there is no need for you to concern yourself with—with any of this," he said, gesticulating toward where the party-goers danced and chatted on, unaware that there was a great miscarriage of justice in their midst.

"But I am concerned, sir," Olivia replied, edging her chair toward his in her enthusiasm. "I cannot stand by while there is someone who is in need of my help." She tried to forget that she herself had been guilty of miscarrying justice when it came to this particular man—after all, she'd been upset by what Bennett had said. How they would all laugh together when it was settled and she and Bennett were married, and Mr. Wolcott had found a bride of his own.

She smiled to herself at the thought.

"You often come to people's rescue, then?" Mr. Wolcott said in a milder tone. It seemed as if he were actually curious, which warmed her heart. And made her realize how few of the people she spoke to seemed to show interest in anything she championed. Except for Pearl, but it was part of being a twin to show interest in things.

"I do." She took a deep breath, wishing she weren't in a constricting evening gown. What if she were called upon to right a wrong? A wrong that required freedom of movement?

She would have to decline because she was elegantly garbed. Not really the type of excuse she would stand for from anyone else, let alone herself.

"I will not allow anyone to suffer because I did not do something, you see, Mr. Wolcott," she explained. "I am fortunate enough to have been born to wealth and privilege. It is my duty to use that position to help those who are less fortunate than I."

"And if they do not want your help?"

The words cut uncomfortably close to what Pearl had said: *These are men you are dealing with, not unfed orphans or gentlewomen who just need a bit of embroidery to brighten their day.*

"I . . ." she began, only to realize she had no idea what to do if someone didn't want her help. She did not think it had happened in the time since she had become aware of injustice, and things that needed doing. By her.

Speaking of which, she had seven shifts to make before the end of the month. And now she had to find Mr. Wolcott a bride. It shouldn't be too difficult. Mr. Wolcott was attractive, no matter his birth.

Plus Pearl was quite good at sewing, so she would likely be able to assist.

"The situation has not come up," she said firmly. Ignoring the image of Pearl's raised brow in her mind.

"Of course not." Was he laughing at her? How dare he? He was just a—well, no, she couldn't think of him that way, not if he was to be her project. Her mission.

"But tell me," she began, hoping she hadn't revealed her thoughts on her face, "what are your most important attributes for a bride?"

She settled back in her chair, clasping her hands in her lap, her eyes focused on him. On that unruly hair that curled down over one eye, giving him an almost piratical look. On how, although he was seated, he looked like he was still moving, even though he was still. As though he was an arrow waiting to be shot straight into someone's heart.

Not hers, of course. And speaking of hearts, he hadn't answered, even though she had given him plenty of opportunity.

"Well?" she demanded, tilting her head to look at him pointedly. "You were going to say?"

DAMN, BUT SHE was likely the most managing female he'd ever met. Not that he'd met that many; the women in his father's household were servants, and he rarely interacted with them. The women he chose for more pleasurable pursuits seldom argued with what he wanted to do to them, since they seemed to enjoy it so much.

But still. He wondered if she would be just as authoritative in more intimate circumstances. He grinned to himself as he imagined it—*caress my breast more slowly, Mr. Wolcott*—then swiftly smoothed his expression so she wouldn't demand to know what he was thinking of.

What had she asked, anyway?

Oh, of course. The kind of woman he wanted for a bride.

He couldn't tell her the first thought that came into his mind—one who was of respectable enough breeding to please his father, but not so aristocratic that she would spend the rest of her life looking down on her husband.

He didn't think such a woman existed anyway.

"The type of woman I desire," he said, mostly to buy himself some time to think of something to say. "She should be intelligent." Because he could not be married to someone who wasn't, although that might further limit his choice. "And interested in a variety of things so we have conversational topics to discuss in the evenings."

She looked at him blankly.

And spoke after a moment. "Is that all you want, Mr. Wolcott?"

Is that all you want?

Well, he wished he could announce that he

didn't want any of it, that he would have to compromise something to find a lady who would marry him. Either she would be dimwitted enough to accept the bastard son of a merchant, or she would be so desperate that she would take marriage to him, which would mean that she hadn't received any other offers.

It did not bode well for him. He returned her gaze, crossing his arms over his chest. He wished he could just stalk away from the conversation, leave her to her managing ways, watch as she tried to lure Bennett into—no, that wouldn't be fair. Not to his friend, even though he had no doubt that Bennett could keep himself out of this woman's thrall.

Although Edward had to ask why his friend was so determined.

"You're asking me what I want in a wife, Lady Olivia, when you should be asking what it would take for a lady to marry me. I suggest," Edward said, "that you compile a list of ladies whose families are in great need of funds. Those are the only types of ladies who would even deign to consider me as a suitor." He took a deep breath. "And if any of those ladies are also intelligent and curious, you will have exceeded my expectations."

Even as irritated as he was with her, and her questions, he couldn't deny that she was deliciously attractive. Her eyes sparkled with a fierce intent, and she was breathing rapidly, likely in outrage, which made her breasts push up against the bodice of her gown. A gown that was exquisitely designed for her, with tiny puffed sleeves and an alluring edging of lace at her neckline that shifted as she moved, making his eyes leap to see if anything more would reveal itself.

Sadly, she was enough of a proper young woman that nothing did, but he couldn't keep himself from looking.

He was nothing if not optimistic.

Only he absolutely wasn't, he had to admit—from the first time he'd noticed he was treated differently from other boys until this very moment, he was suspicious and wary of everyone. Not without cause; this lady herself had called him a bastard before realizing he was acquainted with Bennett. It was only because she was hoping to impress Bennett that she was undertaking this mission to make him respectable in the first place.

"Intelligent and curious. That is what you want in a wife." She sounded disappointed, and he felt a surge of anger rise up.

"I promise you, my lady, that even those requirements will be near impossible to fill."

Her eyes glittered with determination. If only—

No, one of his conditions was that his wife not

look down on him—at least not much—because of his birth. And Lady Olivia made it clear, with every raised eyebrow, each patronizing question, that she did look down on him. He might find her attractive, even alluring, but he would never consider marriage to her. She was too far above him, in her own mind as well as in reality, to waste a moment thinking of her that way.

Besides which, she believed herself to be in love with his closest friend.

"I have never failed when I have resolved to do something, Mr. Wolcott," she announced. For a moment, he almost believed her. "Not only will I get you accepted properly into Society, I will find a suitable lady that you will be pleased to marry."

He felt his lips curl up into a wry grin. "That is a lofty promise, my lady. I will give you a month." He shrugged, feeling the weight of her gaze on his face. "If you can accomplish what you've promised in that time, I will . . ." What could he offer her? He couldn't promise her Bennett. But he did have his wealth. "I will donate one thousand pounds to the charity of your choice."

That would appeal both to her charitable interests and to her assumption that she would succeed at anything she was challenged to do.

She smiled in satisfaction and held her hand to him. "That is a bargain, Mr. Wolcott."

As he took her slim hand in his and shook it to

seal the deal, he found himself—oddly enough—looking forward to the next thirty days, whereas before he had been dreading it.

"You can start tomorrow," Edward said, rising from his seat. If he was going to be presented as a respectable member of Society, he wanted to get good and drunk first. To forget for a moment who he was, and most important, what he was. The bastard son of an indulgent father who didn't see the stings and barbs tossed toward Edward in myriad ways.

"Tomorrow," she agreed.

Chapter 6

Sometimes people do not know what is best for them. It is your duty to show them the way.
LADY OLIVIA'S PARTICULAR GUIDE TO DECORUM

"Olivia!"

Olivia sighed as she heard her mother's voice. She was already having a frustrating morning, what with snarling the thread nearly every time she tried to sew. She couldn't help but realize her entire life was made up of deadlines—she had to deliver shifts by a certain time, respectability and a bride to Mr. Wolcott in a month, and then allow Lord Carson to see the error of his ways and ask for her hand in marriage before her father the duke took his children to the country so he could go hunting.

She did not like hunting.

But these deadlines were all her own fault, brought on by her own determination to do what was right, so she couldn't complain.

Even though you are complaining, Pearl's voice pointed out in her head.

"Coming, Mother," she replied, placing her sewing on the table. She smoothed her gown, picking a few stray threads off her skirts as she walked down the hallway to her mother's sitting room.

"Yes?" she said as she entered, glancing around the room to see what she might have to fix. It was remarkable how many things suddenly needed her attention now that her older sisters were not in residence. She didn't mind being in charge, of course; but she did wish her mother and the household in general were less in need of her attention.

She had wrongs to right and wives to find outside of the home.

"Olivia, what is this I hear about your speaking with that—that person?" her mother asked.

Olivia regarded her mother in confusion. "What person?" Cook was the last person her mother had asked her to speak to, and Olivia couldn't see what her mother's issue might be.

"Mr. Beechcroft's . . . son," she replied in a stiff voice.

The flare of indignant anger rose up in her chest. But despite her mother's casual dismissal of doing anything that required her to think or act, she would not allow Olivia to lecture her.

Olivia had discovered that, to her chagrin, when she had tried to inform her mother about the conditions at the workhouse.

She had learned to escape the house without being entirely clear about where she was going. Her mother was too distracted by her various and multiple thoughts about the weather, her tea, her lady's maid's latest illness, and other extremely important things to bother about where her daughter was going.

Even though her daughter Della had done the same thing, culminating in an elopement with the girls' dancing instructor. You'd think their mother would have begun to pay more attention to what her remaining daughters were doing, but it seemed she just couldn't be bothered.

"Mr. Wolcott?" Olivia replied in a casual tone of voice. She couldn't let her mother know that Mr. Wolcott was her latest project. "Lord Carson introduced us. He is a great friend to Lord Carson," she added, knowing her mother would seize on that point to allow Olivia to keep his acquaintance.

The only thing she and her mother agreed on, actually, was that Olivia should be married to Lord Carson. Persuading her mother that being polite to Mr. Wolcott would speed the betrothal would allow her to work unimpeded on the Wolcott Project.

"Oh, I did not know that," her mother replied, patting the chair next to her. "Come sit down and tell me all about this gentleman. A friend of Lord Carson's, you say? You know your father and I have great expectations of your succeeding where Eleanor . . . did not," she said, her nose wrinkling at the last two words.

If only the rest of Society were as malleable as her mother. Or wanted something as desperately as the duchess wanted this marriage between her and Bennett.

Almost as much as Olivia wanted it.

She sat down, exhaling in relief. "He is well-spoken." Especially when pointing out how grossly she'd misread Bennett's feelings for her. But she wouldn't be sharing that with her mother. Besides which, she would be changing Bennett's mind very soon. "And quite polite, despite being . . ." And then she paused. She couldn't very well say "a bastard" to her mother. "Born as he was," she finished weakly.

Her mother frowned. "But is he respectable? Does he fit in? It would be horrible if anyone thought less of Lord Carson because of his choice of friend."

Does he fit in? No, he doesn't. And not just because of his birth. He stands out, in words and appearance and behavior. Telling me never to let anyone see my pain.

His hair, his looks, his build, were all dangerous. Everything he was combined to become a veritable force, a fearsome storm of fire and emotion and passion.

Not the usual mild type of gentleman Olivia was familiar with. Even Bennett's presence seemed to dim in Mr. Wolcott's company, not that she'd admit that. Beyond the confines of her own mind, that is.

Or perhaps to Pearl. But that was it.

"He is a gentleman," Olivia replied in a firm tone. "He was at school with Lord Carson, and you would never know he was not one of us."

She was keenly aware of a prickling, guilty sensation flowing through her. *Not one of us.* It sounded so condescending, something Pearl would point out to her, even though it wasn't how she meant it.

Although it wouldn't matter how she meant it if he heard it. It sounded terrible.

"As long as you don't get it into your head to fall in love with him or anything," the duchess said, her tone indicating just how ridiculous a proposition that was. Olivia forced an amused smile to her mouth. Did she sound so snobbish when she spoke? The thought made her cringe.

"Being polite to him and allowing him to dance with you every so often is only genteel. Plus I understand his father has quite a lot of money," her mother added, ruining the effect of charity. "And Lord Carson will take it as a compliment that you are so kind to his friend. I had thought he would have asked by now."

"Quite a lot of money," Olivia said hastily, wanting to divert her mother's attention from a proposal from Lord Carson. Soon enough, Olivia promised herself.

"Well, then, as a polite gesture, you can invite him to dine with us when the Marquis of Wheatley comes in a few days. He will even out the table." The duchess made it sound as though it was a grand, beneficent gesture—and it would be, if Mr. Wolcott's father wasn't so rich as to remove the taint of his son's birth.

"Of course," Olivia agreed, even though inside she wasn't certain how to feel. On one hand, she was pleased her mother was being so generous, but she had to admit—this time to only herself, Pearl would not understand—that Mr. Wolcott made her feel all prickly and odd in a way she'd never felt before.

And there was the fact that her mother would likely exhibit the same kind of condescension she'd just expressed, and Olivia didn't want Mr. Wolcott to feel uncomfortable.

That must be the cause of the prickly sensation, she decided. Not because of him, and how she felt around him, but because she was so acutely sensitive to other people's emotions. It was what made her so good when she visited the Society for Poor and Orphaned Children. Sometimes she had to close her eyes when she visited the home, since the suffering was too much for her sensitivity.

And if she were able to secure Mr. Wolcott a place in Society and a bride, she would have gained the society one thousand pounds, which would go a long way toward reducing their suffering. Which would then relieve her nerves.

Speaking of which, she had promised she would start tomorrow, meaning today. "Excuse me, Mother," she said as she stepped toward the door. "I have to go see about things."

Which if her mother were a normal parent would be insufficiently clear, but because the duchess seldom listened to anybody but herself, and even then only listened about half the time, Olivia's vague statement wouldn't be questioned at all.

No wonder Della and then Eleanor had been able to go fall in love and do something about it without anybody noticing. It had worked out wonderfully for Eleanor, now married to Bennett's brother, although not so well for Della, whose last letter had contained the news that her lover—never her husband—had left her and now she had a daughter.

Eleanor had refused Olivia's assistance in helping Della, saying that it might jeopardize the girls' reputations if it were known they were in contact with their scandalous older sister. A refusal that rankled, since Olivia knew she could help if given the chance.

But she should be grateful she hadn't been, since now she had a task that would take all of her time.

"A LADY OLIVIA is here, sir," the butler said with a faint raise of his eyebrow.

The butler, as well as the rest of the staff, had come along with the town house rental. The owners of the property had taken themselves off to the country to recoup their finances following a disastrous turn at the tables by their oldest son. Mr. Beechcroft hadn't quibbled at the price they asked for the property, provided the house came with a full staff.

Edward knew his father had long ago learned to turn a blind eye to perceived slights. He had been a wealthy businessman working with and among the aristocratic elite for too long not to be inured to it.

But Edward still winced every time he caught

one of the upper staff's moue of disdain at having to take direction from people they would not normally be in service to.

He wished he could somehow communicate that they were not so very different from one another; he and his father had none of the breeding required to be in polite society, and his father had come up from the working class to where he was now.

But he supposed that the snobbishness of the upper class was matched by the snobbishness of the people who served them. At least that was how it felt to him.

"Where have you put her?" Edward asked tersely. This would be something for the staff to chew over as well; why was a duke's daughter paying a call on Mr. Beechcroft's natural son? He should have anticipated her foolhardiness and arranged to meet her on neutral ground.

Although there was no neutral ground possible between them, and that was the entire problem. He was not of her world, no matter how much money he had. Nor was she of his; she didn't know what work was, what it was like to be dismissed because of her birth.

"She is in the yellow salon," the butler replied.

Edward nodded, and walked quickly down the hall.

"GOOD AFTERNOON, MY lady." She was standing by the window, her fingers on the sill. She jumped as he spoke, and he wondered what had her thinking so deeply.

"Good afternoon, Mr. Wolcott."

He felt his throat thicken as he looked at her. She was so lovely, so shiningly beautiful, it nearly hurt. She wore a pale cream-colored gown trimmed with green ribbons, and her hair was neatly dressed, pulled away from her face with a few strands artfully falling in front of her ears.

"I hadn't realized when you said we would start tomorrow—that is, today—that you would pay a call here. Are you certain that is appropriate?"

"Of course it is," she said, gesturing to the corner of the room. "I have my sister here with me, and our ladies' maid is taking tea in the kitchen."

Edward glanced to where a young lady was hunched over a book in the corner. A book she quickly covered with her hand as he approached. Interesting.

"I haven't met you yet, have I?" he asked, walking forward to her.

She shook her head, not meeting his eyes. Where her sister was all bright lightness, this lady was a study in contrast—black hair, pale skin, and dark eyes.

"That is my sister Ida. I told her you had a massive library she could visit if she would come here. My family knows the owners of the property, you see, and while I prefer to be doing things, Ida enjoys reading about things."

Edward suppressed a smile at Lady Olivia's dismissal of her sister's academic pursuits.

"Of course, you are welcome to peruse the library. It is just—"

"I know where it is," Lady Ida said, interrupting. She rose and gave a brisk nod to her sister. "You've got half an hour and then we have to go."

Edward watched bemusedly as she marched out the door.

"Well," he said, turning back around to Lady Olivia, "we have half an hour. What can we accomplish in that time?"

WHAT CAN WE accomplish in that time?

For a moment, Olivia just stood and stared at him, his words conjuring up all sorts of things that were not pertinent to why she was there. Images of him taking her in his arms, pressing his mouth against hers, letting her slide her fingers through those unruly curls.

She was in love with Bennett, not his friend. She needed to remember that.

Although perhaps you aren't so in love with him if

you could be so distracted, a voice said in her head. The voice sounded remarkably like Pearl's voice, which annoyed her even further.

"I have a list," she said, drawing a piece of paper from her reticule.

"Of course you do," he replied in a dry tone of voice. Was he laughing at her?

"Are you laughing at me?" she asked. She might as well say aloud what she was thinking. It wasn't as though she had to be the polite young lady around him. She was only with him to fulfill her part of the bargain, not to endear herself to him.

It felt wonderful, if she were being honest with herself. To be honest aloud, unlike the usual softening of tone and opinion she had to force herself into when out in company.

Although she didn't always succeed there, as past encounters showed.

"I think I am," he replied in a surprised tone. "I haven't had much cause to laugh lately, so thank you."

She sat down in the chair closest to her, and gestured for him to take the one opposite. "It's been that bad, has it?" She felt her chest start to burn with her righteous anger.

He sat down, crossing his long legs, momentarily distracting her with wondering just how long they were.

"It's not what you think," he replied, his voice soft. "It doesn't bother me as much as it used to. It's something else." His mouth tightened into a thin line. "It's something I don't feel like discussing."

"Oh." Olivia bit her lip to keep from peppering him with questions, questions he already said he did not wish to answer. But that was the unfortunate thing about her, she already knew; once there was a mystery to be uncovered, or a wrong to be righted, she wouldn't rest—or stop asking questions—until she solved it.

But if he refused to speak with her because she had pressed him too hard, she would never have the satisfaction of seeing him received in Society, nor would he donate a thousand pounds.

Nor would he be happily married.

Nor would *she* be happily married. That was the most important reason of all.

Although that thought didn't please her as much as it should have. This was all for her eventual marriage to Lord Carson. That was why she was doing it, she reminded herself.

"Your list," he said, stretching his hand out. "Can I see it?"

"Yes, of course," she said, holding it out for him to take. His fingers brushed hers during the exchange, and she felt a shiver run through her.

He unfolded the paper and smoothed it out so

he could read it. She watched, fascinated by the firm gesture. His fingers were long and thick, not the gentleman's hands she was accustomed to seeing. His nails were clean, but cut short, likely to be able to write more efficiently. She spotted a dot of ink on his ring finger and smiled to herself.

"A list of potential brides?" he said after a moment, lifting his gaze to hers. "Do you know if they meet my standards? Even though my standards are, as you said, quite limited." He looked back down, his eyebrows drawing together in a frown. "I have been introduced to a few of these ladies already, and I highly doubt if they would wish to be on this list." He looked back up, a rueful smile on his mouth. "And the ones who have not been openly rude are likely just biding their time until they can be."

Olivia felt her cheeks heat. In embarrassment over her fellow Society ladies' despicable behavior, or in having presented the list in the first place, she didn't know. She snatched the paper back from him and crumpled it up in a ball in her hand.

"You have to be open-minded about this," she said, the words spilling out in a rush. "It is not as easy as just selecting an item from a menu."

"But it's your menu," he shot back. "Wasn't that why you came over with this list? To see which lady piqued my interest, even though marriage is not a matter of choosing a name and proceeding?"

"Oh, and what do you know about marriage?" she replied, clapping her hand over her mouth as she realized what she'd said.

His lips curled into a smile devoid of humor. "Exactly. I know nothing of marriage, not having witnessed one in my own life."

Oh no. She'd done it again. Spoken without considering whom she was talking to, a man who'd grown up keenly aware of the stigma of his birth.

She released her hand from her mouth and took a deep breath. "I apologize, Mr. Wolcott. That was—"

"Thoughtless? But also expected?" His voice held a bitter tone that felt as though it was actually stinging her.

"Both," she said quietly. Her cheeks were hot, flushed with embarrassment. And then her whole body followed suit, making it feel as though she were standing next to a hot oven.

"The thing is," she said, licking her lips, which felt suddenly dry, "that you will never be able to find a suitable wife if you believe every single female you meet is likely to reject you."

He raised a brow. "Is that your strategy? Believing anyone you decide upon will wish to have you?"

The words stung. Was it because they were true? She couldn't think about that now. She would not think about that now.

"We're not discussing my situation, Mr. Wolcott." She glanced at the clock in the corner, noting it had already been fifteen minutes. "We don't have much more time before Ida returns, and we should have a plan in place to accomplish your goal."

"*Your* goal," he corrected. "Being properly received in Society is your goal, not mine. I have no hopes of it."

"But you do wish to be married," she retorted. "And in order to find someone, you'll need to overcome the hurdle of your birth."

"Thank you for acknowledging it is a hurdle. Most ladies don't even mention it. They just sniff and look anywhere but at me."

"Goodness, why wouldn't they want to know you? I mean, just look at you!" Of course she spoke without thinking. But then again, it gave her the excuse to just look at him herself.

So tall and handsome and wildly, virilely attractive. That hair of his curling everywhere, as untamed as he seemed to be. And yet he spoke and acted politely, far more assured than many of the young lords she had met in Society. It was just that his politeness seemed to encase someone else entirely different, an outsized man whose passion and intensity might scorch her if she got too close.

She was not going to allow herself to get too close.

Was she?

"You do have a point." He spoke reluctantly, and Olivia tried not to be smugly pleased he had agreed with her. More people should do that in general; it would make her life so much easier. "So what is your suggestion? Beyond making a list of ladies who would be horrified if I came courting?"

Olivia folded her hands in her lap. "I suppose I will have to rethink my tactics."

He nodded at her to continue.

"I will ask if there are families in particularly desperate financial straits, as you suggested earlier. And to those families, we will need to show your good points. To prove that you should be viewed in the same light as any other young gentleman." She couldn't help but look at him again; it felt as though her eyes were drawn to him in a way they had never wanted to look at anything before. Not even Bennett, with whom she was madly in love.

"You and I will appear in company together. I will introduce you to the people I know, and they will come to know you as well."

"Bennett has tried that, you know," he said drily. "How will you succeed where he has not?"

"Well," she said in a prim voice, "Lord Carson is capable in so many ways, but he is not a lady. He doesn't know what ladies find intriguing about gentlemen." He kept his gaze steady on her, making her wish she wasn't too old to squirm in her seat under the scrutiny.

"Because he's not a lady," she repeated, and then his expression relaxed, and it looked almost as though he wanted to laugh.

Chapter 7

In order to achieve great accomplishments, it is important to be greatly confident.

LADY OLIVIA'S PARTICULAR GUIDE TO DECORUM

*E*dward!"

Edward started as he heard his father's voice. He'd been so engrossed in debating with Lady Olivia, he'd forgotten for a few moments about his father. It shouldn't make him feel guilty—his father wouldn't want that—but it did.

But she had thoroughly perplexed him and irked him and fascinated him. And she had made him laugh—when was the last time that had happened?

She and her silly list and her confident assertion that she could succeed where others had failed. He wondered whether Queen Victoria herself would be as regal as Lady Olivia.

He had to admire that, and he had to admire

her. Even if he knew that the two of them would likely be at loggerheads during this entire month.

At the end of which he would not have a bride, nor would he be any more accepted into her world, despite what she thought.

But it would keep his father content, and that was more important than his feeling that his efforts were futile. It didn't matter; nothing mattered except that Mr. Beechcroft's wishes—Edward didn't want to say final wishes—were honored.

And he would also be able to spend time with the most fascinating woman he'd ever met.

He would donate the thousand pounds to whatever cause she wished, no matter what happened; it was only money, he had plenty of it, and he knew whatever cause she championed was likely to be one that helped people less fortunate than she. Which was, barring the queen, everybody.

What must it be like to be the beloved child of a duke? To be accepted wherever she went, treated as though her opinions and presence were always welcome?

"Edward." His father spoke more strongly now, jarring Edward entirely out of his baffling thoughts. Thank goodness.

His father had walked into the room, accompanied by Lady Ida, both of them looking companionable with one another.

"You did not mention we had visitors," his father said, turning his warm smile to Lady Olivia. "And then I was in the library, and scared Lady Ida here."

"I was not scared," Lady Ida interrupted. "Merely startled."

His father rolled his eyes at her, then chucked her under the chin. An action that seemed to startle Lady Ida even more. And again, Edward felt like laughing.

"And then we got to talking, and it seems Lady Ida has interests in some of the same things I have."

"Even though some of his opinions are woefully behind the times," Lady Ida said, but in an amused tone, not as though she were judging.

"So I asked her why she was here in the first place, and she told me her sister was visiting my son. You are Lady Olivia, I presume?"

His father strode up to her, holding his hand out for her to take.

She blinked, then allowed him to enfold her hand in his, offering him a curtsey as she did. "It is a pleasure to meet you, Mr. Beechcroft," she said in a soft tone. Far softer than how she'd spoken to him, Edward noticed.

"Well, I knew we should not interrupt, but then Lady Ida said she had allowed you thirty minutes to discuss whatever it is you are discussing, which is . . . ?" And he trailed off, looking expectantly between Edward and Lady Olivia.

Judging by his expression, it was clear what Mr. Beechcroft thought they were discussing. Edward wanted to tell his father he was entirely and absolutely wrong about that—that Lady Olivia would never deign to even consider him as a suitor—but to mention it would be to hurt his father far more than allowing him to believe the lie would.

"We cannot share that, sir," Lady Olivia said. "It is a secret until it is not."

Now it was Lady Ida's turn to roll her eyes. "Being the very definition of secret, after all."

Lady Olivia dismissed her sister's words with a wave of her hand. "Never mind that." She looked at Edward. "So as we discussed, are you free to take me and my sister out for a carriage ride tomorrow?"

He wanted to laugh at the sheer brazenness of her. Of her assuming he would fall in with her plans just because she wished him to. Although that was what he was going to do, wasn't it? It was far too amusing, and he liked looking at her too much, to deny himself the pleasure.

"I am not going on a carriage ride," Lady Ida said.

"I meant Pearl, not you. I know you won't do anything that isn't sticking your nose in a book."

"Which means you could return here tomorrow," Mr. Beechcroft said in a delighted tone. "I want to ask your opinion of some books I've been thinking of rebinding. Whether they are worth the expense."

Lady Ida smiled a smile of genuine pleasure, and Edward felt his mouth start to gape at how it changed her. She was beautiful, although he wouldn't want to be the one to tell her. No doubt she thought that type of frivolity was beneath her.

"I would love to."

"Well, that is settled then," Lady Olivia said in satisfaction. "We will all come over here. Ida can stay while you take us out in your carriage. You do have a carriage, don't you?"

"Of course we do," Edward's father replied. "We might have a few of them, actually. So you can decide which would be best to go out in."

"That will be wonderful, but I will leave the choosing of the carriage up to Mr. Wolcott." Lady Olivia's expression as she looked at Edward appeared to indicate she had done him a great favor in allowing him to choose which carriage to use.

She really was the most managing female he'd ever encountered. And yet, somehow, he found it oddly endearing.

"Good afternoon, sir, Mr. Wolcott," Lady Olivia said as she marched toward the door, sweeping her sister up with her as she left the room.

Mr. Beechcroft walked after them, but not before turning around with a broad grin for Edward, accompanying his smile with a wink, just in case Edward wasn't clear enough about what his father thought was actually happening.

But if the ruse would keep his father content for a bit, he would continue it. And he would get to spend more time with the thoroughly sure of herself Lady Olivia.

Mr. Beechcroft reentered the room, rubbing his hands together and looking exceptionally pleased.

"Well, my boy, you have already begun to indulge your father's last wish."

Edward winced at his father's words, although the tone in which they were spoken was nearly giddy with glee.

"I have just met Lady Olivia." He turned away from his father, not able to look him in the eye and prevaricate, much less lie to his face. He'd just have to . . . lie by omission. "Bennett introduced us"—*in a manner of speaking, if you count being awkwardly in the room while the lady proposed to my friend an introduction*—"and she donates her time to various causes"—*including mine*—"so I wanted to ask her what effort was in the most need."

And the answer to that was me, and my effort to

find a place in this world that isn't tainted with disdain. Oh, and find a wife while I'm at it.

"Very clever, my lad." Edward heard the chair groan as his father sat. "Ladies have soft hearts, and if they think that a gentleman shares their concern—well, that is a good way to get them interested in you."

"Yes." Edward wished his father wasn't so optimistic about nearly everything—about Edward's place in the world, how people viewed both of them, that young titled ladies would even wish to be married to a bastard. It would make it so much easier to explain the truth when it came time for the truth to be explained.

"Maybe I won't die after all," his father continued, still in that same gleeful tone. "I want to be around to see what your children look like. I wonder if they will get your dark hair? Or take after their mother?"

"You are getting ahead of yourself, Father." Edward turned back around and sat in the chair opposite his father. This, at least, he could say without letting his father know all of his assumptions were false.

"The lady and I have just met, as I said, and you would not want me to take the first offer on the table, would you? It is not good business after all."

His father grinned, then laughed aloud. "You

are my son, that is for certain. Viewing things in such a business-like fashion, even though this is the business of the heart we are concerned with now."

Business of the heart. If only it were just a business and Edward could select what item he wished to own and then pay a certain sum of money to make the transaction.

Unfortunately, it wasn't. Instead, he'd have to go on carriage rides and speak with people who disliked him on principle and pretend that it wasn't ripping him apart inside that his father was dying.

He and Mr. Beechcroft both turned at the sound of footsteps outside in the entryway. The door flung open, and Lady Olivia stepped inside, a few strands of hair coming out from under her bonnet, which was a ridiculous concoction that made Edward wonder if it was deliberate on the part of the hatmaker to have it look like that.

"I forgot to mention that you would be receiving an invitation to dine with us later this week. Lord Carson and the marquis are coming, and it will be a small gathering. And of course you too, Mr. Beechcroft," she added, even though Edward was fairly certain his father would not have been invited if he hadn't been in the room at the time.

"Excellent, we will happily accept, won't we,

Edward?" his father said, rubbing his hands together again in what Edward knew was delight.

"Of course," he replied, bowing toward Lady Olivia.

"Good. I will let my mother know." And then she walked back out of the room, making it feel as though a light had been extinguished when she left.

"And I should go as well." Edward's father walked to the door, still smiling. "The duke and I have met, have done business together, but I have not yet been invited to his home. I have you to thank for that. And Lady Olivia, of course." His smile turned into a grin.

If it made him this happy—well, he'd pretend to court Lady Olivia as much as was necessary. And that way she could work on her own plan. And he would just be happy to watch as she tried to do the impossible.

"He actually agreed to your plan?"

Olivia scowled at the skepticism in her sister's voice.

"He did." Even though he also expressed probably even more skepticism than what Pearl was showing when he questioned her.

It had to work. She had never failed at anything she had decided to do. *Except get Bennett to admit he loves you and wants to marry you.*

But that too would change as soon as he realized the truth of his feelings and that she had been able to help his friend in a way nobody else could. Then he would agree.

"And this is why we are going out with him for a carriage ride?" Pearl asked. "Not that I mind going out for a carriage ride, it is outside, after all. I just want to know what I am supposed to be doing."

"Well, nothing really. We will nod and smile to everyone we know, and introduce Mr. Wolcott to our friends, and then they will see he is an ordinary person whom they should be pleased to call an acquaintance."

"Isn't that what Lord Carson has been doing all this time?"

Pearl was not helping. "You are not helping, Pearl." She might as well be forthright about it.

Olivia took a deep breath, preparing to explain.

"Don't bother trying to convince me." Pearl spoke in a matter-of-fact tone. "It is not as though you are going to, and I've already agreed to go on this carriage ride, so you don't have to anyway. I just want to say that I think some of your causes are misguided."

Olivia's eyes went wide. "Misguided? Helping poor children and orphans is misguided?"

Pearl sighed, shaking her head. Making it appear as though she were decades wiser than her sister, even though they were twins. "It's a good effort, Olivia. But if you don't understand why something is happening, you can't solve it. You can't just go in and give them all shifts," she said, holding up one of the garments she'd been working on, "and have them lead healthy, productive lives. There needs to be more to it."

"What does that have to do with Mr. Wolcott?" Olivia asked, genuinely confused.

"Nothing." Now Pearl just sounded tired. "It's just that I worry about you, about your passion for things that might never change. About how you think you can change whatever you want, just because of who you are. One day you'll find that not to be true, and it will be a revelation to you. But go ahead and parade Mr. Wolcott in the park. That is certain to get people talking about him."

Pearl's words stung, and Olivia sat back as she considered them. Her twin was remarkably and refreshingly honest, and she was often able to ferret out the truth of something before Olivia had. She was the one who'd initially told Olivia about the plight of the poor orphans, after all. That Olivia had seized on the society was due to Pearl as much as to her own conscience.

"Misguided?" she repeated in a quieter tone.

Pearl put her sewing down in her lap to lean over and squeeze her sister's hand. "Your heart is absolutely in the right place, Olivia. I just worry about you."

Olivia felt her eyes start to tear, and she bit her lip in an effort not to cry. Sometimes she forgot that Pearl was just as sensitive as Olivia; she was quieter, and expressed her feelings very rarely, so her thoughts and emotions were easy to over-look.

"Thank you, Pearl. I will be fine. And all it means is that we get to ride in a carriage with a very attractive gentleman." She gave a vigorous nod. "And if it means that some more people find his presence acceptable? Well, that will be a mar-velous bonus." She leaned forward and picked up one of the finished shifts. "Now, let us see how many more of these we can finish before the deadline."

"You mean how many more I can finish," Pearl said drily.

Chapter 8

Do not just go out with no plan; always have a plan, even if your plan is to dazzle onlookers. The plan is the plan.
LADY OLIVIA'S PARTICULAR GUIDE TO DECORUM

*G*ood afternoon," Lady Olivia called to Edward. He spun around to see three of the duke's daughters stepping out of a grand carriage.

Lady Ida nodded at him, then sped up the stairs to enter the house, leaving her sisters outside.

Where Lady Ida was wearing some sort of drab utilitarian clothing, both Lady Olivia and Lady Pearl were faultlessly attired in gowns that made them look like a baker had been spinning sugar, not stopping until he'd created these two.

Their gowns had the requisite amount of lace and frills, but where many ladies looked like overdressed confections, these two were just gloriously and perfectly feminine.

Even though he had a strong preference for one

of the two. He had to say that both ladies were lovely.

Edward hadn't been able to keep himself inside while waiting for the ladies. It just felt so unlike him to sit and wait for something. Usually he went out and got it—whether in business, horses, or hunting—so he felt edgy and restless while staring at the clock.

Standing and waiting was preferable to sitting and waiting, even if neither was preferable at all. But now they had arrived, so he didn't have to wait any longer.

"This is the carriage?" Lady Olivia asked, running her fingers along the rail that ran outside. The carriage was one of four that Edward's father had purchased when the two of them arrived in London; it looked as though it had just come from the coachbuilder, and sparkled nearly as brightly as Olivia's smile.

And when had he come to think of her as just plain Olivia? Even though there was nothing plain about her.

"It is." Edward noticed how Olivia's sister nearly rolled her eyes. At her sister's obvious statement or his obvious confirmation of the obvious? He didn't know, but now he felt foolish.

Again, not something he had ever really felt before. Olivia was playing havoc with his emotions as well as attempting to play havoc with his social and marital status.

"If I may?" Edward said, holding his hand out to Lady Pearl. She smiled in return, a genuine smile that lit up her whole face. Like her twin, she had light hair, but it was darker than Olivia's blond; her eyes were also darker, and she had freckles dotting her nose, making her look entirely adorable. The two looked similar, but not identical. He was relieved he wouldn't have to constantly be wondering which twin he was speaking to. As though he could mistake Olivia's sparkling passion for anyone else, he smiled to himself.

The duke's daughters all seemed to be breathtaking in their own individual ways.

But only one of them made him feel completely and totally alive, as though she'd set fire to his insides, even though he had to admit that sounded entirely unpleasant. But the reality was not; she made him feel the way he did after a particularly satisfying hunt, or when he was in the boxing ring, or doing any kind of physical pursuit.

It was as though she had awoken an animal inside him, one that wanted to exist in a purely visceral way. Even if he was supposed to be behaving like an absolute gentleman.

Dear lord, he was in so much trouble. And yet

he couldn't help but look forward to getting into more.

Lady Pearl settled herself on the seat, and Edward held his hand out to Olivia, anticipating what it would feel like when her fingers were in his.

They were both wearing gloves, of course, but he could have sworn, when she took his hand, that there was nothing but skin between them.

"I think we should go first to Hyde Park," Olivia said as she smoothed her gown at her waist. The feathers and ribbons on her bonnet fluttered as she spoke, moving with each nod of her head. "The best people go there, and so should we."

Edward swung himself up into the seat on the opposite side, an amused smile tugging at his mouth.

"Drive on, Clark," he said, speaking to the coachman. "Hyde Park, if you please."

The carriage was open, suitable only for a few days of the year in England. All the other days it would be too cold, too rainy, or just too cloudy to enjoy.

But today, this extravagant, ridiculous contraption was perfect.

The seats were upholstered in cream-colored leather, with gold buttons anchoring them down. The outside of the carriage was a rich mahogany color, trimmed with a lighter wood rail running all the way around.

The horses were equally matched in splendor, all four bay-colored with black manes and tails.

Edward leaned his head back against the cushions and closed his eyes, relishing the feel of the wind on his face. It was a sunny day, a rarity in London, and he felt both full of care and carefree, if such a dichotomy could be true.

Which of course it couldn't. But it seemed that ever since he'd met Olivia—that is, Lady Olivia—he'd been pulled between wanting to argue furiously with her and wanting to kiss her just as passionately.

"Mr. Wolcott."

Her voice was firm, as it always was.

Edward opened one eye and lowered his chin so he could look at her, opening the other eye as he did. "What is it, Lady Olivia?"

She made a frantic gesture in the air, her expression one of displeasure. "Shouldn't we be discussing things? You're supposed to be asking us how we are enjoying our time in London. And we are supposed to ask you how you find London Society compares to—where do you come from, anyway?"

She looked so outraged at him he wanted to laugh. Whether she was outraged because he was being, in her eyes, impolite, or because she was livid she didn't have all the answers—namely, where he came from—he couldn't say. Likely it was everything, since it was clear Olivia was a woman who wanted to be in control of everything and have all the answers.

What would it look like if she were out of control?

The thought made him shift in his seat. He should not be having such thoughts about her. She was as interested in him as she was in his coachman, although his coachman was likely born of a legitimate union. So perhaps she thought less of him.

"I come from Manchester. My father settled there when he was just starting his empire."

"Oh, and your moth—? Oh!" she exclaimed, her eyes wide.

"My mother, as you might have heard, was the daughter of a large landowner there. They were hoping to marry, but my father was too poor to support them. Her father forbade it. Then I came along, and she died." He shrugged, as though his story didn't matter. Even though of course it did. It had shaped his life, after all.

He wished he could have met his mother, just once. According to his father, his mother had been able to hold him for a few hours after his birth, but then something had gone wrong. And then things had gone even more wrong as his maternal grandfather tried to dump him at an orphanage. It was only due to his father's perseverance and ability to stand up for what he believed in that saved Edward from having no family at all.

His father's perseverance had helped with his business success as well.

"I am so sorry for your loss," Olivia said in a much quieter voice. Pearl nodded in agreement, her eyes bright.

"Thank you. I am very lucky Mr. Beechcroft wanted me. He rescued me from being sent to an orphanage." His father had had to pay Edward's grandfather for the privilege of taking his bastard child, even though it depleted all of Mr. Beechcroft's savings, money he'd been saving for his marriage and to make his way in business.

That fact never failed to make Edward furious, a bitter feeling rising up in his throat at the thought.

He'd never met his grandfather. Nor would he, even though the man lived in the next town over still; how could he meet someone who'd been willing to turn an infant over to an orphanage rather than to his parent?

"Oh my goodness," Olivia said. She reached her hand out as though to touch him, and he felt himself lean toward her, only to snap back when he realized what he was doing. What she was doing.

He didn't know what he'd do if she touched him.

Although parts of his body knew what they wanted him to do.

Which was absolutely why she should never touch him.

"Thank you," he said, turning his head to look anywhere but at her. At her vivacity, at her sympathy, at how much he craved her spark. "I haven't ever known what it was like to have a mother, so I can't say I grew up missing anything. My father did his best to fill whatever gap I might have felt."

"And he never married?" Lady Pearl asked, her tone soft.

Edward shook his head. "I asked him about that once when I was small. He told me he didn't think he could love anybody as he did my mother, nor could he love anybody as much as he did me." Edward felt his lips twist into a half smile. "I think he said it to make me feel at ease in my situation, but I also think it was the truth."

OLIVIA TRIED TO calm herself as they drove toward the park. His story shouldn't have affected her so; she'd heard it before, as soon as word spread that Mr. Beechcroft was being bold enough to bring his illegitimate son with him to London. That the businessman had brought his son into his business so completely that it was impossible for any person doing business with

Beechcroft and Son to avoid meeting Mr. Wolcott.

And since everyone—at least all the gentlemen—did business with Beechcroft and Son, Mr. Wolcott's story was well-known. It must have cost Mr. Beechcroft some business to acknowledge his natural son. It spoke to Mr. Beechcroft's business acumen that he was so wealthy now. Even her father the duke conducted business with Mr. Beechcroft, and her father was averse to any kind of risk, either when it came to his finances or his family.

But she'd only heard gossip and rumors before. Hearing the story from him made her heart hurt. How he set his jaw and relayed the facts as though they didn't matter. As though it wasn't an infant's future that was affected by a father's love, as though Mr. Wolcott wouldn't have grown up alone with no one to care for him, had his father been less determined and less wealthy.

Her throat tightened. She was accustomed to feeling this way when she encountered some of the people affected by her charitable work. But those people were so far removed from her in life; it was as though they weren't of her kind. Which of course they weren't; she was the daughter of a duke, not a penniless child left to fend for itself.

A disconcerting thought crossed her mind:

what if those other individuals were just as much people as Mr. Wolcott here? Had strong emotions and intelligence and the ability to do things, if given the opportunity? What would the world look like then?

Dear lord, she didn't know if her heart could take it.

"Olivia?"

Pearl's voice, and nudge to the shoulder, snapped her out of her thoughts, thank God.

"What?" she said in a snappish voice, then shook her head in apology. "I am sorry, I was thinking about something. What is it, Pearl?"

"Mr. Wolcott is wondering just where in the park we should go. To see and be seen."

"Oh yes." Olivia glanced around, startled to see they were already in the park. How long had she been thinking? That never happened.

Well, she did think, of course, but not so intently.

It was all his fault.

"I believe we should go just over there and then get out and walk a ways. Perhaps feed some of the ducks."

"Because duck feeding is conducive to getting accepted into Society?"

She bristled at his sarcastic tone. Although it did sound ridiculous.

How many things that she said could be

thought of as ridiculous? Was that why Pearl was continually rolling her eyes? And pointing out what she'd said?

"It is." She couldn't waste time on trying to parse out what might or might not be ridiculous. She had a goal. An agenda, and a time in which to accomplish it.

If it meant that he thought she was foolish, well—well, he likely already thought that, given how they'd met. She winced as she recalled picking up the objet d'art and hurling it toward the opposite wall. What if she'd struck him? What if she'd struck Bennett?

And why was the thought of striking Bennett coming as an afterthought to her image of striking him?

It had to be those rakish curls, she thought to herself.

"Park right over there, Clark," Mr. Wolcott said to his coachman. His eyebrow was still raised in skeptical disbelief, but at least he hadn't said they couldn't try her plan.

She really did not like it when people refused to even try her plans. Pearl had refused more often than she had agreed, and it was only because Pearl was her twin that Olivia hadn't stopped talking to her.

That, plus Pearl was her closest confidante, and the one person upon whom Olivia could depend.

"Toss it farther out, Mr. Wolcott."

Olivia stood beside him, her shoulder nudging his arm as she pointed to the middle of the pond. "Do you see? That big one keeps getting all the food, and it's not fair." Her voice rang with righteous anger, and he had to suppress a smile.

Her sister had apparently bored long since, and was now sitting on a bench several feet away, her head bent as she worked on some sort of sewing project. It seemed odd to Edward, but perhaps that was what aristocratic ladies did—go out of doors and do needlework.

He'd have to ask Olivia when she wasn't so riled up about the inequity of duck feeding.

He stretched forward and arced a piece of bread past where the greedy duck swam about, landing just in front of the one Olivia was championing.

The duck fluttered in the water and snatched the bread, gobbling it down even as the greedy duck whirled about in the water in an attempt to get the food.

"You bully!" Olivia had grabbed his arm and was leaning forward herself, her bonnet shielding her face from his view. "It's not fair to take all the food." She turned her head to him. "It's not right." He was startled to see her expression— pained and serious, as though the duck was responsible for all the inequity in the world.

"It's fine, Olivia." He placed his hand over hers, which still rested on his arm. "We took care of that duck. See?" He pointed over her head to where the now-fed duck was swimming, dipping its head in the water and wriggling its tail feathers. "It's fine," he said again.

She looked at him, wide-eyed, as though she didn't fully comprehend what he was saying. And then she blinked and smiled, and he lost his thoughts also.

She was so pretty. Breathtaking, actually, especially when she was passionate about something. Which appeared to be most of the time.

"Thank you."

He felt himself lean toward her, his gaze fixed on her mouth, only to jerk back suddenly as he realized what he'd been about to do. Kiss her. Kiss Lady Olivia, in public, in front of her sister and most of polite Society. Kiss the woman who was in love with his best friend.

He could not have conjured up a speedier way to being drummed out of Society completely than if he had completed his action.

She stared back at him, an unreadable expression on her face. Did she know what he wanted to do? What would she have done if he had kissed her?

He'd never know. He couldn't ever find out.

Instead, he removed her hand from his arm,

reaching down to pick up more bread. An excuse, of course, but it worked to snap him out of the moment.

"Yes, well, thank you for making sure that duck got its fair share."

Her voice was soft. Was it his imagination or was it also a bit shaky?

"Over there." She'd grabbed his arm again and was nodding vigorously, the festoons on her bonnet coming perilously close to his eyes. "That is Lady Cecilia Baxford and her father, Lord Baxford. We should make sure they see us." She let go of him to lift her arm and wave, her whole body shaking with the effort.

She never did things by halves, did she? She was just as upset about the ducks as she was about his position in Society. Did that make him feel more or less special?

"They've seen us, they're coming over."

He turned to see a young lady and an older man stepping carefully on the path toward them. Lady Cecilia's face froze as she looked at Edward, and he found his hands curling into fists at his side.

"Calm down," she whispered, her fingers sliding into his, bringing both of their hands behind his back so Lady Cecilia and her father couldn't see.

It felt delicious, something they were doing

that nobody could see. It did calm him, as she'd intended. But it also made him aware of how right it felt to have her hand in his.

He reluctantly drew his fingers out from hers as she stepped forward to greet the new arrivals.

"Lady Cecilia, how delightful to see you. And Lord Baxford, you are looking well. Allow me to introduce Mr. Wolcott, who has just arrived in London."

Edward caught his breath as he saw the older gentleman realize just who he was and weigh whether or not he should shake his hand.

And exhaled as Lord Baxford stretched his hand out and took Edward's, giving it a weak shake, but a shake nonetheless.

"It is a pleasure, my lady," Lord Baxford said.

"I did not realize you were acquainted with Mr. Wolcott, Lady Olivia," Lady Cecilia said. Was it Edward's imagination, or was her tone somewhat snide?

"But then again your family knows such . . . interesting people."

Not his imagination.

"Yes, we do, don't we?" Olivia replied in a bright tone, as though completely unaware of the other lady's implication. "It is far better to be interesting than entirely predictable, wouldn't you say?"

And not completely unaware, it seemed. Edward wished it wouldn't be entirely rude to tilt his head back and roar with laughter.

As it was, he must have made some sort of amused sound, since Olivia shifted so she could deliver a kick to his foot.

"We've been feeding the ducks," Olivia continued, gesturing to the pond behind them. "It doesn't seem fair, does it, that certain ducks get more food than others simply because of their position in the pond?"

Edward didn't think they were talking about ducks now.

"Eh?" Lord Baxford's expression was puzzled. "Ducks?"

"Ducks, Father." Lady Cecilia took her father's arm. "It was a pleasure to meet you, Mr. Wolcott."

"Likewise, my lady. My lord," Edward said, tilting his head toward the pair. "I will doubtless be seeing you at some event or another. I hope I might be allowed to ask for a dance, my lady?"

There. That was as polite in Society as he could get. He just hoped she wouldn't say no.

"Mr. Wolcott is a good friend of Lord Carson's," Olivia added in the silence following his question.

Lady Cecilia pulled her lips back into a semblance of a smile. Edward had to wonder why Olivia had even bothered with the Baxfords, since it was clear the two ladies did not like one another.

"Lord Carson is a fine gentleman," she said. "I would be pleased to accept your invitation, Mr. Wolcott." She dipped her head in a gracious nod, then walked away on her father's arm.

"That . . . that . . ." Olivia sputtered next to him.

"Greedy duck?" Edward supplied.

She glared at him, then grinned and burst out in laughter, clapping her hand over her mouth, her eyes dancing merrily.

He returned the grin, shoving his hands in his pockets so he wouldn't be tempted to take her in his arms and kiss her laughing mouth.

Even though he was very tempted, so his hands-in-pocket ploy wasn't working. But at least he wasn't acting on his wishes.

Chapter 9

Do not allow yourself to waver from your goals. No matter how rakish the curls.

LADY OLIVIA'S PARTICULAR GUIDE TO DECORUM

*F*or a moment, it seemed as though Mr. Wolcott was going to do something. Something like— well, something that wasn't arguing with her or laughing at her or getting all offended when she said something thoughtless.

Something like kiss her.

Olivia had yet to be kissed; she'd been reserving that honor for Bennett. She'd hoped it would be on the occasion of their betrothal, but that hadn't happened, so obviously the kiss hadn't either.

And for a moment, Olivia had wanted him to kiss her. *Him*, not Bennett. She hadn't thought of Bennett all morning if she were being honest with herself.

What was wrong with her?

She couldn't address that now.

"Why did you bring that lady over here when it is so clear you dislike each other?"

Olivia bristled automatically, then relaxed when she realized he wasn't necessarily criticizing her. He was actually regarding her with an expression of—curiosity? And a kind of warmth?

She hadn't seen that expression from many people before. Most people looked at her with amusement, as he had, or with boredom. Usually when she was regaling them with details of someone less well off.

"Well, it is true that Lady Cecilia and I are not the best of friends," she admitted. Even before she'd seen that lady trying to lure Bennett into her clutches. "But Lord Baxford is a friend of my father's, and I know that he is a notable person to call an acquaintance. I do not like Lady Cecilia as you can tell," she added.

It felt refreshing to share with Mr. Wolcott. To show him she was not perfect, although of course he already knew that, given that the first time they'd met she'd thrown something in the approximate direction of his head. She winced as she recalled it.

"What is it?" he asked, his tone gentle.

She glanced over at Pearl, whom she'd forgotten during this entire time. Thankfully, Pearl was still engrossed in sewing the next-to-last shift, her head bent over her work. She did not want to have to answer if Pearl asked her what she felt about Mr. Wolcott. Mostly because she didn't know herself.

"I wish I hadn't said what I did. When we first met." She looked down as she spoke but tilted her face up when his fingers came under her chin.

She felt her breath hitch as she looked into his dark eyes. She couldn't keep her eyes from drifting over his face, from his strong nose to his mouth. Lord, his mouth.

His upper lip had an indent right in the middle, and she could see the stubble just beginning to come in. She was glad he was clean-shaven, even though variations on facial hair were more in fashion. This way, she got to see the clean lines of his face, to admire how strong his jawline was. How he dragged his lower lip into his mouth and bit it when he was thinking.

He was doing it right now.

"It's fine. You didn't say anything everybody hasn't thought." That he was speaking the truth didn't lessen how bad she felt.

"That's almost worse. I'm supposed to be better than other people. To care more than other people. I *do* care more than other people, I know it is my purpose to fix things."

He shrugged, his index finger sliding along

her skin. Along the underside of her jaw. He must have removed his glove at some point—perhaps while they were feeding the ducks?—because his hand was bare, so she felt his skin on hers. Sending a prickling sensation through her entire body. "People aren't perfect all the time, Olivia." It was the second time he'd used just her name—was he even aware he was being so informal?

This was not the time to remind him of their respective positions. Not that she wanted to, anyway. She liked how her name sounded coming out of his mouth. "It's more important that you recognize your imperfection and try to do better. That's all we can do. Do better."

She swallowed, letting the feeling of his words sink into her bones. *Do better.* Two words, deceptively simple. And yet so difficult to accomplish. But it was a distillation of everything she'd tried to be doing since she recognized the inequality of the world. That not everyone was born a duke's daughter, so not everyone had the privilege she did. And that that privilege didn't mean she had more of a right to basic survival.

"Now what are you thinking about?" His finger was still on her skin, stroking back and forth on her neck. Sliding from her throat to just under her ear and back again, as though she were a cat. She felt like a cat; she wanted to curl into his touch.

"Do better." She shook her head in agreement. "That is all I can do. Do better."

How had they come to this moment? Come to this place where his fingers were on her skin, and she wanted them there? To where she was thinking about leaning up, up toward his mouth, pressing her lips against his?

He took his hand away, and she swayed toward him, missing his touch already.

"Well, we should gather Pearl and go walking a bit more toward there," Olivia said in a bright tone, trying to make it sound as though she were fully invested in walking and seeing and being seen rather than in how much she wished he had kissed her.

There. She'd admitted it. That meant, unfortunately, she would have to discuss it all with Pearl, who would probably say *I told you so* when Olivia revealed how she felt now as opposed to how she thought she'd felt only a few days ago.

She had to push that aside to focus on what needed to be done right now. Namely, introducing Mr. Wolcott to enough people who mattered so that when he next attended a Society function he wouldn't be entirely shunned.

"Let's go," she announced, beginning to walk to the more populous area of the park. Leaving the ducks—and her conflicted feelings—behind as she continued on her current mission.

"I TOOK LADY Olivia and Lady Pearl driving today." Edward paused to rub the nose of one of the horses on display. She wasn't the biggest horse or the fastest, but she was looking at him with an almost earnest expression that tugged at his heart.

He had persuaded Bennett to stop his incessant work for just a few hours to accompany him to Tattersall's. He had Chrysanthemum here, and more horses in the country house, but if he were going to make a showing for himself, he'd have to be suitably equipped in town beyond his mare. He needed horses for the carriage; the ones he'd driven out today were adequate, but not what anyone would expect from him, given his reputation as a gentleman who knew horseflesh.

And he well knew that any indication that he wasn't the absolute best at what he was supposed to be would mean he would be lessened in everybody's eyes. Never mind that there were often extenuating circumstances; nobody would accommodate them because of his birth.

"How do you decide?" Bennett asked, nodding to the filly, who was shoving her nose into Edward's hand.

Edward stopped to think, chewing on his lower

lip as he did when he considered something. "It's a variety of factors," he began, continuing to rub the horse's soft nose. Her breath was warm on his skin. "It's how fast the horse runs, what it looks like, its breeding. And something I can't quite explain, just that I can tell when a horse is a good, biddable animal."

Bennett regarded him with a wry look in his eyes.

Edward stiffened. "It's not like choosing a bride, no matter how similar it sounds."

Bennett shook his head, laughing. Edward resisted the urge to punch him.

The two men continued to walk down the line of horses in the pens for sale.

"How will you choose a bride, then?" Bennett's tone was sincere, and Edward felt himself relax. He couldn't blame Bennett for making light of the situation; he was only doing it to try to make Edward feel better, and Edward did appreciate the effort.

"I suppose it is similar, once I stop and think about it," Edward admitted. He stooped to run his hand down a gelding's leg, feeling how the horse reacted under his touch. "It just sounds so . . . unfeeling to consider breeding, appearance, and biddability as the primary aspects of a wife."

Someone he'd spend the rest of his life with.

Who would bear his children, be his partner in so many things, even though that was not what was traditionally accepted in marriage. It was what he wanted.

He didn't want to have to worry about what he might say, or act like, in front of his wife. He hoped that, when he found the woman he might love, or come to love, that she would be someone who would be his partner. His equal.

Not considering herself his superior because of who he was. God save him from that type of female, even though he strongly suspected most—if not all—of the ladies his father would wish to see him with would view the circumstances of his birth as beneath them.

There had to be someone out there in all of Society who wasn't entirely biased against someone because of how they'd been born.

Although likely not. Look at Olivia, the most passionate arguer for equality he could imagine existed. And yet she too had called him a bastard. And then felt terrible about it, but the thought had been in her mind.

"That is how most of the people in my world— now yours—see marriage. As a likely match between buyer and product for sale, with marks awarded in beauty, personality, and ease of doing as they're told. Wit, if the buyer is more openminded." Bennett sounded as disgusted about it as Edward felt hearing it, but it didn't make his words any less true.

"What about you?" Edward asked his friend. They were almost done with the row of horses; there were three other rows to get through, but Edward knew Bennett would make an excuse to leave before Edward had entirely finished. "What type of lady will be able to wrest you away from your constant work?"

"Since my brother stole my betrothed out from under my nose?" Bennett retorted. He didn't sound bothered by it, and having seen Lord Alexander, Bennett's brother, and his wife, Lady Eleanor, Edward could tell it was a love match. And Bennett, by his own admission, had no time for love. But there had to be something, *someone*, who could get Bennett's attention more than the latest Parliamentary proceedings could.

Perhaps that was why Bennett hadn't even considered Lady Olivia. They were too similar, both fiercely determined to right wrongs and balance injustice. There would be no respite from their respective causes if they were married. It would be relentlessly moral, and not at all the kind of relationship either one of them would truly want, despite what one of the two might have to say.

"I suppose I will have to get married someday. I am my father's heir, after all." Bennett tilted his head to the side in thought. "I would like a lady who is gentle. Soft, almost. Someone who will be a comfort and a pleasure to return to after a long day."

Someone entirely unlike Lady Olivia, Edward thought.

"But that is a long time from now," Bennett said in a weary tone. "There is too much to be done for me to consider anything so frivolous."

Edward had often envied his friend—namely, his friend's legitimate birth—but he had just as often felt sorry for him. That he bore the weight of the world on his shoulders, that his father didn't seem to care much about anything, let alone his eldest son. Edward was eternally grateful that Mr. Beechcroft had been such a remarkable father to him, even though the law would say he wasn't his true father.

"Well, then let's be frivolous for just a bit longer." Edward gestured to the next row of horses. "Give me your opinion on which filly would make the best bride."

Bennett laughed, shaking his head at Edward's nonsense.

Chapter 10

Keep your hands folded and in your lap at all times.

LADY OLIVIA'S PARTICULAR GUIDE TO DECORUM

*W*elcome, my lady, we are delighted to see you again," Miss Saunders said, a warm smile on her face. She gestured with open arms to Olivia. "Look, children, at who is visiting today. It's Lady Olivia."

Olivia nodded to the children, most of whom were staring at her open-mouthed. She'd met Miss Saunders while at the Society for Poor and Orphaned Children and had found herself drawn to the young woman who couldn't be more than a few years older than herself.

Miss Saunders, however, had come from a much different life than Olivia, and it showed in her expression, the worry in her brown eyes. She had come into some money from a distant relative and set up a small school near to the society, teaching a few of the brighter children how to read and write in hopes of eventually getting them out of factory work and into something less dangerous for their small bodies— apprenticeships at London shops, or work in a well-to-do family's home. Some place where gentle manners and a rudimentary education would come in handy.

Olivia came every few weeks to give Miss Saunders a break from teaching. Thus far, it was only Miss Saunders, so the school was only open for a few hours in the afternoon, but Olivia hoped to bring some of her Societal acquaintances to visit once the children were taught well enough to impress the ladies.

Olivia's contribution to the effort was slight, but Miss Saunders was grateful nonetheless, almost too grateful, she felt. Olivia couldn't help but wince when Miss Saunders gushed about her generosity, as though coming to read to such interested, engaged children for an hour or so was a hardship.

Still, it felt good to be wanted.

"Can I take your wrap, my lady?" one of the young girls said in a shy voice.

Olivia smiled at her, beginning to remove her shawl. "Certainly, Mary. That would be splendid."

Mary took the shawl as though it were a precious egg, holding it aloft in two hands and carrying it over to Miss Saunders's desk, laying it on the table carefully, smoothing out whatever creases might be there.

"What have you chosen for me to read today?" Olivia asked once Mary had returned to sit beside her classmates on the wooden benches at one end of the room.

"This one, lady." A small boy stepped forward and handed her a book, its age apparent from the worn cover and spine.

"*Holiday House*," Olivia said as she approached and sat in the chair facing the benches, settling the book on her lap. "I have not read this before."

"It's very good," the same boy said, his eyes bright. "Miss Saunders read it to us, but we wanted you to read it too."

Olivia smiled, a warmth stealing over her at the praise. She was wanted and needed here, more so even than at the society, where she could help but wasn't as directly engaged with the children. Anybody could throw money at something, and she did plenty of that, giving away as much of her spending money as she could to help, but it was something else to give her time, and she found it far more rewarding than just donating a check. Certainly more rewarding than sewing shifts, given how terrible she was at needlework.

She'd never forget that her funds were essential

to helping these children, but she also wanted to feel as though she herself—Lady Olivia—could do something more.

She opened the book and began to read.

> *Laura and Harry Graham could scarcely feel sure that they ever had a mama, because she died while they were yet very young indeed; but Frank, who was some years older, recollected perfectly well what pretty playthings she used to give him, and missed his kind, good mama so extremely, that he one day asked if he might "go to a shop and buy a new mama?"*

And then she had to stop to wipe her eyes because the book, of course, reminded her of him. Of Edward, who didn't remember his mother at all. But he had Mr. Beechcroft, and these children—thus far—had her, so she couldn't allow her sentiments to affect what she was doing for them right now.

"MR. WOLCOTT," OLIVIA's mother began. Olivia felt herself freeze in place, hoping her mother wasn't going to say anything embarrassing. "I am so delighted to find you to be so . . . well, you know," she finished, gesturing toward him.

Please don't ask, please don't ask, please don't ask, Olivia chanted to herself. She had to admit now to feeling sympathy for Pearl, who was often clearly regretting that Olivia had said something.

"So . . . what?" Mr. Wolcott said, raising one of his exceedingly attractive eyebrows. That is, if eyebrows could be considered attractive. Which on Mr. Wolcott they most definitely could.

But he had asked, so she couldn't be thinking about his eyebrows.

The family, the Marquis of Wheatley, Lord Carson, Mr. Beechcroft, and Mr. Wolcott were seated at the duke's dining room table. So far there had been desultory discussion of the weather (damper than one would like), the wine (better than one could expect—it was Spanish, after all, and you know the Spanish), and how crowded the next Society party would be (very).

Olivia was seated beside Lord Carson, as she'd begged her mother. But Mr. Wolcott was seated opposite, and she couldn't seem to keep her eyes off him, even though the presumed love of her life was on her left.

Mr. Beechcroft was on her right, with Ida next to him. The two of them had spent the entire time at dinner speaking of books and such without paying attention to any of the topics. Not that Olivia could blame them; there was only so much one could speak on the weather and the likelihood of rain before one wanted to screech aloud.

But even screeching wouldn't keep her mother from replying to Mr. Wolcott.

"So *acceptable!*" She spoke as though she were delighted to discover he wasn't using his hands to cram food into his mouth. "One would think that you were just another gentleman. I mean, look at you!" she exclaimed, pointing toward him.

Olivia heard Pearl gasp from across the table. She was seated next to Mr. Wolcott, and Olivia had noticed—not without feeling a twinge of something, no it wasn't jealousy—that he had been scrupulously polite to her twin, ensuring she was part of the conversation and making certain she was served.

"I am pleased I have met your criteria for what makes 'just another gentleman.'" Olivia closed her eyes as she heard the bite in his tone.

"My son is more than just another gentleman." Mr. Beechcroft had roused himself out of his conversation with Ida to join the discussion. From the way he spoke, it didn't sound as though he'd registered his son's acerbic tone.

Whether this would all end up with Mr. Wolcott tossing thinly veiled barbs at the duchess, who wouldn't understand them, was still possible, but at least Mr. Beechcroft's wading into the fray might lessen the chance.

"He is not only a fine gentleman, he also is my business partner."

Olivia winced even more. Discussing business at a social event was the height of crass behavior. What would her parents have to say after their guests were gone? Likely her father would grunt disapprovingly, and her mother would dissect every single thing that was said in order to belittle Mr. Wolcott.

Olivia opened her eyes warily, startled to see Mr. Wolcott looking directly at her. What was even more surprising was that his lips were curled into an almost smile. Was it possible he was amused by all of this?

What else might amuse him? Perhaps she should show him her skill in sewing. That might make him chuckle. Or maybe only if she pricked her finger. Or maybe she should make some offhand remark about how magazines were infinitely more readable than books, and step back as Ida's fury emerged in full force.

And then, as her mind was frantically casting about for something to say, he winked at her. Winked. At her.

"I do congratulate myself on having some acumen for business," he said. She was unable to figure out how he might rescue himself and his father without the use of hypnotism. And then wondered if he cared about any of that.

What would it be like not to care?

Although she knew full well he did care—that

was why he was entrusting her to bring his position up in Society. Which he would never do if
he started talking about business in polite conversation.

"I like figuring out the solution to problems."
He leaned back in his chair, looking consum-
mately at ease. Unlike Olivia, who was sitting
bolt upright in her chair, her eyes fixed on his
face.

If Lord Carson had chosen this moment to pro-
fess his love, she didn't think she would be able
to stop staring across the table at Mr. Wolcott.

That didn't mean anything at all. Of course it
didn't.

"What kinds of problems, Mr. Wolcott?" Olivia
heard herself speak almost before she realized
she was doing so. He grinned across the table
at her, and she heard Lord Carson exhale—in
relief?—beside her.

"I am not certain we should be talking about
such things at dinner," Olivia's mother said.

"Oh, Mother, do let him continue." Ida sounded
actually curious, which was perhaps the oddest
part of the evening. Usually she was completely
bored by any and all things that required her
to leave her studies and put on a pretty gown.
Olivia had been startled to see her sister actually smile a few times when speaking with
Mr. Beechcroft.

"It is like a puzzle." As he spoke, his expression brightened, and Olivia felt herself leaning forward to catch every word.

He was remarkably charismatic, that was for certain. That was the only possible explanation for why he fascinated her so. Like a snake charmer, or a mesmerist. Maybe he was hypnotizing her at this very moment.

"There are people, such as your family, who want to have certain things, maintain a certain way of life." She wasn't imagining his sharp tone. And she couldn't help but feel uncomfortable that the tone was warranted, given what her family—and her world in general—thought of him. "My father and I, through our various businesses, have found a way to provide those things while also providing a place for those less fortunate to work. It's a simple equation, although most don't see it that way."

Olivia glanced to see, thankfully, her father engrossed in downing a glass of wine and her mother beaming at Lord Carson. Although that was problematic as well, but something she could consider later.

"I was fortunate enough to invest in a small textiles factory when Edward was quite young," Mr. Beechcroft added. "I saw the future of industry, and eventually I bought the factory outright, then invested as much as I could in finding good workers. I provide reasonable wages, and they make me profitable."

Images of the children in the society made Olivia shake her head in disbelief. "It cannot be that easy. There is not always enough work, or enough *enough*," she said, frustrated by her inability to find the proper words.

Mr. Wolcott's smile deepened, and she felt something flicker inside her. Something warm and responsive to his gaze. "It is not enough. And that is why it is necessary to have people such as you in the world, my lady. People who can point out when something is unjust, or there is a wrong to be righted."

She felt herself start to blush at his referencing their bargain. She didn't dare look over at Pearl, who was no doubt giving her a knowing glance.

"It is very tedious when Olivia takes it into her head to be obsessed about something," the duchess said. Oh dear. Mother had been listening, although there was no guarantee she'd heard or understood everything that was said. Which made what she might say even more terrifying.

"There was the time she could not stop talking about dancing lessons until . . ." And then she gulped because of course their dancing master had run off with their sister Della. But never let it be said the duchess had allowed a potentially embarrassing admission to derail her from her cause. In that, Olivia thought, she took after her mother. Although she wasn't certain now if that was a good thing. In fact, it likely was not.

"And then there was the time right after my dear Eleanor's betrothal to Lord Alexander Raybourn that Olivia would not stop talking about who she was going to marry and what kind of life they would lead." And now Olivia was wishing the parqueted floor would open up beneath her feet and swallow her whole, because she was keenly aware of Lord Carson to her side, his hand halted in midair as he was bringing his glass to his mouth, and Mr. Wolcott's smile fading across from her and Pearl no doubt turning bright red, because her twin felt embarrassment and shame far more than Olivia herself did. And she felt a fair amount of both at the moment.

"Excuse me," she said, pushing away from the table and dropping her napkin on her chair. She turned and fled the room, unable to think of anything but escape. Escape from her mother's words, yes, but also escape from all of these new feelings she had about—about everything.

About everyone.

It was horribly embarrassing, of course, but less so than if she stayed there and felt the weight of all those glances. She might even cry, or pick something up and throw it. Two things she would have thought herself incapable of before. But she'd done one of those things when Bennett had said no, and had come close to the other. It was only Mr. Wolcott's words that had kept her from bursting into tears.

Did she even know herself anymore?

What would it mean, if she didn't know exactly what she wanted to do? Who she wanted to be?

The thought of being unmoored, directionless, was terrifying.

She found herself in the hallway in front of the door to the library.

There weren't any servants around, thank goodness. Nobody to witness how red her cheeks must be, how furiously emotional she looked. She raised her chin as she considered how she could possibly reenter the room without embarking on complete and utter humiliation. A thought that made her wince and lower her gaze to the floor.

"Olivia."

And here he was. She saw his legs in front of her, the long length of them encased in his evening trousers. His hands, restless in front of his body, as though he wished to move them somewhere—to her?—but didn't.

She looked up at him, bracing herself for the

look of contempt she anticipated. After all, she'd already shown herself to him the first time they met, the thought of which should have been the most embarrassing moment ever. Except this one was worse.

Only to see him regarding her with a considerate expression.

He didn't despise her. He wasn't here to mock her or chide her or raise one of those admittedly beautiful eyebrows and make her feel judged.

He was here because—well, she wasn't precisely certain, but she knew it wasn't because he hated her.

And so she knew perfectly well why she did what she did next. She just couldn't have explained any of it to anyone, not even to Pearl. Much less to herself.

But none of that could deter what she wanted to do more than anything.

She raised herself up on her tiptoes, closed her eyes, and leaned up toward his mouth.

And then, after what seemed an excruciating length of time, she pressed her lips against his.

She was kissing him. The bastard.

HE SHOULDN'T BE finding a woman who was apparently suffering from the most supreme humiliation—being casually dismissed by her careless mother—attractive, but so help him, he did.

The way she rose from the table, tossing her napkin in a gesture of fierce emotion. The way the color rose in her cheeks, making her as flushed and rosy as though she had—well. No wonder he found her attractive. Gorgeous. Compelling.

He had no choice, then, but to follow her out of the dining room, tossing his own napkin to the floor as he focused on her, on how she slammed the door to the dining room, stalking to fling herself back up against a door in the hallway. Her bosom heaving delightfully, even if it was in anger.

What would she look like in pleasure?

He thought he might be able to guess, and the thought was intoxicating.

So when she lifted her gaze to his, the gold flecks in her hazel eyes seeming to flash and sparkle as vibrantly as she did, he caught his breath. This was she, the true Olivia, the one whose emotion seemed to reverberate around the room like a claxon.

How had anyone not seen it before?

And then all thoughts ceased as she kissed him, intent in her purpose even if her inexperience betrayed her from the moment her mouth met his.

But it didn't matter because she had wrapped her arms around his neck and tugged him closer, her mouth so soft and wanting, her body also so soft and wanting.

Him hard and wanting.

She broke the kiss, gasping, her hands still around his neck, staring at him as though he was something unknown to her.

Likely he was—a man who wasn't intimidated by her just furor, who found her as charming as she was infuriating.

A man who saw her as a woman, not a young girl overwhelmed by her ideals and passion.

He waited a moment, waited for her to realize what she'd done, to run away, appalled at her own behavior.

And waited as she continued looking at him, a tiny smile curling up one corner of her mouth.

It was that curl that did him in, that made him place his hands on her waist and draw her back to him, lower his mouth to hers and lick the seam of her lips until she gasped, opening to him.

He didn't waste his advantage either, sliding his tongue into her mouth, keenly aware of her body pressed against his.

Keenly aware of his cock growing thicker in his trousers, knowing what he was doing was wrong and shocking—what if someone else came out of the dining room, for God's sake?—

but unable to stop kissing her, shamelessly reveling in how her fingers were tightened in his hair, her breasts pressed against his chest.

He had kissed women before, of course. Just because he was illegitimate didn't mean he was entirely shunned, especially not by ladies, women who saw beyond his birth to his appearance and, sometimes, his wealth.

But he had never felt this shocking, almost primal, feeling that was coiling throughout his entire body. For only a kiss. It was a spectacular kiss, to be sure, but it was only a kiss.

That thought, the idea that this was merely a precursor to something even more stupendous made him pull away from her, knowing if he didn't soon, he would likely have her naked on the floor underneath him in moments.

"My God," he muttered, still holding her waist. "That was—my God," he said again, shaking his head. Unable to find the words.

"Yes," she replied, her cheeks just as flushed as before, the wild spark in her eyes one of desire now, not fury.

Or both. He wouldn't mind seeing her furious desire, as a matter of fact.

"I have to go back," she said, peering over his shoulder toward the dining room. She spoke as though they had a secret, not as though she'd done something of which she was horribly ashamed.

What did it say about him that his first reaction was surprise that she wasn't horribly ashamed? Was he just as class-conscious as the people who derided him for his birth?

Perhaps he would consider all that when he wasn't reeling from the impact of that kiss.

Chapter 11

Be reckless.

LADY OLIVIA'S PARTICULAR GUIDE TO DECORUM

*O*livia, let me come in." Pearl accompanied her words with a few sharp taps at the door.

Olivia twisted up her face as she thought about having to tell Pearl. Because she knew that she would, even though she had tried to pretend she wouldn't, dashing up to her room by herself after dinner was finished. Of course Pearl would know something was wrong, because Olivia never let an opportunity to sigh over Bennett—Lord Carson, that is—go.

Until now. Until she had kissed him. Not the *him* who was Lord Carson, no. The *him* who was Mr. Wolcott, bastard son of the most merchanti-est person she had ever met.

It would be something out of one of the novels she read in secret if it wasn't her real life. What had she been thinking?

She hadn't been thinking, that was the problem. "Olivia!"

Pearl's tone was sharper now, as though her twin were worried about her. And well she should be, but not for the reason Pearl might think—she should worry because Olivia hadn't spent a single second thinking about the gentleman she loved. Who she wanted to spend the rest of her life with doing good things and righting wrongs and having well-bred children.

No, she was spending all of her time thinking about the other one. The Other One. The one who was playing havoc with her mind and her capitalization.

She got herself up off the bed and walked to the door, turning the key in the lock and opening up just enough to allow Pearl to slip inside.

"What are you doing in here, hiding like that?" Pearl looked worried. As she should.

Thinking about kissing the Other One. The One who is not Lord Carson.

"Uh, I was tired?" Olivia winced at how weakly she replied.

Pearl rolled her eyes. Good. At least one of the twins was behaving as usual.

"You are never tired. You are indefatigable, except when it comes to shift making. Speaking of which, I finished the last one, we can take them around to the society tomorrow." Pearl waved her hand in dismissal. "But that is not what is important at the moment." She planted her hands on her hips and squinted balefully at Olivia. "What happened when you ran out into the hallway? Mr. Wolcott dashed after you, and then when you returned, you looked—well, you looked . . ."

"Like I'd been kissed?"

She might as well admit it.

Pearl's eyes went wide, and she reached out and took Olivia's arm, moving them both over to the bed. She pushed Olivia down onto it, then clambered up beside her.

"Mr. Wolcott kissed you? How dare he! I know Father has business dealings with his father, but we cannot keep this quiet. Unless—oh no, do you suppose you'll have to marry him? Maybe you shouldn't say anything about it. I promise to stay close to you anytime we might meet him in public. He won't dare do something so terrible again."

It wasn't so terrible. And she should make certain Pearl knew the truth. "He didn't kiss me."

Pearl's expression showed her confusion.

"I kissed *him*," Olivia clarified. "On the mouth and everything."

She still felt wobbly, even though it had been well over an hour ago. Her mouth was tender, and she would have sworn she could still feel the pressure of his hands at her waist. The way she'd swayed toward him, her breasts brushing his jacket.

Her fingers finally getting to dive into those riotous black curls.

"Oh," Pearl said in a long, surprised exhale. "How was it? And what about Lord Carson?"

Olivia flopped back on the bed, spreading her arms wide. "I don't know! I don't know why I did it—it was just that Mother had said what she had, and he was there opposite looking at me with those dark eyes, and I ran out, and he followed, and he was concerned about me."

And it hadn't felt as though he'd pitied her. Or seen her as a nuisance or a bother or someone who was too loud, too opinionated, too—Olivia.

"I think this is a good thing." Pearl spoke in her most decided tone. "I know you think you want to marry Lord Carson, but how will you know for certain unless you kiss other gentlemen as well?"

Not that she'd kissed Lord Carson in the first place.

Olivia lifted her head to look at Pearl, who was regarding her with that smug "I already told you this" look that made Olivia furious. Mostly because her twin was usually right. Not that Olivia ever admitted that, beyond the confines of her own head.

"So you're suggesting I just go about kissing random gentlemen to ensure that Lord Carson is the one I should marry?" Put that way, it did sound rather enjoyable, but the first—and only—image that came to her mind was of her kissing the Other. Again. And again.

Pearl snorted and rolled her eyes. Quite a gift, to be able to do both simultaneously. "That is not what I am saying, for goodness' sake, Olivia. Just listen to yourself. Kissing random gentlemen." And then she snorted again, likely for some final auditory punctuation on the topic.

"Well, what is your suggestion?"

Pearl tapped Olivia on the leg. "I think you should get to know Mr. Wolcott, since it is apparent that you find him interesting."

Interesting was one way to put it. *Fascinating, handsome,* and *irresistible* were other ways to put it.

Even though, she told herself staunchly, she loved Lord Carson, and she could do the most good by becoming his wife.

Even though, she had to also tell herself, she wasn't feeling the same . . . interest in him since she'd met Mr. Wolcott.

"You're making him respectable, aren't you?" Pearl grinned, a smile that on another person's face might have looked almost wicked. "So you can be unrespectable with him and nobody will be able to tell. He's already unrespectable, at least until you succeed. *If* you succeed."

And if she did succeed, she'd also have to succeed in finding him a bride.

A bride who was willing to accept the hand of a gentleman who wasn't quite a gentleman. A bride who would have the right to slide her fingers through those curls and kiss that gorgeous mouth and—

And then her imagination stopped, because she couldn't continue in that line of thinking. Not without causing some sort of conflagration to her insides.

"That is an excellent idea," Olivia said in a firm voice, ignoring all the sparks of some emotion she did not want to admit to, but which probably rhymed with *mealousy*, that were flowing through her. "As long as it doesn't harm anybody." And as long as nobody found out that she was being unrespectable with him, the bast—even though she'd sworn to herself not to call him that anymore. But if anyone else discovered how friendly she was with him—well, people would say that quickly enough. And she would end up being another one of the Duke's Disgraceful Daughters.

She couldn't allow that.

"I'm so glad you agree." Pearl patted Olivia's leg where she had tapped it, a mysterious smile playing about her lips.

"Mmm," Olivia replied, wondering how she was going to manage her good works, make him respectable, and find him a wife.

And not allow herself to be unrespectable with him any longer.

But now was not the time to doubt herself. She could do all of it. She had to, or she would be just another managing female who tried to do things and failed.

Failure was not an option.

"Mr. Wolcott!"

Edward turned to see her walking toward him, a cheerful expression on her face. As though the last time they'd seen one another she hadn't been making a further mess of his already messy hair and trying to crawl into his jacket.

Hmm. He shouldn't feel piqued, and yet—he did. He wanted her to show the effects of that kiss, to reveal that she knew about their shared secret. Not act as though he was just another guest at a party they happened to both be attending.

"Good evening, Lady Olivia." He bowed, allowing his gaze to travel from the toes of her slippered feet up to her face. Taking his time, letting her know what he was doing.

Rewarded by the flush of pink on her cheeks and the defiant sparkle in her eyes. Damn, but he admired her fire.

"Yes, it is." She swallowed but didn't avert her eyes, meeting his gaze directly. Firmly.

Would she keep her eyes open as he pleasured her?

And now he should look elsewhere, because if he kept staring at her, with all these thoughts in his head, he was bound to embarrass himself with far more than just being illegitimate.

But he couldn't.

"Are you enjoying the party?" she continued, gesturing to the dance floor where several of Society's best people were dancing.

He grimaced, recalling his attempts to dance with Bennett. Whose toes, his friend had informed him, were bruised from the lesson.

"Yes, thank you." *Did you enjoy the kiss?* He wanted to ask. He burned to know if it had affected her as thoroughly as it had him. He wanted to kiss her again, right now. He wanted to hear her theories on duck hierarchy and what was right and wrong in the world.

"Excellent."

A silence fell between them, with her shifting in front of him as though she were feeling awkward but didn't know what to say.

That had to be an unusual circumstance for her. Did that mean she was affected?

And why was he so focused on that?

Oh right. Because kissing her was one of the

most pleasurable things that he'd done, and that included the time he'd spent with a certain widow who'd shown him some innovative tricks and the time he'd beaten the worst of his school tormentors in a horse race by several yards.

He should just admit it to himself—he wanted to kiss her again, slide those wispy sleeves off her shoulders, unbutton her gown, and show her just how very right he could be, so right that there was no possibility it was wrong.

Some of what he was thinking must have shown on his face since her eyes were wide and she was licking her lips.

He wanted to lick her lips.

Damn it, this was not what he should be thinking about at all. She'd probably be horrified that the kiss she'd instigated was resulting in such ideas. Probably she'd gasp as he shrugged off his jacket, rolled up his shirtsleeves, and showed her what a truly legitimate bout of lovemaking felt like.

Damn it.

"Do you want to dance?" He spoke brusquely, sharply, unable to keep his tone polite, given what he really wished he could say.

Can I strip you naked? Could I caress every single exposed inch of you? Will you run your soft, smooth hands all over the rest of me as you did my hair?

"Yes." He started, only to realize she'd responded to what he'd said, not what he'd been thinking.

He held his arm out and she took it, placing her fingertips on his sleeve. Were they trembling?

No, his sparkling warrior queen, his Boadicea, didn't tremble. If anything, he would hope, they were twitching with the urge to touch him again.

They walked to the dance floor, Edward praying he didn't end up placing his substantial weight on her toes. She glanced up at him, and he stumbled, making him smother an oath and clasp the hand that was holding on to him.

"I'm sorry," he muttered. "I haven't had much practice dancing."

He straightened and kept walking, only to pause as he heard a sound coming from his right.

"Are you—are you laughing at me?" he asked in disbelief. He turned to look down into her face, noting the smiling eyes, the wide grin, and the unmistakable sound emerging from her mouth. "You are!"

She nodded, putting her hand over her mouth, her eyes still sparkling.

If only they were alone, and he could draw her into his arms and lower his mouth to hers, taking her laughter as he kissed her lips.

But they weren't; in fact, they were at a Society party, one where nearly everyone probably looked down on him—including her—for the circumstances of his birth.

"It's just that you are, well, *you* and yet there you go, fretting about your dancing ability."

"What do you mean I am *me*?" How did she see him? Was he the intimidator duck, or something else entirely?

She tilted her head and placed her other hand on his sleeve so her hands were folded over one another. It felt inappropriately welcome.

"You stride about as though you know you own the world. Even though, things being what they are . . ." She bit her lip as she stopped speaking, and pink flowed into her cheeks. "That is, the circumstances of your birth might make it seem that you would behave a certain way, and yet you do not. You make certain everyone has to engage with you, no matter what, or you will dismiss them as being beneath you. Rightly, I would add." She nodded firmly to emphasize her words.

He felt his mouth drop open as a flood of emotions flowed through him. That she hadn't hesitated to speak the truth, even though it was awkward; well, that he already knew, but he never failed to be impressed that she was so bold, so persevering. That she recognized how he approached the world, facing it head-on rather than cowering; only Bennett had ever seen that before. And that she admired him for being who he was, even though he wasn't someone to be admired, at least according to the rules of Society.

God, he wanted to kiss her even more now.

"And then you are so adorable to admit that you cannot dance, or at least dance well, and it is so endearing for someone like you to admit to foibles."

Well, now he did not want to kiss her at all. "Adorable?" he said in a growl. "You think I'm adorable?" Of all the things he wished to be seen as—a formidable athlete, a fine judge of horseflesh, an excellent businessman, a gentleman whose birth did not impede his life—he had never wished to be seen as adorable. "And endearing?" he added in an incredulous tone.

"Yes," she replied, smiling as though she knew just how outraged he was. She probably did.

"Let me show you how adorable I am," he muttered, taking her arm and leading her to the dance floor, trying to ignore her laughter as they walked.

Olivia preened to herself as they walked onto the dance floor, Edward's ire positively reverberating through his entire body. In complimenting him, she had inadvertently made him forget—for a moment—who Society thought he was, which was why he was at this party. She had made him remember, she thought, who he truly was. An intelligent, thoughtful, proud man who apparently did not like being called adorable.

His face when she'd said the word! She would cherish the memory of that shocked expression for a long time.

And now they were on the dance floor, and it was a waltz, because of course it was, and his hand was in hers, his other hand at the small of her back, and the music had started, and she forgot everything but the music and him.

"You're not that bad a dancer," she said after a few moments of silence.

"Shh, I'm counting," he replied in a quick tone. "And now I've—"

At which point he trod on her foot.

It didn't hurt that much, just stung a little, since he'd really just stepped on her smallest toe, and had quickly leapt off before she could even register the pain. They weren't dancing any longer, but he still held her in the waltz position, which was not as close as they had been the night before.

Much to her chagrin.

"Are you all right?" He sounded genuinely concerned, and she felt herself melt a little inside. Adorable, indeed.

"I am fine, you barely touched it." To prove her

point, she gave a nod and started to move again, squeezing his hand to get him to continue the dance.

"One, two, three, one, two, three," she counted as he followed her lead.

"No talking," he ordered. "I can't concentrate if you talk."

She pressed her lips together to show her acquiescence and shot a glance at him that she knew spoke louder than whatever words she could say now: *You truly are adorable, and of course I'll stop speaking, you silly man, only I won't stop wanting to laugh.*

You make me laugh.

Has Bennett ever made you laugh?

Olivia nearly turned to see how Pearl could be so close, and then realized she'd just heard her twin's voice in her head.

"You're still laughing at me."

She shot a pointed glance at him as she edged back from within the circle of his arms.

"I'm not going to step on your foot again." His words were exasperated, and she felt a delightful joy at having irritated him so thoroughly. So adorably.

"You can appreciate my being concerned," she replied. "You warned me yourself that you weren't very good at this. You said nothing about possible bodily injury, however."

She narrowed her gaze at him. "I wonder if that is the real reason young ladies might not look favorably at the prospect of having you as a husband. Perhaps they are better informed than I am, and have naturally stayed away."

She shook her head in mock disapproval. "You did not tell me of this impediment to the project, Mr. Wolcott. I might not have taken on the challenge if I knew just what a challenge it was." And then she grinned at him again, wondering just what kind of mischievous spark she had discovered in herself. That he seemed to have unearthed in her.

"If we weren't in the middle of this party," he began, then swallowed and stared determinedly over her head.

Well. That sounded fascinating. She wondered if he were thinking that if they weren't in the middle of this party that he'd grab her even closer and kiss her. Fiercely, with all the passion she knew simmered just underneath his elegant evening clothes.

Speaking of which, she knew he was strong, but she'd felt the force of him as he'd escorted her onto the dance floor. Not to mention how he'd held her in his arms as they kissed. Although she should not be thinking about that.

Still, there was something almost intoxicating about suspecting he had a lot of strength that could be unleashed at any time. Anywhere. With anyone.

Just thinking about it made her shiver.

The music ended, and she curtseyed as he bowed, one of his curls slipping onto his forehead, making her wish she could reach up and smooth it back.

And then muss it all up again? a voice that was most definitely not Pearl's said in her head.

"Thank you for the dance." Even his voice made her shiver—all rich and dark and deep, as though what he was saying wasn't truly what he was saying.

Not that that made any sense.

"Thank you, Mr. Wolcott. You are not that bad a dancer after all. I am sure I can find some eligible young ladies who might be willing to risk their toes for the pleasure."

Although the last thing she wanted—even if she could barely admit it to herself—was for some other young lady to be the recipient of that devastating smile, being held in his powerful arms as he adorably and endearingly counted the beats of the music.

But that was the challenge. And she wanted the money he'd promised for the poor women and children, the thought of whom acted on her emotions like a bucket of cold water.

What was she doing, mooning over him? He wasn't her destiny. Bennett was. With Bennett, she would single-handedly rescue her family's reputation so that Pearl and Ida, at least, could marry well. Perhaps eventually Della could return to London, impossible though that seemed now.

None of that would be possible if she didn't marry Bennett. Never mind getting married to Edward, whose birth would cause yet another scandal.

It was up to her. It was all up to her.

"Can you escort me back to my mother?" she asked, not waiting for his reply as she took his arm.

"Of course."

She took a deep breath as they walked, scanning the room, looking at each single young lady in turn. Too dull, too aware of her own consequence, too irritating, too—curse it. She was never going to win this challenge if she shot down every single possible candidate. It was up to Mr. Wolcott and the lady in question if they suited, wasn't it? She should endeavor to introduce him to every possible female and allow his wealth and undeniable charm do the work.

That settled, she lifted her chin, planning out just who she'd introduce him to and when.

Overcoming her ridiculous fascination with him would be just another test of her perseverance and determination.

"COME IN, MY boy, and tell me about your evening."

Edward turned at the sound of his father's voice, smiling at the now-familiar sequence—he went out, his father waited up for him, and then questioned him intently about who he saw and what he did.

Mr. Beechcroft stood at the entrance to the library, a cozy fire flickering behind him.

Edward handed his coat and hat to the butler and strode after his father, feeling a frown cross his features as he saw how his father labored to sit comfortably.

The tightness in his chest had eased while he had been at the party, but it returned so quickly and forcefully it felt as though he had been punched. What was he doing, attending parties and dancing with sparkling ladies when his father was ill?

Instead of sitting himself, he knelt down in front of his father, looking up at his worn, beloved face. "Why are you up so late? You're supposed to be resting while I am doing all the hard work of finding a woman to marry me." He grinned as he spoke, not wanting to let his father know Edward's reaction when he saw his father's obvious illness.

Mr. Beechcroft smiled in reply, his brown eyes twinkling in delight. At least one of them was happy at the prospect of Edward's marriage. "And how is it going? Did you see your Lady Olivia?"

Edward shook his head and rose, going to sit in the chair opposite. "She is not my Lady Olivia," he said, knowing his father wouldn't care what Edward said if he had gotten something into his head.

It was what made him a brilliant businessman, and a very irritating father—once his brain had seized on an idea, he wouldn't rest until he saw it come to fruition. Hence the various factories that carried the Beechcroft name that had been built despite everyone telling his father his ideas were too grand, that the expenditure wouldn't be worth the eventual minimal profits.

Those people had been wrong. It was one thing, however, when one of his father's ideas made the Beechcroft fortune swell; it was another thing entirely when his father wanted his illegitimate son to marry a lady who would never say yes to his suit, and even if she did, her family would never say yes as well.

But to point out that there were some ladies who were far beyond Edward's reach—regardless of how much wealth and prospects he had—would hurt his father too much. Mr. Beechcroft already felt the sting of Edward's birth far more than Edward himself did.

"Of course she is not." Mr. Beechcroft's tone

made it clear he didn't believe his own words. "It was mere coincidence that you happened to rush out of the dining room the other night just after she did. And of course it didn't mean anything that she spent most of the evening before that looking at you. Did you have something on your face, I wonder?"

Edward didn't respond in words, but he did glare at his father. Who chuckled at seeing his son's expression.

"I stayed up, since you asked, because I was sorting through some papers. I need to get certain business transactions done before—before . . ." And then he paused, letting his words hang there in the silence so that Edward could fill in the blanks.

Before I die.

That sharp pain expanded from Edward's chest through his entire body, and he leaned forward in his chair, staring intently at his father's face. "We shouldn't stay here any longer. Your marital aspirations for me be damned. You should be in the country resting, where we can see your usual doctor. Where you are most comfortable."

His father looked as though he was going to argue, and Edward held his hand up. "Wait. Before you say no, let's talk about it." He held his hand out and began to tick items off on his fingers. "One. You have trusted your own doctor for years. I know you have seen Dr. Bell—that's his name, correct?" he said, waiting for his father's nod, "and that Dr. Bell told you that—" He couldn't say it, even though his father had said it already.

"That I have not long to live."

Edward's breath hitched. "Yes. That. The thing is, you are always saying that any business venture could benefit from having more than one opinion weighing in on it. It seems to me that your health is the most important business venture you've ever dealt with, and I want you to get your own doctor's opinion before you resign yourself to—to . . ."

"Death?" his father supplied in a quiet tone.

Edward nodded, his throat tight.

Mr. Beechcroft leaned back in his chair, wincing as he did so. Because the chair was uncomfortable? Or because he was in so much pain? Edward didn't dare to ask. But Mr. Beechcroft's regular doctor would, and that was entirely the point.

"But if we leave London, you won't have the opportunity to court someone named Lady Olivia," his father said with a grin.

Sometimes Edward wished his father were less jocular.

"If we return to the country and I can see for myself that your health is being taken care of as well as I would wish, I can concentrate on finding a suitable bride," he retorted. "You've often told me it's important to focus on the business at hand. How can I focus on the business of marriage if I am thinking about you and your health? When I know for certain, I will fulfill your wish." He didn't say *your final wish*, but it was clear from his tone what he meant.

His father twisted his lips in thought. "Hmm. And there are some other families still in residence in the country—there are sure to be some eligible young ladies there, so you won't waste time." As though each young lady was interchangeable with another, as long as she came from respectable stock.

His father was certainly single-minded when it came to what he wanted. "Although I do have a preference for that Lady Olivia," he added, confirming just how single-minded he was.

He leaned back in his chair and tilted his head in thought. "I have been thinking about your mother." He looked over at Edward. "I know I haven't told you much about her. It's so hard, even now." His eyes grew distant. "She was so kind and listened to all of my dreams. I knew we would get married, only her father—" And his lips tightened, and he shook his head.

"I'm sorry for your loss."

"And I'm sorry for yours. I wish you could have met her, I wish she could see you now. You resemble her more than me. You've got her father's height and she had dark curls like you do." Mr. Beechcroft shook his head. "If only we could have married, you wouldn't have to—"

Be a bastard, Edward thought to himself.

"Your Lady Olivia reminds me of your mother," his father continued, as though Edward wasn't conflicted enough about everything. "She is generous and intelligent, and she'd be a good wife."

This was one time Edward wished he didn't agree with his father. Because at the moment he couldn't imagine spending a life with any young lady who wasn't opinionated, fierce, passionate, and sparkling.

Unfortunately, he knew how that would end— with her trying to foist some unsuspecting young lady on him in some misguided quest for equality in Society, when they both knew there was nothing of the sort.

Or worse, she'd succeed in marrying him off, and then would resume her chase of Bennett.

How could he allow that to happen to his best friend?

He could not.

"I only want what is best for you," his father said, interrupting his thoughts. "I want you to have what I never did." His eyes got a distant expression. "I did think about marrying, but any other woman just didn't compare. And there was you to take care of." He smiled at Edward, a smile that revealed all of the love he had for his son. "All right," he said, waving his hand in the air. "I know you won't stop pestering me until I agree—you're like me in that way, you know," he said with a smile, "so we will return to our country home at the end of the week."

"Long enough for you to see your regular doctor and take his advice?" Edward knew how slippery his father could be when it came to his words. The man was renowned in business circles, at least, for saying things that seemed to indicate one course, only to mean something entirely different when it came to a closer examination.

"Yes. I will stay in the country until things are resolved."

Edward narrowed his gaze at his father, wondering what he was missing in the somewhat vague words. But he didn't want to spend time arguing about it when his father should be resting, so he merely nodded.

"I'll make all the preparations," he said.

Taking his father back home was the right thing to do. Even though it meant he wouldn't be able to watch Lady Olivia fail in her attempt to make him into a respectable member of Society. Even though he wouldn't watch as she introduced him to various young ladies who would probably rather swallow their dance cards then waltz with him.

Even though he wouldn't be able to kiss her again, watch as she argued vociferously in defense of one of her causes.

But it wasn't about him. He owed everything to his father, and he was going to sacrifice everything. A week or so ago, that sacrifice had been to try to gain acceptance into Society. Now it was to spend the rest of his life with a lady who could tolerate him.

"But you must meet him, Miss Hunter. I insist." Olivia smiled at the young lady opposite her, trying to look reassuring. Judging by the expression on the other lady's face, it was more likely she had on what Pearl liked to call her "You Must Do What I Say" Face. "Mr. Wolcott has just come to town and doesn't know that many people. I told our mutual acquaintance Lord Carson that I would endeavor to expand his circle of friends." She glanced over to where Mr. Wolcott stood, slightly outside the various groups of people sipping beverages while eviscerating one another's reputations. He stuck out from among all of them, a tall, dark, arrogantly curled gentleman whose face bore its usual distant expression.

Was it her imagination, or did he look slightly wistful?

"But Mr. Wolcott is Mr. Beechcroft's—" And then Miss Hunter paused, holding her hand up to her mouth as though she couldn't possibly utter the word that was in both of their minds.

Bastard.

"Well, he is," Olivia said in a terse voice. "That is true. Mr. Beechcroft has taken Mr. Wolcott in and recognized him as his own. Would you have preferred he left him in an orphanage? Because I promise you, those places are not ones where any child should be left."

The instinctual sorrow she felt when she considered those places, and those children, threatened to overwhelm her for a moment. Miss Hunter had likely never visited an orphanage, and likely had no idea what children who weren't in their own privileged position faced.

But Olivia did. And she was glad that Mr. Wolcott had managed to avoid that future, even though it meant he would have to meet ladies such as Miss Hunter, who looked terrified at the thought of meeting someone of Mr. Wolcott's birth. Miss Hunter's own family included a spendthrift brother, which was why the family was in straitened circumstances and why Olivia had chosen her. But he was legitimately born, so that meant he was more important and accepted than Mr. Wolcott.

But it was not the time to get angry at someone's

naïveté. "Please, Miss Hunter." Olivia glanced over again, sighing in relief. "And look, Lord Carson has joined him. I can introduce you to both of them."

"Well, in that case," Miss Hunter said, nodding her head in agreement.

The two ladies walked to where Mr. Wolcott and Lord Carson stood, Mr. Wolcott's eyes traveling over her body in a lazy assessment that made her skin prickle.

Which made her angry, because why was he daring to look at her that way, when he knew perfectly well that they should not have kissed and it was only an unfortunate emotional moment that they should both regret?

That Olivia did not regret it was her own problem, and something with which she berated herself at various hours of the day. It was like a clock chiming, it was so regular.

Oh! Time to regret one of the best experiences of my life!

"Lady Olivia," Lord Carson said as they approached. "It is lovely to see you this evening."

"And you, my lord," Olivia said, dipping into a curtsey. Trying not to assess Mr. Wolcott the same way he'd done to her. Though it was admittedly difficult, what with his being all tall and spectacularly and elegantly dressed, the messy disarray of his curls the only item not presented to perfection, which made him seem even more handsome.

"And may I present Miss Hunter? She is making her debut this year. Lord Carson, this is Miss Hunter. Mr. Wolcott, Miss Hunter."

They made their various "pleased to meet you's" and other pleasantries until an awkward silence fell over them.

Did she have to do all the work?

She did. Suppressing a roll of her eyes, she began to speak.

Chapter 12

Don't think too much about things that are in the past. Look only to the future.
LADY OLIVIA'S PARTICULAR GUIDE TO DECORUM

The party is delightful, don't you think?"

She had on her most sparkling expression, and yet Edward could tell it was forced. At least, he hoped it was forced. Because if some of her brain wasn't currently reviewing the details of that passionate kiss, he would have to reassess his kissing skills. Which he'd been assured were very good.

"And the music." She nodded encouragingly at them in turn, her expression faltering as she looked at him. *Say something*, her eyes seemed to express.

Well, he couldn't deny any of her wishes. Not when she wished to kiss him, and not now when she was so desperate for him to meet this wispy young lady whose presence he'd barely noticed, his attention having been taken so much with her.

"The music is indeed glorious," he agreed. He held his hand to her. "Would you care to more fully experience it and dance with me?"

Her gaze darted angrily between him and Miss Hunter, and he wished it were acceptable to lean his head back and laugh at her obvious discomfiture.

It was not, however, so he just clamped his jaw so he wouldn't laugh and let his hand dangle out there, a physical reminder of what he'd just asked her.

"Fine," she said in a terse voice, taking his hand. "Let us dance."

"And Miss Hunter, could I persuade you to dance?" Edward heard Bennett say behind them as they walked onto the dance floor.

He could feel how rigidly angry she was, and wondered just what it was about her ire that made him so . . . delighted.

When he was concentrating on her, on her emotions, he felt the warmth and heat of them spread all over him, like a blanket that nonetheless prickled.

He probably shouldn't tell her she reminded him of a prickly blanket.

Nor, honestly, should they dance together, because with her being all stiff and irritated, and him being the dancer he was, he would likely end up stepping thoroughly on her pride as well as her feet.

Instead—"Come out here for a moment," he said, guiding her to the windows that opened onto the terrace. She didn't argue, for once, but let him walk her quickly out into the night.

It was blissfully quiet out here, a welcome relief from the societal cacophony of inside. Not for the first time, he wished his father wasn't so set on his joining this world—he didn't particularly like it, or the people who were in it. He'd much prefer to be useful or entertained, whether that meant working on furthering his father's business ventures or galloping one of his horses while on the hunt in the country.

"Why are we out here? Why didn't you ask Miss Hunter to dance rather than me? That was the point, you know," she said in an aggrieved tone, folding her arms over her chest and glaring up at him.

A deliciously prickly sparkling blanket.

It was unfortunate he was going to be leaving at the end of the week.

"I do know," he said, reaching out and pulling one of her arms away from her body and taking her hand in his. She kept the other arm locked around herself, and he wondered if she knew just how tempted he was to remove that and pull her close against him. "I didn't want to lead Miss Hunter on in any way." Which was laughable, since the lady would likely be appalled to think that he was even possible as a suitor. "Because I am leaving London at the end of the week. I know I am thus depriving you of your opportunity to win our challenge, make me entirely respectable, and find me a bride." God help him. "So I will, of course, honor the commitment I made to you and donate a thousand pounds to the charity of your choice."

Her expression got both piqued and angry, and he watched as she tried to figure out what to say in reply.

He wished it would be *Well then, kiss me again, you idiot*, but he strongly suspected it would not.

"But why?"

He hadn't expected her to sound so—so *lost*. As though she were truly going to miss him.

"I—have to," he began, and then heard the words rush out of him, as though he wasn't in control of speaking them at all. "I have to take care of my father. He's—he's been given some news about his health, and he has said he will return home so we can see his usual doctor. I can't let him stay here in London just because . . ."

"Because he wants you to succeed?" she finished in a soft voice. "He is a good father—he only wants the best for you. I don't understand why so many people have a problem with a father wanting the best for his son."

Her voice was returning to its normal fierce tone, for which he was grateful. A comforting, soft-voiced Lady Olivia would be so out of his experience he might just break down and sob in her arms, which wouldn't do either of them any good. Especially with his leaving.

"I am sorry to hear your father is not in the best of health." She bit her lip. "It makes sense that you would want to leave town as soon as possible. You are a good son for making sure he takes care of himself," she said. "I appreciate your living up to your part of the challenge. I have no doubt that if you were to stay for the full month, I would succeed, however." She lifted her chin as she spoke, and it was as though he could feel her confidence in his own body.

It was breathtaking. It was likely a good thing he was leaving, if he thought about it. He was too intrigued by her, too intent on watching the expressions play over her face, wanting to feel the warmth of her sparkle. *Everywhere.*

"I have no doubt that you believe that, Lady Olivia." He couldn't keep the skepticism out of his voice; after all, she was one lady, albeit a fierce one, and he was standing among all the politely born ladies and gentlemen whose only experience with situations like his were to hold their noses and cross to the other side of the well-bred street.

"You are maddening," she said, but it didn't sound as though she were maddened by him. Or not entirely maddened by him, that is; she was looking at him with a slight smile on her mouth, as though she also found him amusing.

"But at least I was able to persuade you I am a decent enough gentleman," he said, allowing himself to step closer to her so he could look straight into her eyes, gauge her feelings by how she was regarding him. "And for that, Lady Olivia, I am eternally grateful."

"Oh, damn you," she replied, then slid her arms around his neck and drew his mouth down to hers.

SHE WAS KISSING him again. And this time, she didn't have any excuse except that she wanted to. He froze for a moment, and she had a sudden anxious feeling that he would draw away, an embarrassed expression on his face, and inform her that kissing her was not what he actually wanted to do. That he'd done it the other evening because he'd felt sympathy for her.

But then she felt his hands grasp her waist firmly, and he drew her to him just as firmly so their bodies were pressed up against one another. And he was kissing her passionately, ruthlessly, as though she were a woman who was able to withstand the force of him.

And she was. What was more, she inhaled the force of him, wanting to participate just as fully in this kiss as he was. Learning the taste of his mouth with her tongue, sliding her hands over his shoulders and down his back, flexing her fingers so she could make out his impressive musculature.

Even his back was strong. That shouldn't surprise her, but it did.

Eventually, her hands returned to the front of his body, and she found her palms running over his chest, wishing she could reach underneath his clothing to touch his skin. Nice though his clothing felt, she imagined he would feel even nicer.

His hands were still at her waist, but his fingers had tightened, and she wondered if he was struggling with the urge to touch her as she was touching him. If she weren't so intent on kissing him so thoroughly, she'd draw back for a moment and tell him, *Yes, please, do touch me in those places that suddenly seem to be clamoring for your fingers.* But she wouldn't, because if she withdrew, he would stop kissing her, and what was more important, she would stop kissing him, and she didn't want that. Not at all.

The fact that he was leaving shouldn't make her feel so alone. But it did. And kissing him helped, at least for right now, at this moment.

Then she heard a noise and leapt back from him, glancing around guiltily, hoping nobody had seen them.

"I—" he began, then took one of the hands that had been at her waist and pushed the curls off his forehead. "I did not mean to allow that to happen again."

"You did not mean for this to happen again?" She rolled her eyes at him, wondering how she'd missed that he was such a dolt. A handsome, curly-haired dolt, but a dolt nonetheless.

"You are not the one who did all this," she said, gesturing to the space between them. "Let me tell you once and forever, Mr. Wolcott," she continued, emphasizing his name with a raise of her eyebrow, "there is no one who is in control of me. I chose to kiss you, not the other way around. And may I say, I regret my action, if you were going to claim responsibility for it. But it was my action, not yours." She drew herself up to her full height, which was still, unfortunately for her, many inches shorter than his, and planted her hands on her hips. Her mother would be appalled at how common Olivia appeared right now, but that didn't matter. Not when he thought that he had bestowed a kiss on her, as though she were some pitiful supplicant. Was that how he saw her?

"I see I've annoyed you, Olivia." His voice was amused, and of course that irked her further. "I merely wished to draw the blame onto myself, since I know you do not truly wish to kiss me. Because you wish—" And he stopped, a pained expression on his face.

Because you wish you were kissing Bennett, her mind supplied. Even though Bennett—Lord Carson—hadn't crossed her mind once, and she would need to examine that more thoroughly later. But meanwhile . . . "Draw the blame onto yourself?" She stepped forward, raising one hand to point a finger at his chest. The chest that had been so intriguing to her just a few minutes ago. "As though I am not responsible for what I do? As though someone might accuse me of something untoward, and you would have to take the blame because of who you are? A man?"

She accompanied the last word with a poke to his body, making him stumble back, likely from surprise since the poke wasn't that hard.

"A bastard." He spoke in a quiet tone, and she felt the whoosh of shame flow through her on hearing his words. Hearing the pain and guilt, yes, of his acknowledging what he was—in his own eyes, as well as Society's.

She dropped her hand as though she had been touching a red-hot poker, twisting her hands together in front of her so she wouldn't do anything more foolish like touch him comfortingly or, God forbid, kiss him again.

"You are not that," she said in a furious whisper. "You should not and will not be defined by your birth. And your saying something like that just deflects from what it is that you were saying in the first place—that I was not responsible for my actions because I was not in control. Let me assure you, Mr. Wolcott—*Edward*—that I am entirely in control."

"Are you?" he asked, a dangerous tone in his voice. A tone that nonetheless made her shudder in an entirely good way.

"Are you in control when I do this?" and he accompanied his words by drawing her forward back into his arms, and she couldn't help herself— she raised her arms and wrapped her hands around his neck, stepping closer to him still.

"Or when I do this?" he said in a whisper, his breath on her cheek, his mouth lowering to hers.

"Or this?" he finished as he pressed his lips against hers in a firm, intense, and yes, completely controlling manner.

Dear lord, she might swoon. Or be discovered. Or lose control.

She wished she were horrified at any of the ideas. But she was absolutely not.

Chapter 13

Follow your heart, or the body part that seems as though it is in the most need.

LADY OLIVIA'S PARTICULAR GUIDE

TO BEING RECKLESS

*E*dward had wanted to show her how she could lose control as thoroughly as he, but it didn't manifest itself that way.

She was probably still irritated by his words, since she kissed him ruthlessly, sliding her tongue into his mouth, holding his upper arms in a furious grip.

As though to battle him in who could make the other lose control first.

It might be me, a voice said in his head.

He stood there, returning her savage kisses with his own. Running his hand down to the small of her back, and lower still, to cup the soft curve of her arse, to pull her up against him, his cock rising up in his trousers to press against her body.

She was magnificent, and he wanted to devour her. Or let her devour him, he didn't care which. He was egalitarian in that way; as long as complete and total ravishment happened, he was fine with it.

He drew his other hand behind her as well and yanked his gloves off, dropping them to the ground. Then he returned his hand to her curves, but brought his other hand to her neck, sliding his fingers down to touch her collarbone, her upper chest, until he was able to cup her breast in his palm.

He felt her shudder at his touch, and he wanted to grin at how reactive she was. If she hadn't wanted this, she would have made it absolutely and totally clear—her fury at his attempt to own what had happened between them showed him that. So he didn't hesitate, running his fingertip up at the edge of her evening gown, dipping it into her bodice to touch the warm softness of her breast. To reach two fingers in now to touch her nipple, its hard point a testament to what she was feeling now. What she wanted now.

Dear God, he wanted to fuck her. Or no, he wanted to make love to her, long, slow, and thoroughly. He wouldn't be satisfied with a mere fuck, a moment where he could explode and have it all be done with. He wanted to savor her, run his tongue over each and every part of her, learn what made her sigh and quiver and scream his name.

She broke the kiss, leaning back to look up at him, a dazed expression in her eyes. Likely the same one was in his.

"What is happening here?" she asked. "I—my God, I've never," and then she shook her head as though to clear it. His fingers still in her gown, his cock no doubt tenting his trousers. Surely she must feel it pressed against her?

"What is happening, Olivia, is something that cannot happen again." Edward sighed and leaned his forehead against hers, removing his fingers from her bodice and his hand from her arse. Putting his hands gently at her waist. "I am leaving. We likely won't see one another again." He placed a kiss on her forehead. "It has been a pleasure. Far more than I can, or should, say."

He stepped back, and gestured toward the ballroom. "You should probably precede me, since I am in no state to enter polite society at the moment." Which was a discreet way to mention his erection, and hopefully she would understand.

She darted a glance down—well, then, she did understand—and bit her lip. "Yes, of course. If you'll excuse me," she said, as though they had just parted from a waltz, not the most passionate and intense interlude he'd ever had. She squared her shoulders, gave him one last rueful smile, and returned to the ballroom, not once looking back at him.

Leaving him bereft, with a massive cockstand, and a heart full of ache and longing.

"WE'RE SUPPOSED TO deliver the shifts today. Or had you forgotten?"

Pearl's voice roused Olivia out of an uncharacteristic bout of introspection. Normally she thought about the things she was aware of and was trying to solve.

But now she was also thinking about the man she knew about and absolutely could not solve, and she suspected she would be thinking on that topic for a good long time.

And she would never see him again.

"Olivia?" Now Pearl sounded concerned.

"Yes, of course," Olivia replied, trying to return to her usual efficient tone. "We can deliver the shifts and we can also stop in to see the children."

"We've been too busy with all these parties," Pearl said, making it sound as though she would rank parties just below stubbing one's toe or drinking cold tea. Though for Pearl they were; she was too shy, too restless, to want to sit in a room filled with people she barely knew and likely wouldn't want to.

If only Society had more energetic events, possibly held outside, Pearl would be a lot happier. But until the best families decided Mayday poles and dances held in fields were the most appropriate way for them to show their being at the top of the social world, that likely wouldn't happen.

Though the thought of some of those ridiculous lords in over-snug trousers trying to waltz among bales of hay was rather amusing.

"We should never be too busy to take care of people who need it," Olivia replied. Feeling her chin lift in her usual stance of combat.

It was only Pearl, but she couldn't allow her skills to diminish. She never knew when some misguided man would tell her that children much preferred to work than have to go to school, and she would have to show him—in explicit and excruciating detail—why he was wrong.

"Of course not," Pearl replied drily. "Oh no, look!"

She held up the topmost shift on the pile, which was now shredded at the neck with a few cat hairs indicating what had happened. "I thought I reminded you to put those in a box so the kittens couldn't get to them." She turned to look at Olivia. "You're not normally this careless. Is something going on? Something I should know about?"

"Uh," Olivia began, only to stop when Pearl's

face lit up and she flung the shift back on the pile to run over to Olivia's bed and hug her.

"Something did happen! What happened? Did you finally realize you don't really love Lord Carson? Was it when you were spending time with Mr. Wolcott? Did you fall in love with Mr. Wolcott? I have to say, I prefer him to Lord Carson. Lord Carson is always so serious and preoccupied. If you ask him a question like 'Do you want sugar in your tea?' you get the feeling you've just interrupted the course of progressive history. With Mr. Wolcott, he always seems as though he is grateful you've asked him about how he takes his tea."

Olivia bit her lip at Pearl's statement; obviously Mr. Wolcott was grateful because so few people treated him with courtesy. Or the kind of discourtesy with which she had shown him last night. She couldn't keep herself from wincing at the memory of it.

"There was something." Pearl narrowed her eyes at her sister. "You have to tell me. Or I'll ask Ida to pretend we're in chancery, and she can be the magistrate. You know you can't withstand Ida asking questions."

The thought made Olivia flinch. No, she did not want her most analytical sister asking questions that would reveal that Olivia had basically thrown herself at Mr. Wolcott. Well, thrown her lips at his lips, to be more accurate.

She leaned over to look under her bed, locating two of the four kittens and scooping them up into her lap—they protested with ridiculously cute meows.

One of them, Snapper, began to knead her gown, his tiny claws getting stuck in the embroidery of her day gown. She kept extracting him from it, and he didn't seem to be ruining anything—yet—and the joy of having two little furballs of love on her lap was worth a slight disarray of her gown, which was the one she kept for visits to the lesser neighborhoods she visited anyway.

The other kitten curled up into a ball on her thigh and promptly fell asleep, Olivia scratching its head.

"Yes, they are very sweet, but you cannot evade the questions through the use of feline subterfuge."

Olivia looked at Pearl in surprise. "Have you been spending more time with Ida lately? 'Feline subterfuge' sounds like something she would say in court, actually."

Pearl laughed. "No, I was just reading *The Mystery of the Urn*, or one of those kinds of books, and I thought I'd try speaking that way in real life." Her expression became haughty. "Do you surmise I would be sufficiently able to persuade those persons of lesser intelligence and education of my undeniable ability to counteract any such attempt by another cat or cat-like animal to ravage ladies' unmentionables?"

"You mean convince people you can keep the cats away from the rest of the shifts?" Olivia replied, laughing at Pearl's absurdity. "I think so. Have at it, sister."

Pearl got off the bed to take the shifts out of the cats' way, and then returned to the bed, crossing her arms over her chest. "And now you have to tell me."

She did. She would have to. It often felt as though something hadn't truly happened unless she could tell her twin all about it.

They would have to discuss that in the future if or when one of them got married. But meanwhile, Olivia could tell her twin most of this.

"I kissed him."

Pearl nodded slowly, encouraging Olivia to continue. "You kissed Mr. Wolcott, to be clear. You did not kiss Lord Carson."

"No. Not yet." And maybe not ever, if what Pearl was suggesting and Olivia herself had wondered was true. Had she fallen out of love with Bennett? Had she ever been in love with him at all?

"What kind of kiss was it? The kind that says, 'Thank you for the dance, I've had one glass too many of champagne, and there's your cheek'?"

But judging by the way Pearl said it, she knew perfectly well it wasn't that kind of kiss.

"How would you know anything about any kisses at all?" Olivia glared at her sister, whose expression did not change.

Pearl was very good at keeping her own counsel. Nor would she be deterred when she had questions. "No, not that kind of kiss." How could she put it? She settled herself cross-legged on the bed, dislodging the sleepy kitty, which growled and then went right back to sleep. The other kitten was playing with a ribbon on her gown.

"You know how when you're reading one of those novels like that mystery one? And it's so good and so enthralling, and you can't believe the things that are happening in it. And you're rushing so fast to read it, only you don't want it to ever end, since then it will be over."

"Ooohhh," Pearl replied in a soft exhale. "That sounds wonderful."

"It was." Olivia lowered her face to stick her nose into Snapper's fur. As much for the kitten's cuteness as so Pearl couldn't see her expression right then. Because she was fairly certain it would reveal a certain amount of regret, and her fascinated wish to do it again, and confusion about just how she felt now about everything.

And Pearl would see it all and would no doubt

have something to say about it. For a relatively quiet person, Pearl could definitely talk a lot.

"So does that mean he is courting you? Are you the respectable lady who will marry him and make him respectable too?"

The thought should have occurred to her before, what with the kissing and all, but it simply hadn't. She straightened like a shot, a few cat hairs wafting about in the air in front of her nose, and stared at Pearl.

"No, of course not."

"Because you still think you're going to marry Lord Carson?" Pearl asked in a gentle tone. The one she used right before she gave Olivia some hard truths.

Olivia thought she knew the truths already, so perhaps they could skip that part.

"I don't think that any longer." Now it was Pearl's turn to look surprised.

It felt as though Olivia's world was shifting, again. She'd thought for so long that she would marry Bennett—Lord Carson—that admitting it wasn't true felt as revelatory as when she had realized there was more to life than parties and gowns.

She licked her lips, which had become dry. "I think if I am so easily able to kiss somebody like Mr. Wolcott without thinking of Lord Carson, then it is probably true that I am not, actually, in love with Lord Carson after all." *Dear lord. I am not in love with Bennett. I might never have been in love with Bennett.*

Who am I? Who will I be?

The thoughts came fast, making her feel as though she were spinning in a circle, her brain going faster and faster until she couldn't think anymore.

Pearl's eyes widened as Olivia spoke, and then she smiled, a warm smile that felt lit up from the inside. "Oh, thank goodness. I was worried I was going to have to toss you over a horse and gallop away from the church with you. You can't marry him—that's clear enough."

Olivia couldn't help the pique in her tone. "Clear enough? Why is it clear enough? Because he is handsome and intelligent and wants to do the right things and is of our world and was supposed to marry Eleanor until his brother stole her?"

Pearl rolled her eyes. "Look, you and I agreeing on this very important matter—the matter of your future life—does not mean you should be defensive about it. It does happen, our agreeing sometimes." She gestured to the kittens in Olivia's lap. "We agreed these little ones should be saved from the Robinsons' gardener, although we still don't know what we're going to do with them. They should be running around free somewhere, not stuck in our rooms in London."

Olivia grinned at the thought that popped into her head, making Pearl look at her suspiciously.

"I have an idea," she said.

Chapter 14

Offer gifts chosen for the recipient, not for the giver.

LADY OLIVIA'S PARTICULAR GUIDE
TO BEING RECKLESS

*O*livia approached the front door not with anxiety—she was never anxious; she always knew just what she was doing and why. No cause for concern, ever.

But she had to admit to feeling a little off. Whether it was that she'd realized she didn't actually love the love of her life, or that the last time she'd seen Mr. Wolcott was supposed to have been the *last* time she'd see him.

And that same last time was also the last time she'd kissed him, and then he'd kissed her, and everything was a muddle, and she didn't know what to think anymore, so it was not surprising she felt a little off. Which was a vast understatement of how confused and lost she felt.

Besides which, she had two wriggling kittens tucked into her jacket, and even her ability to withstand discomfort in the service of doing good was having trouble against all those tiny kitten claws.

And since she had snuck out without even Pearl in attendance, she wasn't certain how to knock on the door. Not without dislodging the kittens.

She was very grateful she hadn't had to drive herself, at least.

She raised her arm and rammed her elbow into the wooden door, grimacing at the shooting pain that went all the way up into her shoulder.

But she did hear steps approaching so, as she frequently told Pearl, the pain was worth the effort.

The door swung wide to reveal a butler whose expression of surprise was quickly replaced with the bland assurance Olivia associated with most butlers.

"I am Lady Olivia, here to see Mr. Wolcott. They haven't gone yet, have they?" she asked, trying to peer around the butler's substantial form in the doorway.

"I will inquire," he replied, his sharp gaze likely taking in that she was alone and therefore perhaps not entirely respectable.

Her parents' phaeton was at the bottom of the steps, but the butler likely couldn't trust it belonged to her. She appreciated how strict he was to his duty, but she did wish he'd asked her in so she could sit down and remove Scamp and Mr. Whiskers from her jacket.

The door snapped back open again in minutes, only now it was Edward opening it. He glanced around, a protectively angry look on his face, and yanked her inside, slamming the door behind them.

The kittens did not like the sudden noise and movement, so Olivia let out a shriek that was far louder than she would have liked.

"Did I hurt you?" he asked, his expression now concerned.

"No, it's—do you have a place we can talk in private?" Because the butler was still in the hallway, and there was a footman or two standing around as though waiting for something. If they weren't careful, they'd each get a kitten, and she didn't think that was the type of task they had been hired for.

"Yes, in here," he said, taking her arm more gently now and guiding her to the same room she'd been in the time she'd visited before. When she'd made that list and he'd talked about how it hurt. Even though he hadn't directly talked about how it hurt, Society's condemnation of him, but she could understand what he was truly saying.

It was her empathy that got her into these situations, after all.

"Tea, please," he said to the butler, closing the door just enough to ensure nobody could hear, but leaving it wide enough so that no impropriety could take place.

Unfortunately.

"Would you care to sit down?" he asked, gesturing to one of the chairs in front of the fireplace.

She shook her head no, then sat down in the sofa right underneath the window. Sitting down carefully, so as not to startle her traveling companions.

"I thought last night—I thought we weren't going to see one another again." He spoke in an exceedingly polite tone, enunciating clearly, which made Olivia want to smile even as she wanted to cry about it all.

"Well, yes, but then I recalled that you hadn't yet given me the thousand pounds you promised. And I thought of something I could give to you that would perhaps make the country even more enjoyable." And with that she slipped her hand inside her jacket and withdrew Mr. Whiskers, with Scamp following quickly behind.

They wasted no time in vaulting off her lap to go sniff the legs of the sofa.

He was frozen in place, his eyes pinned to the kittens.

"You brought me . . . cats?" he said in disbelief.

"Not cats, silly." Did he know nothing? "They are kittens, and Pearl and I rescued them from our neighbor. There are two more, but I didn't think you would want all four."

He lifted his head to look at her. "I don't want any of them, Olivia." He sounded outraged, and she had a twinge of doubt. Was it possible he wouldn't want them? But he didn't know them. He just had to give them a chance.

"Oh, you do," she contradicted in a knowing tone of voice. "Kittens are delightful creatures, they don't need much care. Just some food and a place to, you know."

"You brought me kittens." It sounded as though he was having difficulty processing her generosity.

"I did." Olivia removed her hat, placing it on the sofa beside her. "They can't stay in our house—my mother will have a fit if she discovers them." That her mother hadn't yet figured out that there were additional residents in the town house was testament to just how self-absorbed the duchess was. Olivia thought she might safely house a marching band prone to practicing at all hours without her mother noticing, but she didn't want to share that detail with Edward.

Not that that was the only reason. "I know we

might not see one another again, and I wanted you to have them as a way to remember me."

"It's unlikely I will forget you." His tone was both amused and wry, and she wondered how he would recall her, later on, when the kittens had grown up and he had—well, she couldn't think about that.

Olivia heard a noise in the hallway, and quickly scooped up the kittens, holding them up against her chest.

"Tea, sir," the butler said as he walked in with one of the footmen who was bearing a large silver tray. The butler directed the footman where to place it, and Olivia could have sworn she saw the man's eyebrow raise just barely as he took in the sight of two wriggling kittens in Olivia's arms.

He seemed to be a very good butler.

"Is there anything else?" he asked, this time his gaze flickering more obviously toward Olivia and what she held.

"I suppose a saucer of milk would be useful." Edward spoke in a grumpy tone, but at least he was already providing the kittens with sustenance.

"Excellent, sir," the butler said, nodding to the footman.

The two servants walked out as Edward resumed his staring at Olivia. And not the "you are the most beautiful creature I've ever seen" kind of staring. More the "what insanity have you brought into my life, you crazy creature" kind of way.

"I can accept your draft for the thousand pounds because I'm supposing that you don't just have it lying around, even though I do know you are fabulously wealthy."

Olivia returned the kittens to the floor, then leaned forward to the tea things. Like everything she'd seen thus far in the house, the set was perfect, clearly very expensive, and lacking any kind of individuality. "Did you or your father choose the furnishings? Likely not, since I wouldn't think you would have enough time to do so, plus it is generally considered a lady's domain, and you don't have a lady in residence." She picked up one of the teacups, marveling at the thinness of the bone china, the delicate flowers painted on the side.

She set the teacup down on its saucer and poured tea. "Milk? Sugar?" she asked, looking up at him.

"Nothing." He bent over to pick the teacup up and went and sat in one of the chairs opposite her sofa, keeping his gaze on the floor so he wouldn't step on the kittens, she supposed.

She made her own tea, and then leaned back against the sofa. Most ladies wouldn't dare allow their bodies to relax against a sofa back, but she was already behaving shockingly—visiting the illegitimate son of a wealthy merchant without a chaperone—so she thought that being comfortable was the least of her infractions.

"Why would you even think I'd want kittens?"

She rolled her eyes, taking a sip from her cup. "You're still worried about the kittens? I promise, they are lovely little creatures. You'll fall in love in no time. Mr. Whiskers, he is the one with the long whiskers—obviously—he is the most adventurous of the four, so I thought he would suit you the best. Since you are also prone to adventure. Scamp, she is the snuggliest. She just wants pets and I thought that would suit you as well, since I know you have a generous heart."

"A generous heart?" He raised an eyebrow, an amused look on his face. At least he wasn't continuing to ask her about the kittens.

Because honestly, she wasn't sure why she had thought they would be the perfect things to give him. Just that she'd known, with some bone-deep certainty, that he would love having them, and they would love being had by him.

She was not speaking about herself, of course. Never that.

And besides, when and if they were to cross one another's path again, she could ask him how they were doing, and then they wouldn't have to spend time on other topics, such as *Why did you kiss me?* and *Why don't you consider being my bride?*

Oh. Well. She hadn't really thought about that last point. It would be ridiculous, anyway. He tolerated kissing her, but it was clear he found her overbearing, managing, and too opinionated.

He wasn't wrong, but those were the things Olivia liked about herself. She *liked* knowing just what she should do, and doing it. That others didn't immediately fall in with her plans showed their lack of comprehension of just what was at stake.

"I am not generous because I am about to give you a thousand pounds," he continued, leaning forward to place his teacup on the table between them. He'd drunk it all already.

"Sir?"

It was the butler again, this time holding a small bowl presumably filled with milk. Even the china deemed suitable for a cat was delicate and clearly expensive.

"Just on the floor next to the sofa."

The butler nodded, placing the bowl down with as much butlerly aplomb as he could. Olivia had to admit she admired his sangfroid.

"Nothing else, thank you," Edward said. The butler nodded and left the room while the kittens ran over to investigate the bowl, starting to slurp the milk, making Olivia giggle.

"Look, aren't they adorable? Come over here, Edward, and see." She froze as she realized she'd just used his given name—how had that happened? It wasn't as though they were more than acquaintances, if you forgot about the two times they'd kissed.

Oh, if you just forget about those times, you barely know one another. It was Pearl's voice in her head, of course. Being sarcastic, because of course they were more than acquaintances.

That's right—you are friends, Pearl said.

"Hush," she muttered.

"I didn't say anything."

"No, I—" And she turned to look at him, now seated beside her on the sofa. His curls all unruly and riotous, one corner of his mouth pulled up as though he found something amusing but didn't want to admit to smiling.

"Edward! Edward, are you here?"

Olivia spun around to look at the door while Edward rose to call out into the hallway. "In here, Father," he said.

He glanced back at her, an aggrieved expression on his face. "And now you're going to have to explain why you're here, and he's going to think something else entirely. Honestly, Olivia, do you ever consider your actions?"

It was on the tip of her tongue to say of course she did, that she considered things far more than most people, but then Mr. Beechcroft had stepped into the room, accompanied by Ida.

"What are you doing here?" Ida asked, not sounding at all pleased to find her older sister at the house.

"I could ask the same of you," Olivia retorted, only to realize how foolish that was—Ida was here, of course, because she wanted to be. Ida never did anything she didn't want to, so if she was here, it was because it suited her in some way.

Olivia shared her sister's single-mindedness, but Olivia's own focus was not on books or philosophical conversation, but on what could, and should, be done.

Because if she didn't, she didn't trust that anybody else would.

Just thinking about what might happen to the poor and orphaned children if Olivia weren't there to help them—well, it was enough to bring the sting of tears to her eyes. Not that she ever cried. But her eyes definitely stung.

"Mr. Beechcroft has asked me to help catalogue the library. The owners of the house have quite an impressive collection. Not that they likely know much about it," Ida sniffed, since of course nobody could possibly be as well-informed as she was.

"I'll be visiting the library after Mr. Beechcroft and Mr. Wolcott depart for the country. That way, when they return, the catalogue will be finished. I believe there are some unearthed gems hiding there." She sounded excited, which startled Olivia. Her sister was so seldom enthusiastic about anything.

When they return. But from what Edward had intimated, they wouldn't be returning. At least—Mr. Beechcroft wouldn't.

She couldn't keep herself from glancing at Edward, wishing there were some way she could ease his heartache. But that would require more than just arriving to do some good; this was literally about life and death, and the love a son had for his father.

That moved her as profoundly as seeing any type of injustice in the world. She'd never seen that kind of love before—after all, her father communicated in grunts and growls, and her mother didn't communicate as much as unleash a steady stream of commentary. It humbled her.

Which was remarkable since, as Pearl was fond of saying, Olivia was never humbled. But now? Having realized that Lord Carson was not for her, that she would miss seeing Edward, miss being in his presence, and miss seeing Mr. Beechcroft's clear pride in his son?

She was humbled.

"Ida, since you're here, would you want to accompany me home?"

Ida looked surprised, likely because Olivia seldom asked for Ida's participation in anything. But Olivia should try harder with her sister. She should try harder to understand people who weren't her. She should try harder to figure out what it was she truly wanted also.

Because it wasn't Lord Carson, and it wasn't spending time at parties, and it wasn't being more honorable than everyone else.

Although that did have its appeal.

She wasn't certain what it was she did want. But she had a terrible suspicion it was a tall, strong gentleman with gorgeous curls, a devastating smile, and a wicked sense of humor.

A gentleman who was far beyond her in his honor, and yet would be seen as someone far below, were she to even imagine such a thing happening.

"Thank you for asking," Ida replied, sounding honestly grateful. "I will just go get my things. Mr. Beechcroft, do leave that atlas if you can. I can send it down to you in a week or so, after I've had a chance to review it."

Mr. Beechcroft smiled as he patted Ida's hand. "Of course, my capable assistant. I am so glad we have made the acquaintance of the duke's daughters. We will miss you when we leave town."

"Oh, let me go get what I owe you, Lady Olivia," Edward said. He walked into another room off the hallway, reappearing with a piece of paper in his hand. His draft for the thousand pounds, she presumed.

She took it from him and tucked it into her pocket without looking at it. Looking, instead, into his dark eyes and Mr. Beechcroft's cheerful visage.

Olivia felt a lump rise in her throat and wished she were brave enough—yes, she wasn't brave enough, at least not right now—to tell Edward that she felt something toward him. That it was more than just pique or natural curiosity or frustration.

But she didn't know what it was.

Or who she was. Or what he thought about her.

It felt, suddenly, as though nothing mattered. That thought terrified her more than anything.

Chapter 15

Listen to your heart. And if your heart seems to be saying the wrong thing, listen to your sister.

LADY OLIVIA'S PARTICULAR GUIDE

TO BEING RECKLESS

*I*t is unfortunate that we have to leave town, my boy," Mr. Beechcroft said as the carriage pulled away from the town house. He leaned back against the seat cushions and placed his hands on his stomach. "But I do have to admit that I am feeling better about the decision. I worry that Dr. Bell was too hasty in his diagnosis. I am feeling quite well, if tired. But London will do that to you."

Edward nodded without looking at his father; his attention was on the two kittens, both of which were trying to escape the basket they'd been put into for the journey. The housekeeper seemed to be perturbed at having been asked to provide a basket for this purpose. Edward shared her perturbation, but he couldn't just abandon them. Not when she had given them to him.

"She gave you kittens?" Mr. Beechcroft said for at least the hundredth time. It seemed his father was as perplexed by the choice of Olivia's gift as Edward himself was.

"She did." Edward drew Mr. Whiskers out of the basket and tucked him up against his shirtfront. "Lady Olivia has a penchant for rescuing strays." *Like me*, he thought to himself with a smile. "I believe she thought she could improve the kittens' lives by finding them new homes." Thank goodness she hadn't brought all of the kittens.

Edward's father leaned forward with his hands out. "I can take the other one. I don't want it to feel abandoned."

Of course not. Edward himself was proof of that—close to three decades ago, Mr. Beechcroft had had the chance to shrug off his responsibilities, and he had chosen to own up to them. Edward had never once felt abandoned, even though he had felt many other things.

"Here you go. I believe the animal's name is Scamp." Edward handed the kitten over to his father, wincing as tiny claws dug in.

"There, there," Mr. Beechcroft said, smiling

down at the kitten. "You are going to like being in the country. Much better than London."

"You'll enjoy it better too, if I'm not mistaken," Edward said.

Mr. Beechcroft paused in the middle of petting Scamp to look at his son. "You're going to miss London though, if I'm not mistaken."

Edward felt his chest tighten. He was. He was going to miss seeing her, needling her on her outrage, watching her champion ducks and bastards alike. Kissing her.

Yet he knew she would never be for him, knew she still believed herself in love with his best friend.

Which meant he knew full well it was a good thing he wouldn't be seeing her any longer. Even though it hurt.

The pain would ebb, and eventually she'd find someone—not Bennett—to marry, and Bennett would let him know, and Edward could pretend it didn't hurt.

"We'll go see your doctor the day after we arrive home."

"And depending on what he says, perhaps we will return to London after all." Apparently Mr. Beechcroft was not to be deterred.

He should just talk about it then, since his father wouldn't relent until he had heard firsthand how his son felt.

"I know you want what is best for me," he began, knowing that that was the absolute truth. "And I know you think that marriage to a respectable female is what is best for me. And that, perhaps, I have grown fond of Lady Olivia." And aggravated and amused and enchanted.

"But the thing is, I have no desire to marry anyone until I know your health has been taken care of as best it can. I don't know why I let you convince me otherwise. Why we stayed in London for as long as we did when we should have returned home so you could rest and see your usual doctor." Edward grimaced. "That is, I do know why I let you convince me otherwise. Because you are remarkably persuasive, as all your business partners know. But I shouldn't have listened. And Lady Olivia is, unfortunately, persuaded that she cares for—for another," he said, stumbling over the phrasing. His father liked Bennett well enough, but Edward didn't trust his father wouldn't take Olivia's purported feelings for Bennett as an affront.

"I know you could persuade her she cares for you," his father replied. "If you wanted her to."

If I wanted her to.

Did he want her to? What did it matter, anyway? There was no possibility of his seeing her again. His first and only concern was his father, not whether Lady Olivia could be persuaded to fall in love with a bastard like him.

"Perhaps," he replied, leaning back in his seat, closing his eyes, and tucking Mr. Whiskers under his chin.

"THANK YOU FOR your visit, ladies." The matron of the home never seemed to be as honored by Olivia and Pearl's visits as Olivia might have wished. In fact, she might have possibly spotted the lady suppressing exasperation when Olivia was merely trying to point out a better way of doing things.

But today, Olivia knew, would be different. And that was because she had Edward's draft tucked in her pocket, and she was going to present it after she and Pearl had donated the shifts.

She didn't want the shifts to get short shrift, after all. And then nearly guffawed at her own joke.

It was a good thing she did feel like laughing— Pearl had commented that for the last few days Olivia had seemed like a faint copy of herself. Not smiling, not managing, arguing only a little when their mother had insisted Olivia adored shirred eggs, when it was actually Pearl.

She knew just why she was feeling so out-of-sorts, and she did not like it one bit. Even though she did like him, the Other, more than one bit. And that was the problem.

She missed him. She kept going to parties and glancing around for him before remembering he wasn't there. That he was off being an honorable son, even though the world would say he was dishonorable. Olivia knew better. As usual.

"You can put the parcels just there," the matron said, gesturing to a corner of the room where it looked like a hundred shifts had been placed already. Olivia felt her mouth open into an O of surprise, and glanced over at Pearl, who was glaring back at her.

Of course. Because Pearl had done the most work on the shifts, and Olivia had believed their donation to be essential, when it appeared that, in fact, they were not.

"Well, you certainly have a great number of contributions," Olivia said.

"Yes, well, it seems that many ladies are desirous of assisting the society with their good works," the matron replied, her tone indicating that Olivia was just one among many.

Naturally, Olivia felt like bristling. But did the next best thing, which was withdraw Edward's draft from her pocket. "This is one good work that I believe will be unique," she said, unable to keep a smug tone from her voice.

Even she knew she sounded pompous, and

she wished Edward were here to take her down
a peg.

Perhaps kiss her as well.

But mostly take her down a peg.

Even though she was lying to herself about her
preferences for what he might do.

"Gracious, that is a generous donation." The
matron looked at Olivia with a newfound admiration in her gaze. "We will be able to do so
many good things with these funds. Thank you
so much, Lady Olivia."

Olivia began to speak as she felt Pearl's furious
nudge in her side. She frowned at her twin—of
course she was going to mention Mr. Wolcott, she
didn't need Pearl to remind her—and returned
to the matron. "I am merely an emissary for this
good deed, Miss—" And then she paused, because she always forgot the woman's name.

"Miss Pettyworth," Pearl supplied. Pearl was
always better at paying attention to things like
people's names and what they did and their favorite foods and the like.

Did that mean Olivia was more like their mother?

The thought—the near truth of it—made her
want to shout and proclaim how very much unlike her mother she was, only—only she wasn't.

"Miss Pettyworth," she echoed instead, promising herself she wouldn't forget the name. "A

friend of mine, a Mr. Wolcott, is actually the benefactor. He would be here himself, only—"

Only he returned to the country to ensure his father would get the best care, leaving Society's whirl and the promise of an advantageous marriage to do so.

Even though, she had to admit, those things never seemed to hold an appeal for him.

"Mr. Wolcott." Miss Pettyworth nodded. "He seems a most excellent and generous gentleman."

Olivia's throat got thick. "He is."

"I will ask the children to work on a thank-you card to send him. We'll be able to afford more pencils and paper for them now."

Olivia felt even worse at those words—that these children didn't have pencils and paper, things she took for granted, just because of whom they were born to. That she did have such things because of whom she was born to, not who she was as a person.

It made her angry, that same righteous anger that had begun to consume her when she saw things as they were, not as she wanted them to be. But that anger was tempered now, now that she knew that people born into unfortunate circumstances could be just as flawed and wonderful as anybody else.

Because of him.

"That is lovely to hear," Pearl said, taking Olivia's arm. "And we'll be leaving so you can return to helping the children."

"Yes, of course." Olivia allowed Pearl to pull her down the hallway and out into the street, where their father's carriage waited. One of the footmen opened the door, and she got inside, wondering just what was happening to her.

"Are you all right?" Pearl asked as she climbed up to sit beside her twin.

It seemed Pearl was wondering what had happened to her too.

"I don't know." And she didn't, but she did. Although she didn't want to admit it all to herself.

"Are you feeling sick? We don't have to go to the party tonight, we can just stay home. We haven't done that in such a long time, not since the Season began, and we can have supper sent to our rooms and play with the kittens."

It sounded heavenly, which was not something Olivia would have said three months or even three weeks ago. Then she would have been too consumed with finding a way to run into Lord Carson, to impress upon him how responsible and civic-minded she was.

Now she just wanted to stay home with Pearl and nuzzle kitten fur. Given that the thing she most wanted to do—the person she most wanted to see—was in the country, and she wasn't likely to ever see him again. Her sister and kittens were an adequate substitution.

"Yes, please," Olivia said, taking Pearl's hand in hers. "And perhaps tonight we can talk about something you want to talk about. Like shirred eggs or being outdoors or if there are any gentlemen who have caught your fancy."

Pearl's eyes widened, and she blinked rapidly, as though staving off tears. "That sounds wonderful. I never thought you—" And she stopped talking, shaking her head in surprise, holding Olivia's hand tight in her own.

Chapter 16

Think about others as you think about your-self.

LADY OLIVIA'S PARTICULAR GUIDE
TO BEING RECKLESS

Olivia!"

Olivia dislodged Snapper from her lap when she heard her mother's voice.

It had been a week since Edward had left London, and although Olivia continued to be as busy as ever—overseeing all the tasks her mother did not wish to (which were most of them), visiting her various charities to make sure that things were going as she thought they should be, and spending time out of doors with Pearl—she felt as though she had lost a fragment of her interest in, well, everything.

The only thing that was a joyful discovery was focusing on Pearl. That night together they'd spent sipping chocolate and playing with the kittens as Pearl shyly, and then more enthusiastically, shared what it was she loved most. Her sister was more than just her sister. She was a person with her own wants, desires, and interests.

It had been a revelation, although it had also been a revelation about how horrible Olivia felt when she realized it'd taken her more than twenty years to discover the revelation in the first place.

"Coming, Mother."

She went downstairs, wondering what task her mother was going to set for her now—yesterday it had been to do a complete inventory of the linens, even though their housekeeper was more than capable, and the day before she had had to discuss the intricacies of what type of response to send to a lady who shouldn't be encouraged in being friends with the duchess, but wasn't to be discouraged either.

It was all so mundane and trivial, and Olivia wished she could be as rude as Ida and just raise an eyebrow and then do whatever it was she wanted. Or be as quiet and unassuming as Pearl so that their mother would overlook her.

But neither was the case.

She walked slowly into her mother's particular room where the duchess was ensconced on her favorite chair, her lady's maid darning something behind her.

"Olivia, come here." The duchess held her hand outstretched, and Olivia faltered; her mother seldom actually wanted her daughter, she just wanted her daughter to do things.

It was with a wary feeling, therefore, that she took her mother's hand and allowed her to guide her to the seat beside the duchess's chair.

"Do look. I've had a lovely invitation." The duchess picked up a letter on the table beside her and waved it in front of Olivia's face, too fast for Olivia to look, as her mother wanted her to.

"I would love to look, Mother, but I cannot see it." She might as well try to imitate Ida in the viewing of letters, at least. And besides, her mother never noticed blunt speaking, what with usually not noticing anyone but herself speaking anyway.

"Here," the duchess said, dropping the letter on Olivia's lap. "It is from Lord Carson—it is an invite to the country for hunting and shooting and lovely walks."

Obviating the need for Olivia to actually look at the letter since it seemed her mother had summarized it. Still, Olivia opened it, glancing at Lord Carson's distinctive bold slashes that passed for handwriting.

It was as her mother said—an invitation to the country for a visit, nothing beyond that.

It was what she would have shrieked in joy about only a few weeks ago, back when she thought she loved Lord Carson.

But she didn't think she did now. Did she?

"Lord Carson included directions to the house, so thoughtful of him. Of course I've accepted. Your father and I wish you to marry Lord Carson since Eleanor was so ungracious as to fall in love with his brother," she said with a sniff, as though Eleanor had deliberately chosen to thwart their parents.

Which she might have; Olivia didn't know, not having asked her. Not having asked any of her sisters much about anything.

Was it normal to feel this sense of shame for not asking questions? For assuming things? For thinking she knew everything already?

But that wasn't important now. What was important was that they were going to the country, all of them, and Lord Carson would be there, and what if he had decided he was in love with *her*?

"It is up to you to marry respectably now. I thought Lord Carson would have proposed by now, so it is a relief to receive this invitation. He must want to take care of it in the country. So much fresh air and such," her mother added, as though the level of oxygen mattered when it came to proposals.

Olivia felt her chest tighten, as though she couldn't breathe. Perhaps her mother was on to something.

But that would mean her mother was correct in something, and that had yet to happen, although the duchess's determination never wavered.

Chapter 17

Ask more questions even if you think you know the answers. The answers might surprise you.

LADY OLIVIA'S PARTICULAR GUIDE
TO BEING RECKLESS

"You've done what?" Edward said, his tone increasing in volume so it was remarkably close to a shout.

His father did not seem perturbed. In fact, he grinned a little more.

"I've asked your friend Lord Carson to invite the Duke and Duchess of Marymount and their daughters here for a visit. He'll be coming as well. Only for a few weeks." His father blinked innocently at him. Even though Edward knew that blink wasn't innocent at all. "I thought you might enjoy seeing your closest London acquaintances since you insisted we leave so suddenly."

Edward couldn't speak. Or he could, but then

it would be to rail against his father, when he knew Mr. Beechcroft was only doing something he thought was good. But he didn't know. He couldn't know what it would be like to see her again. To see her launch herself at Bennett all over again, all of it made even worse now that he knew what her mouth tasted like. How she felt in his arms.

"And since the doctor has said I am much improved, I thought it would be a delightful diversion. I will certainly take those walks the doctor recommends if I can take them with Lady Ida. She has the most interesting ideas on all sorts of things. If I had had a daughter, I would imagine she would be very like Lady Ida." His father smiled. Edward was grateful to at least one of the duke's daughters, then.

"Coming here. Bennett and the duke and duchess and Lady Ida and Lady Pearl and—" And her. "And Lady Olivia," he finished.

"Yes, all of them. I am going to leave it up to you what entertainments we offer to the young ladies. I will take the duke shooting, and then we can have a hunt."

His father punctuated his words with a nod, placing his hands over his stomach in apparent satisfaction.

I am not satisfied, Edward wished he could say. *You have invited them here, her here, and she is the last person I want to see. Mostly because she is the first person I want to see, and yet she is not for me. No matter what you might think.*

But his father was only following his own internal reasoning, and likely it seemed to all make sense inside Mr. Beechcroft's brain: an attractive, eligible young lady appeared to be intrigued by Edward, and so the two of them must be put into the same general vicinity so things could progress.

That was how Mr. Beechcroft thought about industry and workers, after all. And that strategy had worked in his business, at least.

But this was the business of the heart, to use his father's phrasing.

"When do they arrive?" Edward was surprised to discover his voice sounded almost as it always did. If a bit more strained.

"A week or so, perhaps. Lord Carson wasn't certain about the arrangements." Mr. Beechcroft shrugged, the nonchalant gesture belying the crafty look in his eye. "I told him we would be here, no matter when they came. Since I have to stay here under the doctor's care, as you told me." His blasted father then had the temerity to grin slyly, as though he knew just how he had bound Edward up with his own worries.

Not for the first time, Edward stood in awe of his father's prowess as a skilled negotiator. Albeit now he was negotiating with his son's future, and Edward suspected that the results would not be to Mr. Beechcroft's liking.

Nor to his—seeing her married to his best friend, having to watch as they exchanged vows, had their first kiss (although not her first kiss, after all), bore children, spent holidays and social events with one another.

Thank goodness he would be able to sequester himself in the country so that there was no possibility Bennett could invite him to any proper event. Though he knew Bennett—and Lady Olivia, for that matter—would refuse to bend to Society's strictures and still invite him.

Damn it all. And not only was she about to invade his tenuous peace, but his father had orchestrated it.

"LORD CARSON WILL no doubt enjoy seeing you in that shepherdess costume we packed," Olivia's mother said, beaming as she looked at her daughter.

They had spent three days preparing for the trip to the country, Olivia being called on to manage everything from deciding whether or not they had to bring the silver (*You know how I hate stirring my tea with a tablespoon.*) to how many changes of clothing they all needed (*No, we don't need our warmest clothing. It is spring, after all.*).

She had been run ragged as Pearl played with the kittens and Ida looked on, unamused.

And now they were in the carriage, heading to the marquis's country estate where Lord Carson would be waiting.

Waiting to tell Olivia he'd changed his mind? That he wanted to marry her after all?

What would she say?

"You're thinking about it again," Pearl said in a quiet voice, leaning in so that neither their mother nor Ida could hear. "You don't know he's changed his mind. You don't know how you'll feel if he does change his mind. You don't know anything."

And that was the problem. That, for once in her life, Olivia didn't know anything. Not a thing. She didn't know how she felt about Bennett, she didn't know how he felt about her, she didn't know whether or not she would get married before Pearl, she didn't know what she felt about Mr. Wolcott. Edward.

Although she did almost sort of know. And that was something she couldn't even admit to herself.

She felt so topsy-turvy as to be almost seasick.

"But why would he arrange this if he didn't want to marry me?" Olivia asked Pearl for perhaps the hundredth time. "What other reason could there be for him to have his family leave London and go to the country if not to propose?"

Pearl rolled her eyes. Not that Olivia was looking at her twin to confirm that, just that she heard the huff of air that always accompanied Pearl's eye rolls. And then there were her words. "Not everything is about you, Olivia. Lord Carson is very engaged in politics and the government and Father does have some say in things, even if what he says is mostly grunts." And then Pearl giggled, and that made Olivia laugh too, and she forgot— for the moment, at least—all about whether or not Lord Carson was going to make her most ardent wishes of a month ago come true.

Even though those were not the wishes she had now.

"WELL THANK GOODNESS we'll be there soon," the duchess said, sounding as aggrieved as if she'd spent ten days traveling in a farmer's hay-filled cart rather than two days in a carriage upholstered in silk. "I am fatigued to death of all this bouncing around. You'd think they would have smoothed out the roads or something, how is this even civilized?" And then she glanced around at her daughters, all of whom were in varying degrees of trying not to laugh. Even Ida.

The duke had taken a separate carriage, since

the ladies took up all the room in one. But he
would have done that even if there had been
plenty of room—it was clear he did not like
spending time with the ladies of his family,
which begged the question as to why he had
brought so many of them into the world.

Now that Eleanor was married and Della had
run off and was in disgrace, that number was
down to three, but adding in the duchess made it
seem more like twenty-three.

"I wonder, Olivia, if we shouldn't have brought
the linens after all. You know how sensitive I am
to scratchy bedsheets." The duchess gave a vigorous nod. "Bedsheets are truly the most essential
item for any person living in the world today."

Olivia grimaced, thinking of all the things that
families who weren't ducal would put above non-
scratchy bedsheets—food, heat, lodging, clothing. The true essentials.

"And tea. If we didn't have tea we would be sav-
ages," the duchess continued. "How else would
we be able to communicate with one another?"
As though the imbibing of tea was the essential
element of communication.

"So you're saying that the only things people
truly need in this world are quality bed linens
and tea?" Ida asked, her tone sharply sarcastic.

Their mother smiled in approval at her youn-
gest daughter. "That's exactly what I am saying!"

she said in a delighted tone. "I never think you are paying attention to me, dear."

"So says the woman who doesn't even know how we take our essential beverages," Pearl murmured to Olivia, who smothered a giggle.

It had been a long-running bet as to when—or even if—the duchess would finally prepare one of her daughter's cups of tea the way the daughter actually preferred it.

The closest thus far was Ida, who took her tea with nothing in it. But at the last minute the duchess had added a lemon, and all of the sisters had had to stifle groans of disappointment.

"Oh, I don't always pay attention to you, Mother," Ida replied, and Olivia held her breath, wondering just what Ida was going to say—her sister was nearly as liable to say something shockingly direct as their mother, only in a more intelligent fashion. "But it has gotten too dark for me to read any longer. When will we be there, anyway?"

Olivia looked out of the carriage window, squinting to make out a long line of trees in the distance. "It looks as though we are on property, not on the road any longer. Judging by the way the trees are managed." She had to say she approved of the symmetry; trees left to their own devices were more likely to be wayward.

"I would imagine Mr. Beechcroft has enough

money to purchase proper bedsheets," their mother continued.

"Mr. Beechcroft?" Olivia said, feeling her stomach constrict. "You mean the marquis, surely?"

Olivia could see the duchess's head shaking no, and then felt her mother reach across to pat her on the knee. As though she were a child.

"We are going to Mr. Beechcroft's estate. Why would you think we were going anywhere else? You haven't been listening to me either, Olivia." The duchess turned to look out the window. "I see the lights of the house now. We should be there in a matter of minutes."

Olivia sat back against the cushions, feeling her body stiffen in shock. Pearl took her hand and squeezed it, but Olivia barely noticed because of all the emotions coursing through her.

Mr. Beechcroft's house. Which meant he would be there.

"Will Lord Carson even be there, Mother?" Olivia asked, hearing the tension in her voice.

"Yes, he arranged it. Honestly, Olivia, you cannot imagine we would go visiting Mr. Beechcroft just to see him. Have I not raised you properly at all? This is the moment all your dreams will come true! You'll be engaged to Lord Carson and then I can focus on getting Pearl and Ida married."

"Don't bother on my account," Ida said drily.

"Ida, did you know where we were going?" Had she just assumed things and everyone else knew otherwise?

"No, but I am pleased. Mr. Beechcroft is an excellent conversationalist. I am looking forward to resuming our discussion of books and ideas." Ida did sound pleased, not aghast or startled or any of the things Olivia was feeling. Of course. Ida just saw the chance to continue her intellectual discussions—she wasn't thinking about the physical interactions that might or might not happen.

Dear lord.

"And we are here! Girls, make sure you shake out your skirts as we exit the carriage. Not that Mr. Beechcroft is someone we have to concern ourselves with. But Lord Carson will be here, and we do have to worry about him."

It would be fine. She would see Mr. Wolcott and they would be civil toward one another and Lord Carson would propose and she—she didn't know what she would do.

She felt a suffocating squeeze suspiciously near her heart.

"Are you all right?" Pearl whispered as the coach slowed to a stop.

"No," Olivia replied. "Not at all."

It was the truth. She wasn't all right. But she was Lady Olivia, champion of the oppressed, a duke's daughter, a person who had literally been trained from birth to be gracious in awkward situations.

And this certainly counted as an awkward situation.

"WELCOME!" EDWARD'S FATHER said as the carriage door opened and the ladies began to emerge. Edward cursed himself for looking so eagerly to see her, but that didn't stop him from doing so.

And there she was. Her face was set, almost angry, and he could see the flare of red on her cheeks even in the darkness.

What had happened to upset her so?

He felt a surge of protectiveness well up inside his chest. He wanted to go find whoever it was who had made her react this way and do something about it. He wanted to hold her, to tell her it would be fine, that he was there.

But he couldn't. He didn't have the right, he most certainly didn't have her permission, and he would likely be rejected if he even intimated that that was how he felt.

"You have an enormous house," the duchess said, her voice indicating she was surprised.

"I do!" Mr. Beechcroft said in satisfaction. "I commissioned it when Edward first came to live with me. I wanted it to be the biggest house in the area, and it remains so, even after twenty-five years."

Edward wished his father didn't sound so proud, as though he were bragging. Which he absolutely was. It made him sound like what he was—a merchant who had so much money that people in a social status above his were forced to acknowledge him. To visit him at his country house.

And now Edward was doing just what he'd always thought proper Society did—judging people on their politeness, their fitness to be in company with. He was as misguided as Lady Olivia.

Another thing they had in common.

His father took the duchess's arm to lead her into the house, chattering away about the amenities he'd had installed—the private water closets, the plumbing, the innovations in heating. Things the duchess likely did not care at all about.

He had to push that aside. He would not be ashamed of his father or who his father was. Especially since his father would not be here for much longer.

"Lady Pearl, Lady Ida, Lady Olivia," he began, noting the concerned look on Lady Pearl's face and how eagerly Lady Ida was looking at the house—likely anticipating how large the library must be if the house itself was so big. Not looking at her, in case her expression was still so raw, so he wouldn't embarrass himself or her by demanding to know what was wrong. How he could fix it.

"Thank you for inviting us," she replied, and he could hear the strain in her voice. "You do have a lovely home."

"It is my father's," Edward corrected, then felt like an ass for being so sharp.

"Could we go inside?" Lady Ida said, her tone making it clear he was an ass for making them wait outside for so long.

"Of course, please." And he held his arm out toward them, with Lady Pearl and eventually Olivia taking one each.

Lady Ida had already started up the stairs, her soft slippers seeming to march as she went.

"Bennett arrives tomorrow," Edward said, speaking to Olivia. Wishing his friend wasn't always prompt, but knowing it was inevitable no matter when he arrived.

"I see," Olivia said, not sounding at all the way he would have expected her to.

"Mrs. Hodgkins has set up tea in the drawing room, if you would care for refreshment before retiring for the evening."

"That would be wonderful," Lady Pearl said. "Please thank her for us."

Edward brought them into the drawing room,

scanning the area for any signs of poor taste in design or anything that might betray his father's origins. And then hated himself all over again for it.

Thankfully, the drawing room—like the rest of the house—was tastefully decorated, giving the duchess and the rest of her family no cause for thinking Mr. Beechcroft was vulgar. Beyond his own admittedly lower-class heritage.

"Duchess, will you pour?" Mr. Beechcroft asked, gesturing to the silver tea service laid out on one of the mahogany tables. The silver sparkled so much it seemed to light up the room, which was already lit with sconces and low lamps.

Lady Olivia put her hand over her mother's as the duchess stretched her hand to the teapot. "I can do it, Mother. You should rest after our journey." And she didn't wait for the duchess's reply before beginning, fixing a cup for her mother and handing it to her, then looking expectantly at Mr. Beechcroft.

"Your tea, Father," Edward prompted. "How do you take your tea?"

Mr. Beechcroft clapped his hands together, his eyes lit with pleasure. "Milk and plenty of sugar please," he exclaimed.

OLIVIA SMILED AT him as she prepared his tea. What would it be like to have Mr. Beechcroft as a father? It would certainly be a lot more cheerful, she could say that. And he spoke to his child, didn't just grunt from behind a newspaper. Edward was so lucky in that way. Although if Mr. Beechcroft hadn't been who he was, Edward would have grown up in a foundling home, probably forced to wear something Olivia had sewn.

That would be a terrible situation, even without including Olivia's inability to be a seamstress.

"And now let me serve you ladies," Mr. Beechcroft said, putting his teacup down on the table beside him. A table, Olivia could see, decorated with tiny globes on axes, each delicately made and painted in a variety of vibrant hues.

"Those are lovely," Olivia exclaimed, getting up from her seat to crouch in front of the table. "Where did you get them?"

She reached out a tentative finger to touch one, setting the globe to gently spinning.

Mr. Beechcroft blushed and ducked his head. "I make them, actually."

"In one of your factories?" Olivia put her finger on England; there was probably enough room for two of her fingertips on their country, but not much more.

"No, I make them myself. By hand," Mr. Beechcroft explained.

Olivia heard the whoosh of skirts behind her,

and then Ida planted herself next to her sister, her intense gaze on the globes.

There were five of them, all in varying sizes and color schemes, all meticulously crafted.

"This is incredible, Mr. Beechcroft," Ida said. Olivia blinked in surprise; she'd never heard such an approving tone from her sister before. "You'll have to let me watch you make one."

"Better than that, my lady," he replied. "You'll help me make them. I have not been able to interest Edward in my little hobby," he said, glancing toward Mr. Wolcott, "and I do so love to talk while I work. The kittens are good listeners but don't often reply." And then he laughed at his own joke.

"The kittens! I'd forgotten they'd be here. Where are they? Can we see them?" The twins had had to leave the other two kittens behind at the duke's London town house since their mother didn't know about them being there, but certainly would if they were all traveling in a carriage together. Their maids had promised to watch over them, which probably meant they would be getting spoiled by the entire staff.

"Mr. Whiskers is likely sleeping on my father's chair, while Scamp is terrorizing my hunting dogs." Edward sounded both indulgent and disgruntled, which made Olivia want to giggle.

"I would like to see your library, sir," Ida said bluntly. "And if Mr. Whiskers is there, I imagine Pearl and Olivia would like to as well."

"No tea, then?" Mr. Beechcroft said.

"I need to rest," the duchess said, standing up from her chair. Her lady's maid, who'd been discreetly waiting behind her, bustled up to rewrap the duchess's shawl around her shoulders. "I look forward to seeing what entertainment you have planned for tomorrow, Mr. Beechcroft." She paused, a tiny frown creasing between her eyebrows. "You haven't mentioned if the duke has arrived."

"Not yet, Your Grace," Mr. Beechcroft said. Olivia felt guilty for being relieved he knew the correct way to address her mother, and then berated herself again for being a snob.

"He might have stayed in the village. The Four-in-Hand Arms is quite a tidy little inn."

The duchess's reply was a sniff, indicating much more than mere words could. Namely, that the duke would never stay at an establishment where common people could be found. Olivia wondered just how her mother had talked him into this trip. Or perhaps he, like her, thought they were going to the marquis's estate?

What if he was there now? She felt her eyes widen at the thought. If it was only Lord Carson here, he couldn't properly propose, not without her father in attendance.

She hoped her father was just as mistaken as she had been, although she felt for the poor staff at the marquis's estate, which was not expecting anyone for a visit.

But if it kept Lord Carson from making good on the implicit promise found in his having arranged this trip, she would try not to feel too bad.

The duchess and her maid left the room, the duchess still remarking on how surprisingly nice she found Mr. Beechcroft's estate.

"Did she think we'd have workers on machines in the ballroom? Or perhaps piles of money lying around in the hallway waiting to be counted?" Edward said, low in her ear. She could tell he was joking, only—

"It's entirely possible," she replied with a sigh. "Mother is not the most diplomatic of people."

"Duchesses seldom have to be," he said. "But you didn't think that. That's all that matters."

No, I didn't. But then again, I didn't have time to think about it, since I hadn't known we were coming here.

Olivia waited as Mr. Beechcroft took Ida's and Pearl's arms to lead them to the library. She didn't miss Mr. Beechcroft's sly look as she stood beside Edward, and she wished she could tell him he was completely misguided. There was no way she and Edward would ever—he wouldn't, he had his father to take care of, and not only that, her parents would never accept him as a suitor, and she—

She loved him.

No, wait. She loved him? Oh no, that was the worst possible thing that could have happened. She felt her knees buckle as her thoughts struck her, and he grabbed her wrist to hold her up before she fell.

"Are you all right?" The concern in his voice—like when he had followed her out of the dining room after that embarrassing moment—made her want to weep. Even though she was not a woman who wept. That he was worried about her when he was the bastard, the one whom Society would never accept, the one who was being asked to marry, preferably a woman who wouldn't look down on him.

"I am fine, thank you, Mr. Wolcott." Her throat felt thick with emotion. With love.

Dear lord. What was she going to do?

"I didn't get a chance to thank you for the kittens." He held her arm as they walked slowly down the hallway. He sounded sincere, which surprised her.

"I got the impression you weren't all that happy with me giving them to you," Olivia replied, try-

ing not to just say everything she was feeling—
*I think I've fallen in love with you, in fact I know I
have*—instead of talking about kittens and tea
and perhaps later on the likelihood of rain.

Exciting topics that were—except for the
kittens—perfectly acceptable in Society.

"I wasn't, not at first." He chuckled, the low
rumble sending a sizzle of something through
Olivia's body. "But then my father fell in love with
them, Mr. Whiskers in particular, and it is such a
delight watching him play with them. I don't remember the last time he actually played. He does
his globes, and he takes time to look at books, but
he doesn't seem to have unadulterated fun."

"And you?" Olivia asked, looking up at him.
He had gotten no less handsome since the last
time she'd seen him—those dark curls moving
on his shoulders, his strong nose and sharp eyebrows making him look as dangerous as he was.
"Do you ever have unadulterated fun?"

His sudden intake of breath let her know she
had hit a sore spot. One she couldn't resist poking again. She was suffering through the pangs
of her own unrequited love, she didn't see why
she couldn't make him suffer as well, albeit for
an entirely different reason.

"Fun. Like when you take a walk without
knowing where you're going, or sing your favorite songs until your voice is hoarse."

"Hunting provides a certain sort of fun."

She was nodding when the words hit her—"Hunting? What do you hunt?"

He shrugged, and she felt his gesture in her body as well. "Foxes. Well, the dogs hunt the foxes, and we chase after them."

"Foxes? I know that farmers don't like foxes because they steal chickens, I can understand that, but I hardly think you're managing poultry here." She looked around the hallway they seemed to have stopped in, her gaze taking in the various paintings—all clearly originals—decorating the walls, the delicate chairs lining the walls, the thick carpet under their feet.

"No, no chickens here," he replied in an amused tone. "We do have your favorite type of bird, however: ducks. There's a pond at the back of the house we can go to see if there are any injustices being committed."

"You're laughing at me," she said accusingly.

"As though you haven't laughed at me?" he said, arching one of those dark eyebrows at her.

"That was different! Because—because—"

"Because it was you, and you are a duke's daughter? A lady who should never be viewed as anything but a lady?" He stepped in close to her, so close she could see his dark pupils, see the faint lines at the edges of his eyes. "I see you as a woman, Olivia, like it or not." His words skittered over her skin, making it feel as though he were touching her. Burrowing inside her. A woman. She didn't know what it would be like to be just a woman.

He reached his fingers up and smoothed the hair next to her ear, his finger brushing her skin. She trembled. Not with his touch, although that was an element of it; but at his assertion that he saw her entirely differently from everyone else.

Was that why she had fallen in love with him?

"I am a woman," she said, lifting her chin as she spoke. A movement that brought her mouth closer to his, which she wasn't certain was intentional or not. "I am a woman who is more and less than a duke's daughter." She swallowed hard against the lump in her throat. "And I can't believe nobody has ever seen me before. But you have."

"I have," he said, murmuring low, so softly she could barely hear him. "That's why I wish you hadn't come here. It's—it's impossible to see you, to be near you, without—"

"Without what?" she asked, now deliberately lifting her feet so she stood on her toes, enabling her face to get that much closer to his.

So what if Lord Carson was on his way here to propose? So what if Edward was the illegitimate son of a merchant who had the extreme good fortune of having good taste? What mattered was right here, right now.

"The library," he said in a husky voice, nodding over her head. Before she did something stupid, like kiss him again. *He doesn't want you to kiss him again*, a voice yelled in her head.

Mortified, she turned to see her sisters and Mr. Beechcroft within, Pearl and Ida standing over a desk that looked as though it was Mr. Beechcroft's globe-making desk, and Mr. Beechcroft himself looking directly at them.

What would have happened if she had acted on her impulses and kissed him? Mr. Beechcroft would have seen, which would mean that Ida and Pearl would have seen, and then Edward would have had to propose, even though he didn't want to, and she couldn't allow him to. Lord Carson would be devastated, and her parents would never allow her to leave the house.

It was a very good thing he didn't want to kiss her after all. That kiss might have entirely ruined her life.

Chapter 18

Say what you mean. Unless what you mean will upend your entire life. In which case, you should probably shout.

LADY OLIVIA'S PARTICULAR GUIDE
TO BEING RECKLESS

*H*aving her here, right beside him, was nearly too much. Nearly. She looked even better and brighter than he'd recalled, her expression constantly curious, her mere presence making it feel as though his world was off-balance. It was odd to see her here in his home; she'd visited the London town house, of course, but that wasn't where he lived, the place that he felt connected to.

But he did feel that here. He'd been brought here after his mother died, when his father claimed him, and he'd come to know the place as home. It was large, it was extravagant, it was a physical display of his father's business acumen, and he loved it.

Thank goodness the suggestion to view the library had been made, or he would have taken her off to one of the numerous quiet corners in this behemoth of a house and kissed her senseless.

It almost looked as though she wanted that too; her face had been lifted just so, and there was a sensual anticipatory gleam in her eye that made all different parts of his body react.

But thank goodness he hadn't kissed her—or her him—since his father and her sisters were all in plain sight.

"The library, as you can see, houses a vast collection, from books on industry and business to my father's collection of maps and globes and atlases." Edward could see Lady Ida already eagerly pulling books off shelves and discussing them with his father.

Mr. Beechcroft was a generally happy person, but his expression at this moment was one of delight. Edward was still livid that his father and possibly Bennett had enabled this surprise visit, but at least his father got some benefit out of it.

He couldn't think it could be anything more. He couldn't become invigorated in her presence— even though he was—he had to believe the worst would happen, because if he even thought about it, he would begin to hope, and that way would lead to despair.

"Mr. Wolcott, what books are your favorites?"

Why did she have to engage him in conversation? Didn't she know what she was doing to him?

No, because he hadn't told her. But he'd shown her, hadn't he? Or were his kisses not passionate enough, or perhaps he'd kept his expression as guarded as he'd hoped?

What would happen if he did show her? Explicitly, and with her full consent so she could make her own decision?

The thought was appealing, and not just because it meant he would touch her soft skin. Kiss that mouth and caress her body. Feel how she responded to his touch, and how she made him shake when she was near.

The thought was so appealing, in fact, that it took all of his will not to just walk over to her, pick her up, and hoist her up on his shoulders.

As it was, he had to turn and pretend to examine a book so his erection wasn't so obvious. And he had to spend weeks in the same house with her.

"Mr. Wolcott?"

She'd come to stand next to him, her face tilted up to his, her expression guarded, but also mischievous. As though she were baiting a bear. A bear named Edward.

"Yes, Lady Olivia. My favorite books." He took her arm and led her over to one of the corners of the room, the one that offered the most privacy. "Why do you ask?"

Because if she was just taunting him, poking at the bear inside him, he needed to know now so he could shut down whatever feelings were swirling inside.

"I want to know more about you," she said in a quiet, sincere tone. "I know who you think you are. I know who you appear to be. But I don't know you as well as I wish to."

"And why do you wish it?"

He froze as she opened her mouth to respond, snapping it shut after a moment.

"Why are you here?" he asked after what seemed like an eternity of silence.

"I didn't know we were coming!" she said in a very non-Olivia type of squeak. "Mother said, and I assumed, that we were going to the marquis's estate. Not here."

He felt as though she'd punched him in the chest.

"But I didn't want to go there either," she continued, the color in her cheeks rising. "I don't know what to think anymore."

And she sounded so unlike the sparkling blazing Lady Olivia that he grabbed her hand and dragged her back out into the hallway, shutting the door behind them.

"Where are you taking me?" she squeaked

again as he pulled her down the hallway, not caring if Olivia's sisters were aghast in the room behind them.

He knew how his father would respond, so he didn't have to worry on that score.

"Here," he said, thrusting her into one of the rooms where his father's business managers came for meetings. He closed the door quietly, so nobody could hear where they were.

It was a small, sparsely decorated room, suitable for meetings with people who might otherwise get overwhelmed at the genteel opulence on display in the rest of the house.

He sat down on the chair where the managers usually sat and hauled her onto his lap, curling his hand possessively over her waist, holding her in place. Even though she could get up at any time—his holding her was mostly for him.

Because she knew he wouldn't do anything she wasn't willing to do herself.

"Well," she said, exhaling so gustily a piece of hair flew up into her eye. "That was unexpected."

He grinned at first, and then burst into laughter. "It was. I think I am taking on the more unfortunate habits of that forceful duck. Taking what I want no matter what is fair. I know this isn't fair," he said. "And I know that you are greatly concerned with fairness."

She swatted his arm, and then leaned against

his chest. It felt too good. "It's fair if there is an equal give and take."

"I don't think it will be fair if I sit on you," he said, arching his brow.

"Not that," she replied, sliding her hands around his neck. "But this."

How many times had she kissed him? It had to be at least three now, though it would never be enough.

This time, though, wasn't outside on a terrace or in a hallway. They were in their own private world, albeit a world inside his house with their relatives only a few yards away. But still, the door was shut and they were alone, and her mouth was on his, and her hands were moving in his hair, sliding along his scalp, making him want to have her touch him everywhere.

Especially there. The part that was standing up and taking notice of her actions. The part she was sitting on.

He drew her close and kissed her, pulling her closer against his chest, shifting her so his cock was just under her delectable bottom.

She had to feel it. She had to know what she was doing to him.

And then she leaned closer, her breasts pushing against him, his cock throbbing in delicious agony. She placed one hand on his chest, sliding it under his jacket, over his waistcoat, her fingers beginning to work the buttons free.

He broke the kiss, gasping, and moved his hand to the bottom of his waistcoat, undoing the buttons furiously, meeting her fingers in the middle. Within seconds, he'd managed to shrug off his jacket, tossing it to the ground, his waistcoat following, and then they were both tugging on his shirt. She drew it up over his head and he was momentarily blinded, and then saw her face as she threw the shirt in the air, heedless of where it would land.

She was grinning, and he smiled back, and then—thank God—her hands were on his skin, her palms sliding all over him, her gaze focused on his face, on his reactions.

She slid her fingers over his nipple and he closed his eyes, letting the sensation of her touch be all that he felt.

"That seems as though it is particularly interesting," she said with a hint of laughter in her voice.

"It is, Olivia, and you should never stop doing it."

The words came out before he could think, and then he felt her reaction as she withdrew her hands and shifted, then got off his lap entirely.

Fuck. He shouldn't have reminded her about it, that this was something that not only should they not be doing now, but that it was something they would never be doing in the future.

Because, according to her, she would be married to his best friend, and this would all be a painful, embarrassing memory.

"I should go back."

He opened his eyes, wincing as he saw the look on her face. A look he couldn't entirely gauge, but looked suspiciously like regret, anger, and shame.

"I'm sorry, I didn't mean—this is entirely my fault."

She raised one of her eyebrows in that proud Olivia look he couldn't help but admire. Even if she was currently staring him down, not an errant duck or a snobbish lord.

"I had just as much to do with all of this as you. To say it is your fault is to deny my part in it, as though I am just a puppet for your—your lustful behaviors." The color was high on her cheeks, and he felt himself starting to laugh, but smothered it.

But of course she noticed.

"And now you are laughing at me—again, might I say?" She planted her fists on her hips and glared at him, but he could see the glimmer of humor in her eyes.

Perhaps she thought this was funny as well, but of course her maidenly demeanor and upbringing meant she absolutely must not indicate she did.

"No, of course not." He rose, grimacing as his still erect cock brushed against the front of his trousers. Leaning over to pick up his discarded shirt and putting it on, then grabbing his waistcoat and jacket from the floor.

Was her expression wistful as he put his clothing back on? Or was that just his hope?

They didn't speak, and he didn't trust himself to touch her, so he opened the door for her and gestured for her to go ahead, unable to keep from looking at her back as she walked quickly down the hallway back to the library.

If this was what they ended up doing after only an hour of being together, what would happen when they were in one another's company for weeks on end?

Thank God—or goddamn it—Bennett was arriving tomorrow.

Chapter 19

If you don't trust yourself, get your sister's advice.

LADY OLIVIA'S PARTICULAR GUIDE
TO BEING RECKLESS

*A*gain?" Pearl sounded incredulous, and Olivia had to admit her twin had reason to.

They were in Pearl's bedroom, having endured a dinner party with their mother dominating the conversation and their father glowering at the food (he was not a good traveler) as Olivia tried not to look at Edward, and it appeared Edward was trying not to look at her.

Ida and Mr. Beechcroft were the only ones who seemed to have a pleasant dinner.

The bedrooms, as could be expected, were enormous. Pearl's was decorated in varying shades of silver and grey, with vases of bright pink roses scattered on nearly every available surface.

It was far more opulent than their own house, but it managed to remain tasteful, which was a neat trick, Olivia thought.

Her own room was gold and green, and she wondered if Edward had decided on the rooms, since her coloring matched the room's shades.

Or she was thinking too much of herself.

"Olivia. Again?" Pearl repeated in a firmer tone.

"Uh . . . yes?" she replied, sounding hesitant. Not at all like herself.

Then again, nothing about this was like herself. First was the fact that, yes, she had to admit—in the privacy of her own mind—she loved him.

Damn it.

And that she did not want to marry Bennett. But what kind of good could she do if she were just Lady Olivia, the most Disgraceful of the Duke's Daughters? The one who had refused to marry the man she had been chasing in order to marry his best friend?

And, dear lord, what would that do to Lord Carson? How would he feel if his best friend were to marry the woman he had decided he should, indeed, marry?

"I think I should leave England and go help people somewhere." She blurted it out before she could think, but as soon as she thought about it, it made perfect sense.

"Help people somewhere?" Pearl rolled her eyes. Apparently it didn't make perfect sense after all. "Are you running away?"

"Absolutely not!" Olivia replied sharply.

And then she took a deep breath and spoke again. "Never mind. I am. That is, I'm not. I had a momentary weakness, but I will not." She heard her voice tremble. "Pearl, what am I to do?"

Pearl didn't answer, but instead got up from her chair and sank down on the rug in front of Olivia's chair, resting her arms on Olivia's knees. She looked up at her with an expression that managed to convey both compassion and "I told you so."

It was a remarkable gift her sister had.

"You always know what to do. You will figure it out. What does your heart say?"

"My heart." Olivia felt her throat get thick. "My heart tells me I love him."

Pearl smiled, a warm, loving smile that made her whole face light up. "That is the Olivia I know."

"But I was so adamant about marrying Lord Carson! And I don't even know if Edward would want to marry me."

Pearl shrugged. "Why don't you ask him?"

Olivia blinked. Ask him? Ask him how he felt about her? Ask him if he wanted to marry her?

Well, it couldn't go any worse than the last time she had asked someone to marry her. Could it?

What if it did?

But what if it didn't?

"I will. I'll ask him." And if he said yes? Well, then, she would already be engaged, and Lord Carson wouldn't even have the chance to propose.

But on the other hand, if he didn't feel the same way.

Her heart hurt. Her lungs hurt too from all the agitated breathing she was doing.

Because Lord Carson was arriving tomorrow, and everyone—possibly including him—was expecting her to want to marry him, not this Other gentleman who wasn't truly a gentleman.

And the ways in which he wasn't a gentleman were so very lovely. She let her mind wander back to that kiss in the office, how she'd felt, quite clearly, the result of it just under her bottom.

If she were as ladylike as she'd always thought, the idea of all of that should terrify her.

Instead, it had quite the opposite reaction. She wanted to explore more, she wanted to explore him.

She wanted.

"Olivia?" Pearl's voice snapped her out of her reverie. "What are you thinking about? Because you have the most interesting expression right now." Her sister's wry tone let her know that she had a strong suspicion of what Olivia was thinking about, and Olivia grinned in reply.

She would ask him.

"Mr. Wolcott, the other party has arrived. Lord Carson is in the drawing room, and I have taken the liberty of showing the marquis his rooms. He wanted to rest after the journey—he said he would join everyone for tea."

Edward rose from his chair, wishing he weren't conflicted about Bennett's arrival. Bennett was his best friend, his only friend, truth be told, and Edward should not have presumed with Lady Olivia.

Even though she had, in fact, presumed first.

But it was the gentleman's responsibility to maintain decorum, and he had absolutely not.

He would have to ask Bennett if his feelings toward Olivia had changed. If he should push all his own feelings about the lady to the back of his mind, to lock them down and never think of them again.

It was the right thing to do, even though he dreaded the answer.

"There you are." Bennett stepped into the office, the very same room where—but he could not think about that.

"Your butler told me to wait in that drawing room, but I knew I would find you here."

Bennett, damn him, looked as though he'd stepped off the House of Commons floor—perfectly clothed, looking refreshed with no outward signs he had journeyed several hours from London, and traveling a lot faster than the other guests.

"I was just told you were here. I am sorry I wasn't at the door to greet you." Edward sounded awkward and stiff to his own ears, and Bennett raised an eyebrow in reply.

"At the door to greet me? What nonsense are you talking about?"

He couldn't let these questions drift around his mind any longer. He had to know.

"Why are you here?"

Bennett didn't reply right away, but his eyebrow rose even more. He unbuttoned his jacket and sat down, gesturing for Edward to sit as well.

"I am here, you blockhead, because your father invited us." Bennett crossed his arms over his chest. "Are you saying you wish we hadn't come?"

"Did you know"—he took a deep breath, knowing he was about to start this conversation and find out for certain—"that the Duke of Marymount's family is here as well?"

Bennett's eyes widened, and Edward felt a sagging relief.

"No! Oh no, that is not good," he said, jumping up from his seat and beginning to pace around the small office. "Edward, why would your father not tell us? Unless my father knows—I wouldn't put it past him to have planned all of this. He is still determined to marry me off to one of the duke's daughters." Bennett shook his head, his expression haunted.

So it was clear that Bennett had no idea she would be here and was clearly horrified at the prospect. He shouldn't have doubted his friend. But his confusing and admittedly physical relationship with Olivia had made him question everything. Including his best friend.

"You're going to have to help me," Bennett said, sounding desperate. "In such close quarters I won't be able to maintain a distance from her. You're going to have to distract her."

Edward swallowed the delighted noise he felt bubbling in his chest, merely nodding in reply. "Of course. Whatever I can do."

He suspected that Lady Olivia was not quite as determined as she had been to marry Bennett; if she was, then that put their kissing interludes into quite a different light, and he didn't think she was that person. When she pursued something, she was intent and focused; she wouldn't just dally with him casually. He knew that. What he didn't know, what he'd have to discover, was how deep her feelings ran.

But now, at least, he knew that his best friend was definitely not interested in her in the same way Edward was.

"Thank you. I know you like her; it's clear from how you look at one another. You rushed after her during that dinner at the duke's house. What happened, anyway?"

He probably shouldn't tell Bennett precisely what happened; Olivia's sister was married to Bennett's brother, and perhaps Bennett would insist that Edward do the right thing and propose.

"Uh, I just wanted to check on her. Her mother had just profoundly embarrassed her, and she'd already had a recent embarrassment," he said, nodding toward Bennett to indicate he meant the rejected proposal. "And she is, or was, trying to help me. It felt like the right thing to do."

And then there was the kiss, which was also the right thing to do. At the time, at least.

Bennett clapped a hand on Edward's shoulder. "Of course you reacted that way. Just like you did when anyone was teased in school."

Edward nodded, wishing he felt more honorable and less like rushing to her room at that very moment and kissing her senseless. Again.

"Well, I should go prepare myself for this visit." Bennett winced as he spoke, and Edward realized just how ridiculous his concerns about his friend's feelings were. He was beyond muddled.

"I will do my utmost to prevent a betrothal, or

even a suspicion of one. I promise." *For myself as much as for you*, Edward thought.

THE GOOD THING about her arrival was that he had momentarily forgotten his concern for his father, and his father's health.

That concern was revived as soon as his father's usual doctor came to see his patient.

Edward waited impatiently outside of his father's door as the examination continued for close to an hour.

What could possibly be taking so long?

At last, the door opened, and Dr. Martin stepped out, his expression neutral.

"Well?" Edward said, not able to wait a moment for the man to begin speaking.

The doctor shifted his bag from one hand to the other, and Edward resisted the urge to grab him by the shoulders so he could shake the information from him.

"You should go speak to him," Dr. Martin said slowly. "But it is my belief that the London doctor was incorrect in his diagnosis. Your father is ill, yes, but it isn't something that will take him from you unexpectedly. He just needs time to rest, a much better diet, and I've written a prescription for some medications that will hasten his return to good health."

The doctor tipped his hat to Edward, seem-

ingly unaware that with just a few words he had
lightened Edward's heart so much that he wished
now he could grab the man by his shoulders so
he could kiss him.

He did not. "Thank you," Edward called after
the doctor, who was already hurrying down the
stairs. He tapped on his father's door, stepping
inside without waiting for his father's call to
enter.

Mr. Beechcroft was lying in his bed, looking as
tired as Edward had seen him.

"Ah, Edward!" Mr. Beechcroft said in a weary
voice. "You've spoken to the doctor? You've heard?"

Edward came to sit on the edge of his father's
bed, taking his hand. He looked down at it, at
the fingers that still managed to look as though
they did manual labor, even though it had been
years since his father had done anything like that
himself.

"Yes, I spoke to him. It's something else? Not
something life threatening?"

Mr. Beechcroft grinned, his face lighting up despite his obvious fatigue. "That's right! Dr. Bell, it
seems, was over-hasty in predicting my demise."
He scowled. "But I will have to modify my diet,
it seems. Gruel and such."

Edward patted his father's hand. "I don't think
it will be that drastic, Father. Cook will be able to
make something that will be good for you and be

tasty. And you're going to have to rest, to hand over more of your day-to-day business to me."

Mr. Beechcroft sighed in reluctant acceptance. "I suppose." He peered at Edward, tightening his grip on his son's hand. "I still want the same thing, though. Don't think that just because I'm not going to die right away you can forget about what you promised."

Edward raised his eyebrow at his father. Of course the consummate businessman would want him to honor a promise he made in a different situation.

"Don't look at me like that," Mr. Beechcroft said in a mock growl. "It is not as though you don't want it also. I have seen how you regard Lady Olivia."

And now that his father was not, in fact, going to die, he wouldn't be under the same pressure to marry. He'd have to tell Lady Olivia—he wouldn't want her to continue thinking his father was in ill health—but then she would know he wasn't under such pressure to marry.

So if she were even slightly inclined to be interested in him, she wouldn't have the same incentive. She could just wait until she realized she felt differently.

"Lady Olivia might still be determined to marry Bennett, Father," Edward explained. "Although Bennett most definitely does not wish to marry her."

Mr. Beechcroft beamed. "So there is no impediment to your marrying her! Go on, my boy, I believe in you." His father finished his words with a worrisome cough, and Edward released his hand, rising as he did so.

"You should rest. I will go see to our guests. I know you won't miss dinner, and I will speak with Cook about the meal."

Mr. Beechcroft's expression revealed just what he thought about all of that. "Ask Lady Ida to come see me in about an hour? We were having the most interesting discussion, and I want to get her opinion on some of the globes I've been working on."

"Of course." Edward would not be able to stop his father from working entirely, but he could ensure it was work that wouldn't tax him too much.

He walked out of the room, feeling even lighter than when he'd entered. He might not have any idea of what his own future would hold, but at least he would have his father for a bit longer.

Chapter 20

I have no idea anymore.

LADY OLIVIA'S PARTICULAR GUIDE
TO BEING RECKLESS

*H*unting? You'll be sending dogs after innocent foxes?"

Olivia directed her question at Edward across the breakfast, who met her gaze with a wry smile.

Olivia had slept restlessly, her dreams filled with images of him and how he'd looked when she'd stepped away from him. Waking up to hug the idea that she loved him close to her chest, only to feel devastated as she realized she had no idea what to do about it.

Ask him, Pearl had said. It sounded so simple—and it had been when she'd asked Bennett the same thing—but she had no idea what Edward might say.

Which was entirely the reason she should ask, she heard an irritated Pearl say in her head.

"Hunting is one of the nation's most revered traditions," the duke said, making all of his daughters stare at him in surprise. It was an entire sentence not punctuated with a grunt, after all. "Mr. Wolcott's skill in judging horses is well-known, and I for one, want to see his expertise firsthand."

The duchess didn't seem to notice that her normally recalcitrant husband had seen fit to utter an entirety of two sentences. "Yes, hunting is one of the things that makes life worth living, after all," she said, even though she'd never hunted in her life.

"Like bedsheets and tea?" Ida muttered so that only Olivia could hear.

Olivia clapped her hand over her mouth so she wouldn't laugh, and caught him looking at her. Again.

She'd have to talk to him soon; she couldn't keep wondering what was in his thoughts.

"What are your objections to the hunt, Lady Olivia?" Edward asked.

As though he didn't know. Did he enjoy seeing her get self-righteous? Perhaps he did, though nobody else ever seemed to like it.

"I find it reprehensible that people will set dogs on a fox that just wants to take care of its family and live its life, all for the sake of sport. It's not even sporting, honestly. I mean, there is one fox and how many hounds? And how many people on horses adding to the cacophony?"

"So you would be fine with it if the odds were more even?" Edward asked, still with that smirk on his face. "When we release the hounds, perhaps we could release an equal number of foxes?"

"That is not what I am saying at all," she replied, feeling her cheeks start to burn. As they always did when she was encountering injustice. "It's not fair."

There was a moment of silence, or there would have been if the duke hadn't grunted disapprovingly.

"I understand what you are saying, Lady Olivia," Edward said at last, the wry smirk no longer on his face, but something—something warmer.

Something that made a tiny glimmer of hope kindle inside her. Perhaps this conversation would go a bit better than the last time she'd asked a gentleman what he thought of her.

"Instead why don't we take the horses out without the hounds? We could go for a vigorous gallop rather than chasing down foxes." Edward nodded toward Olivia. "I know how you feel about fairness in the animal kingdom."

"Thank you," Olivia said in a soft voice. Quite unlike her usual tone, but then again, nothing about her now was usual.

"And then when we've returned, perhaps you

would like to take a walk to the village?" This time it was clear Edward was speaking to her, although the invitation was a general one.

"I would love to," Olivia said.

Her sisters agreed also, although their mother demurred, perhaps because that would mean she might miss tea.

So perhaps later on she would be able to speak with him. About her and him and them and all the things she had barely allowed herself to admit within the confines of her own head.

Now THAT HIS father was no longer in imminent danger of perishing, Edward could fully concentrate on the thing—or more specifically the person—that brought him the most enjoyment in life.

He knew when he'd mentioned hunting that she would speak up against it. He found himself savoring how her voice rose in volume, as did the color in her cheeks. How her eyes flashed furiously as she argued in defense of the foxes.

It had been easy to agree to what she said. It was a pleasure, actually. To accede to her wishes in something so minor when it would bring her so much satisfaction.

"Mr. Wolcott, how many people live in the village?"

Her voice brought him out of his thoughts, and

he turned his head to smile at her, conscious of her arm on his left. Her sister Lady Pearl was on his right-hand side, while their other sister Lady Ida strode ahead, looking back with an aggrieved expression at how slow the rest of the party was.

Edward wasn't assuming that; she had called out a few times for them to hurry up, but her sisters had told her they would walk at their own pace, thank you very much.

"I am not certain," he replied, doing a quick tally in his head. "Perhaps five hundred? I don't go into town much, not unless I am meeting one of our representatives at the Lamb and Flag. The local inn," he explained.

"And do the children attend school?" she demanded, clearly already spoiling for a fight.

"Oh, for goodness' sake, Olivia, of course there is a school," Pearl said dismissively. "They're not barbarians."

"I didn't say that!"

"You implied it," her twin pointed out.

"You need to ask questions, even obvious ones, to make certain everything is as it should be," Olivia replied in her most autocratic tone.

"Of course you do," Edward said, patting her arm.

"Now you're being condescending."

Edward took a deep breath. "You're right. I am. I apologize."

"Apology accepted," she said in a low tone.

"Thank you," he said, equally quietly.

The more he got to know her, the more he realized how vulnerable she was, despite her headstrong determination to be on the right side at all times.

It must be very difficult for her to always be on the alert for injustice. From ducks to foxes to impoverished children, it was all equally important.

Perhaps he should be asking her if she had ever had any unadulterated fun.

"I believe that today is market day in the village. I haven't been for some time, but as far as I recall, it's a festive occasion. And," he said, making a grand gesture of consulting his pocket watch, "it should be late enough so that the children are no longer in school."

She swatted him on the arm, but he could see her smiling out of the corner of his eye.

"I have some pin money, perhaps we can buy something," Pearl said in an excited tone.

"I do as well, although I cannot think of anything I would want that is more important than someone else's comfort."

"Oh, do give it a rest," Pearl said. "Can't you just have fun without worrying about people?"

"No," she said. He hurt for her, that she felt she had to be so vigilant all the time.

No wonder she kissed him so often—she was probably desperate for something that would take her mind off her constant monitoring of potentially unjust situations.

They walked the rest of the way in silence, him wishing he could get her to ease up on her worries without having to compromise her.

OLIVIA KNEW SHE was being unpleasant. Pearl only ever wanted the best for her, but she was finding it impossible to concentrate on anything with him so close. Her hand looped through his arm, his body right next to hers.

"I used to come to the village once a week when I was young," he said in an abrupt tone of voice. As though he wasn't accustomed to telling anybody anything. "The people who lived there knew who I was and didn't treat me any differently. Neither as though I were more important or less." He chuckled. "Maybe because I was twelve years old and skinny as a rail, and yet I know I always looked as though I were ready to punch someone."

The image was sweet, in its own odd way—a young Edward blustering through the world, keenly aware of his birth and determined not to let anyone stop him from being who he was.

Except he had come to her world to be more than he was. Only, if he were to be accepted by her world, he would have to end up being less. Marrying a woman who was less, because she had agreed to marry him. Having to watch his behavior all the time so nobody could accuse him of living up to his origins rather than his upbringing.

"It must be exhausting," she said, feeling the ache inside her. Like her own type of fatigue, only his wasn't born out of injustice for others. But injustice for himself. Something he couldn't escape by attending a party or laughing with siblings—he didn't have any, that she knew of—or playing with kittens.

Or kissing. Although maybe that was why he had responded so fiercely when she kissed him. Because he was trying to escape, not because of how he actually felt about her.

The thought was lowering, but she deserved to think that. She'd spent so long thinking she was above others because of how she thought about them—as though they needed her attention and care. Bennett didn't want her attention; she could admit that to herself now. Did Edward?

She would have to ask.

She was opening her mouth to do just that when they turned a corner and walked into the heart of the village. Ida and Pearl were already there, already clapping their hands as a trio of musicians played some sort of lively tune.

A few grubby children were dancing at the outskirts of the circle, and Olivia felt that familiar tug grip her. The urge to help, to do something, to show that she cared.

"Do you have any money?" she asked him.

He frowned, puzzled, and then nodded. "A bit. I am to purchase some new pens for my father."

"Can I have it?"

She didn't wait for his reply; she just held her hand out, palm out.

He shook his head, withdrawing his wallet from his inside pocket. He extracted a few bills and placed them on her hand.

"Is that all you have?" she demanded.

He shook his head again and withdrew some change, placing that on top of the paper.

"Excellent," she said, curling her fingers around the money and turning, the fierce flood of doing good making her whole body heat.

WHAT WAS SHE doing? Edward wondered as he watched her stalk toward the tables set up for the market. He saw her go and speak, apparently fervently, to a few of the merchants, gesticulating in that vibrant Olivia way he'd come to love.

Love?

That word caught him up short, only to blind-side him with the veracity of it. Love. He loved her.

How had he denied it to himself for so long?

He loved her, his prickly, sparkling, vibrant firebrand, who barged into situations and demanded justice—for ducks, for women, for foxes. For him.

Love. It wasn't something he'd thought he'd ever have, certainly not with someone like her—a duke's daughter. A lady who, in normal circumstances, would scorn what he had to tell her.

But these were not normal circumstances. Not at all.

He felt off-balance, and yet righted, now that he knew what he was suffering under. Love. The greatest toppler of nations and gentlemen the world had ever known.

And now Olivia, his love, was gesturing to the town, waving his money in the air, a fiery blush on her cheeks as she seemed to be arguing passionately for—

"But I want to buy everything for the children!"

The children in question had stopped dancing, likely because the musicians had stopped playing, and everyone else was frozen as Olivia whirled around to look at the crowd.

Most of whom were looking back at her with disdain.

Oh no.

"We aren't in need of your charity, miss," one of the women said. The other women nodded their heads in fervent agreement.

"And nobody asked you to come here and wave your cash around," a merchant selling fruit added in a belligerent tone.

He waited for her to crumple, but of course she didn't. Because she was Olivia, and she did not crumple.

Instead, she did what she always did; rush in and fight.

"But it's not charity. I want to help!" She glanced around the crowd, her shoulders thrown back, her chin raised. Looking every inch a pampered aristocrat condescending to people who were beneath her. Who didn't know any better.

Except they did. "Your kind of help isn't wanted," another of the women said, waving her arm in dismissal. "You think you can just come in here and pay for everything and it will be fine." The woman stepped forward. "And it was fine, until you came. Do you think we can't take care of our own? Do you think we need your help?" And she finished her sentence by spitting on the ground in front of Olivia.

Edward winced, restraining himself from going to her. His presence would just exacerbate the situation; he knew full well Olivia could take care of herself, and he also knew neither she nor the townspeople would welcome his interference.

Olivia took a step forward also so that only a few feet separated her from the woman who was still glaring at her.

"Don't you want to be fed and nurtured?" she asked in a low, almost desperate voice. "I just want to help," she continued, shaking her head.

The woman folded her arms over her chest, her gesture giving a clear answer to Olivia's question.

Olivia's cheeks were flame red, and she continued to face the woman, but he could read that, for the first time, she was suffering from defeat.

How must that feel for Olivia? Treasured duke's daughter that she was?

Edward also felt compassion for the people in the crowd—he knew the villagers, none of them were starving, none were in need of the kind of desperate help Olivia was offering. They didn't fit the role that Olivia expected them to play; in her world, people were either bullies or oppressed. These people were neither.

His father had made sure of that, actually, having set up various means of assistance through his years of living in proximity to the village.

Of course Olivia didn't know that. Didn't know any of that, but then again, she hadn't asked. If she had asked if the townspeople would be receptive to the kind of lofty charity she was attempting, he would have given her a firm refusal, and perhaps—just perhaps—she would have conceded that for once her help was not needed.

But it was too late.

He stepped forward, reaching her in a few quick strides, taking her arm and drawing her away from the table, her face frozen, her expression confused.

"I just wanted," she began, and he took her hand and drew it through his arm, pulling her close to his body. As he did so, he made eye contact with Lady Pearl, who was regarding her twin with a rueful expression. Maybe Lady Pearl had anticipated that one day her sister's help wouldn't be wanted?

Lady Ida glanced between the twins, her expression pained, eventually taking Pearl's hand in hers and stroking it in sympathy.

The sisters walked toward them as he escorted Olivia back the way they'd come, his money still clutched in her hand, her head bowed, her gaze on the ground.

Chapter 21

Everything you thought you knew is wrong.
LADY OLIVIA'S PARTICULAR GUIDE
TO BEING RECKLESS

*O*livia's heart felt bruised as she allowed Edward to walk her away from the village. When she had seen the children, the idea had been so clear—help them however she could, with what means she had at her disposal.

The means were in Edward's wallet, and the help would be to offer the children some food. But the merchants had declined the offer, as though she had no right to make it, and the children had just stared at her when she tried to ask them about it.

And then one of the children's mothers had glared at her and stepped over to the children, her chin lifted proudly.

And then—and then she had been publicly humiliated. When all she wanted was to help.

"Are you all right?" he asked in a low voice.

She bit her lip and raised her chin. "I am fine," she said, even though her voice was wobbly.

"You were trying to do the right thing," Lady Pearl said, coming up to Olivia's other side. Ida walked behind them.

"I was. They just didn't want my help." Olivia spoke wonderingly, as though she found it difficult to believe.

And of course to her it was.

"Not everybody wants help, Olivia." Edward had hold of her arm, and he felt her jerk away at his words.

She stopped and spun to look at him, a high wash of color on her cheekbones. "But they don't always know! They might be in need of things, those children could be hungry, and they wouldn't know! Or they're too proud," she said in a bitter tone.

Edward shook his head slowly. "But I know. I do know about them, and this situation. It's not like the ducks, Olivia. The townspeople are perfectly happy and are doing quite well. But you just assumed, since you are determined to see injustice and inequity everywhere, that those people were suffering. But if you had asked . . ." And he let his words trail off, waiting to see her reaction.

Her expression froze, and then he saw her blink

as though processing her thoughts. She bit her lip, and he wondered for a moment if she would cry—but of course she wouldn't, she was Olivia.

His beautiful, brave, headstrong, foolhardy, proud Olivia.

"I should have asked," she said at last.

And then he fell even more in love with her.

"Olivia?" Lady Pearl said, tapping her sister on the arm. "We should start walking, it looks as though it might rain."

Olivia shook her head. "Go ahead, you two. Mr. Wolcott will walk with me." Then her eyes went wide, and she shook her head. "Though I should have asked, shouldn't I?"

"You don't have to ask," Edward replied, seeing Lady Pearl's mouth open as she heard his words.

"We'll just be going along then," Pearl said, a knowing look in her eye. She took Lady Ida's arm as the two started walking briskly back, Pearl bending her head close to her sister's and whispering furiously.

Leaving them alone.

Edward glanced up at the sky. Sure enough, there were some clouds forming.

"I believe your sister is correct. It looks as though it's going to rain."

Olivia shrugged. "It doesn't matter. I can't control everything. I definitely cannot control the weather." She sounded deflated, and Edward suppressed the urge to take her in his arms. He would enjoy that—and she might as well—but the most important thing now was to restore her confidence.

Instead, he raised his eyebrow at her. "You can't? Lady Olivia, you wound me." He clapped his hand on his heart and staggered back as though struck. And then righted himself and grinned. "It's fine. You suffered a humiliation just now. It just proves you're human."

She snorted. "I have always been human, Edward." She looked up at him, her eyes vividly bright in the increasing greyness of the sky. "I wanted to be more than just me, Lady Olivia. One of the duke's daughters, a lady who would do just as she was supposed to."

"And you have." He stepped toward her, putting his hands on her arms and tugging her forward to him. "You are remarkable, Olivia. You are brave and strong and I admire you. Even if you can be stubborn and rush into things without heed."

Her lips curled into a rueful smile. "That is true." She slid her fingers up his arms and curled her fingers into his hair. "I find that I like rushing into things," she said.

So of course he had no choice by then but to kiss her.

WAS THERE ANYTHING better than being kissed by Edward?

Well, perhaps. Although none of that had happened yet, so she couldn't answer for certain.

They were standing out on the road, for goodness' sake, where anyone could see them. Not that they'd seen a soul until they went into town—into that blasted village filled with people who very definitely did not want her assistance—so it likely didn't matter.

He slid his tongue into her mouth, and she opened her lips to accept him, loving how delicious it felt, how her whole body was starting to tingle.

His hands were stroking her back, up and down, and she moved even closer into his body, putting her hands on his side, underneath his coat, sliding her fingers on his body.

She'd seen what he looked like underneath his clothing. She wanted to see it all again—his firm, muscled chest, his broad shoulders, the sprinkling of hair on his chest. She wanted to run her fingers all over him. Yes, there too.

There where she felt him pressed against her.

She wanted more.

She drew her head back and looked at him, noting his heavy-lidded gaze, his deep inhalation of breath, his intense focus on her.

"It's going to rain. We should find shelter."

He looked at her as though he didn't understand at first, then nodded, a wry smile on his mouth.

"I know just where to go. We can stay there until the storm passes."

He took her arm and they ran, ran down the narrow path hand in hand, her heart beating against her ribs, her thoughts filled with a tumult of emotions—*I love him, I don't know who I am, I want this, I want him, I want, I want, I want.*

They ran until she was breathless, and she lagged behind as he pulled her along. They came to the outskirts of Mr. Beechcroft's property, where Olivia saw a small shed with shutters.

"There," he said, slowing his pace and walking briskly. "It's where the gardeners keep their tools, but they won't be working today."

She bit her lip and looked up at him.

"But if you have changed your mind, and you want to return to the house, we can do that as well," he said, his eyes intent on her face.

"No. I want this." *I want you.*

He smiled, and turned to open the door, allowing her to step inside ahead of him.

The shed was spare and tidy, a variety of what she assumed were gardening tools hanging on the walls. There was a pile of cloth bags in one corner, and a few chairs set in front of a rough, wood-hewn table.

The room was dark, and it felt immediately more intimate. As though only they existed here, in this moment. He was Edward and she was Olivia, and that was all there was to them.

He shut the door and turned to her, taking her in his arms again and lowering his mouth to her lips.

She didn't hesitate, but opened her lips to slide her tongue into his mouth, placing her palms on his chest and stroking the firm muscles she felt underneath his clothing.

She needed to see him again.

She reached up to push his jacket off his shoulders, sliding the sleeves off his arms without breaking the kiss.

It was awkward, it probably looked ridiculous, but she didn't care about that. She just wanted him.

He smiled under her mouth, and she felt a chuckle in her chest.

Who knew kissing could be so fun?

He withdrew for a moment so he could remove his jacket entirely, tossing it onto one of the wooden chairs.

She raised an eyebrow and looked pointedly at his waistcoat. "That too, please," she said in her most commanding manner.

"Have I mentioned how much I like it when you tell me what to do?" he replied, grinning wickedly as his fingers went to his buttons. He undid them rapidly, far faster than she would have done, and soon enough his waistcoat was lying on top of his jacket, leaving him only in his shirt and trousers.

He paused as his hands went to the fabric of his shirt.

"Why are you stopping? I want it off now," she said, noting how breathily she spoke. How urgently she wanted him to take his shirt off so she could see him—just him—again.

He nodded toward her. "I expect there to be some reciprocity in this arrangement. We are equal, are we not? We all deserve what each other has?"

She felt her lips curve into a rueful smile. "When I have spoken like that in the past, I did not mean about this," she said, gesturing in the space between them.

"But it is fair, isn't it? That we each be given a chance?" He drew the tails of his shirt out of his trousers, exposing a bare swath of skin.

There was enough light in the shed, thankfully, for her to see the trail of hair that led down his skin into his trousers.

To there.

"I suppose in the interest of equality," she said, turning around so she had her back to him.

His fingers went immediately to the buttons on the back of her dress, and he worked quickly, his warm breath on the nape of her neck. A curl tickling her skin as he bent toward her.

A few minutes later—there were far too many buttons, Olivia decided—he'd tugged her sleeves down and she finished the work as his hands went to her waist to push her gown down.

She stepped out of the fabric as he leaned over to pick the gown up, folding it carefully, his eyes averted from her as he placed it on the other chair.

And then he was looking at her, and she caught her breath at the intensity of his gaze. She felt hot all over, even though she was standing in her shift and corset, and the air was cool.

Her fingers went to the ties of her corset, and she tried to undo them, but her hands were shaking.

"Here, let me," he said, a knowing smile on his mouth.

She reached for his shirt, tugging him closer as she felt his fingers brush her upper neck, lower, and then her breast.

Oh. That felt incredible, and yet there were still layers of fabric between them. What would it be like when his bare palm was on her skin?

She swallowed against the thickness of her throat.

"Off," she said, drawing her fingers, still holding the bunched fabric of his shirt up.

"Likewise," he muttered, removing her corset and putting it on top of his waistcoat.

Leaving her in her shift.

He pulled his shirt over his head and dropped it to the floor, apparently not caring any longer about keeping his clothing tidy.

She licked her lips as she looked at him, his chest broad and muscled, his shoulders wide, his waist narrow.

He looked like a statue of some proud warrior, and yet he was warm, and living and breathing directly in front of her.

She placed her palm on his chest again, sighing in satisfaction as she felt his warm skin. She slid her fingers over his nipple, smiling as she heard his intake of breath. Doing it again just because it brought both of them pleasure.

He grabbed hold of her wrists and drew her arms around his body, placing her hands at the small of his back.

This brought their bodies together, but because he was so much taller than she, they were face to chest instead of chest to chest. She rose up on her tiptoes and buried her nose into his neck, placing kisses on his skin as she slid her hands up and down his back.

Suddenly she felt him hoist her up so their mouths met again, and he was kissing her savagely, ruthlessly, and she loved every moment of it. His tongue possessing her mouth, his hands wrapped around her, his body holding her close.

Lower still, a certain part of him making its presence known. Feeling that pressure created a soft ache inside, a warm, prickly feeling dancing on her skin.

And then his hand was curled around her breast, his finger finding her nipple. He ran his palm over it and she gasped as the sensation flowed through her body.

"You like that," he murmured against her mouth. It wasn't a question.

"Mmm," she replied, sliding her fingers from the small of his back to rest on his hipbones.

"Are you certain about this?" he asked, pressing forward there so it was clear what he meant.

"Mmm-hmm," she said, holding her breath as she put her hand right there, right where he was so large and firm and—and large.

"God, Olivia, you're killing me," he said, only he didn't sound in pain.

"Oh?" she replied, rubbing her hand over him. He groaned, and then quickly picked her up, carrying her to the pile of bags in the corner, letting her down to lie against the coarse cloth.

Standing in front of her, his mixed expression showed desire, curiosity, and concern.

Still concerned, even though she was here and was a full participant in what they were doing.

His hands were at his waistband—they stilled as he waited.

"Go ahead," she said, sitting up to reach to the hem of her shift, starting to pull it up her legs.

"No," he replied, a sly smile playing on his lips. "I want to do that. Wait for me."

He undid the placket of his trousers quickly, shucking the pants off his legs with remarkable speed, leaving him only in his smallclothes.

His male part stood proudly out from his body, seeming as though it was aimed right at her. She nearly giggled at how it looked, as though it were something he had stuck on himself at a right angle.

"Is something amusing?"

She began to shake her head no, then nodded. "It's just so—so there," she said, pointing to the object in question.

He grinned as his hand went there, grasping it and sliding his hand up and down, his gaze intent on her.

"Oh," she said in a soft voice as she watched. His hand moved in a steady rhythm, his other hand sliding over his chest.

There was something so sensual about watching him, but she wanted to be the one to touch him.

"Weren't you going to remove this?" she said as she plucked at the hem of her shift.

He immediately lowered himself beside her, his fingers on her skin, on the shift, lifting it up her body and over her head.

"I wanted to take my time doing that," he said, his eyes traveling all over her body, "but I couldn't wait. I'm too impatient."

She swallowed and put her hands on his shoulders to bring his body alongside hers.

They lay facing one another, his member pressing against her belly, his gaze on her mouth.

"I want this, Edward," she said in a soft voice as she slid her hands down his body to grip him as he had.

"Gladly," he replied, releasing his hold of her to slide his smallclothes off so they were both naked, lying on the cloth bags in a darkened shed.

The rain had started, and there was a pleasant low hum from the drops falling on the roof.

It felt even more as though only they existed in the world. It was a precious, wonderful moment she never wanted to stop, even though she knew its end was inevitable.

But meanwhile, she could savor it. Savor him.

And this. All of this.

Chapter 22

Act on your desires.

LADY OLIVIA'S PARTICULAR GUIDE
TO BEING RECKLESS

*E*dward held his breath as Olivia touched him. His cock throbbed, hard and insistent, in her hand.

She ran her fingers up and down his shaft, tentatively at first, and then curling her hand around him in a delicious grip.

"That's it," he said, his fingers splayed out on her skin just below her waist. "A little tighter," he said, and she held him tighter, making him groan his satisfaction.

"This isn't hurting you?" she said, more in observation than a question.

"No," he said, sliding his fingers down her belly to where his cock most wanted to be. She gasped and stilled her hand, and he paused as well.

"Go on," she said, adjusting her hips so that she was more open to him. He put his fingers into her nether curls and then slid his fingers through, finding her already warm and wet.

"Oh," she moaned, laying her head back against the bags, moving her body restlessly as he rubbed the little nub at the top of her sex.

"You like this," he said, leaning forward to lick her neck, then up to her ear, and then he found her mouth, plunging his tongue inside as forcefully as his cock wanted to be inside of her.

She returned to stroking him, and he urged himself into her hand, relishing the friction and how he could feel her breathing get faster as both of their hands moved on one another.

She was quivering under his touch, and he tried to focus on her, focus on her pleasure, on feeling how her body changed the closer he brought her to her peak.

Because she was heading for it, he could tell— her nipples poked sharply against his chest, her breathing was rapid, her grip on his cock was tight.

He lifted his mouth from hers and looked at her, at her eyes unfocused and lost in desire, at her moist lips and flushed cheeks.

He'd thought her beautiful before, but in the throes of passion, she was glorious. Truly the sparkling woman he'd been enchanted by after that regrettable proposal.

And then her eyes closed, and she cried out,

her whole body stiffening as she clenched her legs around his hand. He could feel the pulse and tremor of her orgasm, and he slowed his hand, petting her there as she gradually emerged from the bliss.

"Oh my," she said at last, opening her eyes to look at him. She looked dazed, likely as dazed as he felt.

"Oh my indeed," he replied, smiling in satisfaction.

She took a deep breath, and then she blinked slowly. "I didn't know."

"You hadn't—?" The thought that she might not have found a way to pleasure herself was surprising. His fierce warrior queen not doing for herself what he had just done for her?

"No, I . . ." And then she blushed more vividly, and he felt a ridiculous swelling in his chest at realizing he'd given her her first orgasm.

Although that wasn't absolutely correct; he would not have had the opportunity had she not been so willing, so open, and so receptive to his touch.

"You must be," she said in a halting voice, her eyes darting down to where his cock pressed into her side.

"Yes, but we can wait." He placed his hand on top of hers, which was still holding him in a loose grip. "Although if you feel as though you are up to it," he said, a teasing suggestion in his voice.

"Of course I am," she said in her usual strong tone. And she began to stroke him up and down again, making him shudder. He was so close, he was—

"We should think about marriage."

The words snapped him out of his sensual haze. "What?"

She shrugged, looking almost abashed. Which would be odd if their entire circumstances weren't so odd. "Your father wants you to be married. I know he is ill, and I know how much you love him."

Nothing about if she loved him.

"My eyes were opened this afternoon," she said in a low voice. It sounded to him as though she were shouting. "I can't do everything I want. I want to be able to do as much as I can. Together we can do so much, and you can help guide me, since you know these people so much better than I do."

His mouth gaped open at her. His cock still in her hand, his heart, apparently, not worth mentioning.

"And this way your father will be happy, and we can continue all of this." And she released him to gesture around them, the ridiculousness of the situation making him snort.

"All of this?" No mention of how she felt about

him. Just that she had become aware she couldn't do all of it—whatever it was—by herself anymore because she needed some sort of lower-class interpreter, which he was ideally suited for, what with being a bastard. That's how she thought of him, wasn't it? She'd never stopped thinking that way.

"Yes, all of this." She took a deep breath and raised her chin in that way he'd thought he loved. "I know that it only makes sense for us to get married."

He raised himself onto his elbow to glare down at her. "It only makes sense for us to get married?" he repeated. He rose and found his smallclothes, putting them on hastily, finding his discarded trousers and putting them on as well. She hadn't moved, just stared up at him with a confused expression. "You said precisely the same thing to Bennett. And it worked out just as well." He took a deep breath, trying to calm himself. "As it happens, my father is much improved. I have plenty of time to find myself a wife. Hopefully one who won't look down on me because of my birth, who loves me as I love her"—dear God, he loved her, why did she have to be so careless— "and who isn't just reacting because she got her feelings hurt."

He regretted those last words as soon as he'd said them, but it was too late to take them back. Her eyes widened, and she got up as well, still entirely unclothed, her whole body seeming to seethe with indignation.

But she was no more indignant than he was.

He leaned over and picked up her shift, which he held out to her. She snatched it out of his hands and tossed it over her head, angrily adjusting the fabric around her body.

"I did not propose because I got my feelings hurt." She planted her fists on her hips. "I proposed because I know it would help you enormously if you were to marry one of the duke's daughters. Because I know how much you care for your father, and I know he would be pleased to welcome me as his daughter-in-law. Because this"—and she extended her hand to encompass both of them and whatever had just occurred— "keeps happening, and I don't want to lose it. I don't want to lose you."

She stopped speaking abruptly, clamping her mouth closed.

"You don't want to lose me." He swallowed against the tide of emotion in his chest. "But you don't want to keep me. Or you only wanted me when it seemed your assessment of yourself fell. Would you have asked me to marry you before this afternoon? Before you discovered you weren't the invincible do-gooder you believe yourself to be?"

"I'm not the one who constantly thinks the

worst of themselves because of the accident of their birth." Her words cut to his heart because in some way he knew they were true.

"But you're the daughter of a duke, as you say. So you've never had to think anything but the best of yourself. Until now."

She took a deep breath and opened her mouth again, then shook her head and stepped past him to where her corset and gown lay on the chair.

He didn't know what was happening. Why they had gone so quickly from her pleasure to their mutual displeasure. How she had possibly thought that now was the right time to discuss all of this?

He watched as she picked up her corset and put it back on, tying the laces with unsteady fingers. He stopped himself from going to help, knowing his help wouldn't be wanted.

Not now.

Eventually she just shook her head in disgust, leaving a few dangling strings, and picked up her gown, holding it up so she could put it back on.

Shaking her body to adjust the fabric, then biting her lip as she tried to reach around to her back.

"Let me," he said in a quiet voice. He walked to where she stood and did up the buttons, trying not to touch her skin.

"Thank you."

She turned her head, keeping her gaze on the

floor. "I am glad your father is feeling better. I will try to persuade my mother"—and then she chuckled drily—"to go earlier than we'd planned."

She didn't say anything else, just picked up the skirts of her gown and opened the door, closing it softly behind herself as she left him alone.

He walked to the door also, but didn't open it, instead slamming his fist against the wall in frustration.

He loved her. That wouldn't change.

But he'd never be with her again.

Chapter 23

Say what you mean.

LADY OLIVIA'S PARTICULAR GUIDE
TO BEING RECKLESS

*O*livia walked slowly back to the house despite the ongoing rain, reliving every moment of what had just happened. How had it all gone wrong?

There was that amazing feeling as he did whatever he did with his fingers, and then she'd thought that she should just say what she was thinking. Only she probably shouldn't have.

She winced as she realized how she must have sounded—presuming he would know more about some people than she because of his birth. And yes, that was true, but that was because she had been so sheltered until recently. Not because his birth was so much lower than hers.

Although it was, and to ignore that would be disingenuous.

Had she told him she loved him?

She reviewed what she'd said, and the sick horror started to grow as she considered her words. No wonder he was angry. She had been, even if inadvertently, proud and condescending. She hadn't told him she loved him.

Instead, she'd focused on what they could accomplish together—the things *she* wanted to accomplish—and that his father would be pleased.

Mentioning, as though it was secondary, the incendiary attraction between them.

Damn it.

She felt tears start to prickle her eyes, and she wiped them away with the back of her hand. Lady Olivia Howlett did not cry.

Except she was crying.

Damn it again.

She spied a small terrace and a door that led back into the house. Hopefully it would be unlocked, and she could slip inside and gather herself together so that nobody would know anything was amiss.

Keeping her head down, she walked briskly up the three stairs to the stone terrace, reaching her hand forward for the doorknob.

Please—"Ah," she said with satisfaction as the door swung open, and she stepped inside.

Her eyes blinked against the sudden brightness of candles, and she wavered, trying to focus on the room.

"Olivia?"

It was Ida, sitting on the floor with an enormous book spread out on her lap.

"Hello," Olivia replied, her voice wavering. "I didn't mean . . ." And she trailed off, not sure what she didn't mean. Or did mean anymore.

"You're not all right." It wasn't a question. The tears threatened to come again, and she looked up at the ceiling, trying to calm herself. She heard the rustle of material as Ida got up to stand in front of her.

"Olivia." Ida had hold of her chin and was pulling her face down.

Her sister was very close to her. Physically, not figuratively. Ida was so distant at times, it almost seemed as though she wanted to keep herself apart from her ridiculous family.

Olivia couldn't blame her most of the time. Their family was ridiculous—one sister eloping with the dancing master, the other sister refusing to marry Bennett. Her falling in love with a man who was only barely admitted to Society because of his vast amounts of money. Not that Ida knew about the falling in love part, but she had to suspect it, at least.

Ida was nothing if not intelligent and observant.

"What happened?"

Ida drew her over to sit down on the sofa

placed in front of the fire—so similar to the first time she'd met Edward that she nearly sobbed aloud—and made her sit, taking Olivia's hands in hers.

"I know I'm not Pearl, but you need help now, and Pearl stayed behind to make sure you made it home." Ida straightened her shoulders and nodded. "Which you did, but Pearl hasn't come back yet. No idea where she got up to in this rain. So you're going to have to tell me what is wrong."

It felt so odd to be confiding in Ida, and yet Olivia found herself telling her as much as she'd ever told Pearl—about trying to help Edward gain respectability, finding him a bride, realizing he intrigued her. Not sharing precisely what had happened in the shed, but Ida's penetrating gaze let Olivia know her sister had figured it out.

At the end, Ida looked puzzled. "It sounds as though you told him what should be done, but not how you feel. Shouldn't you have done that?"

The clear directness of Ida's words made Olivia want to laugh and cry at the same time. It was so simple, wasn't it? She should just tell him, and then see what he said.

"Thank you," she said as the door opened to admit Pearl.

"There you are!" Pearl exclaimed. "I waited, just

in case you needed to talk." She frowned, stepping forward to lower her head to stare at Olivia. "You do need to talk."

"She does need to talk, but not to either one of us," Ida said in a brisk tone. "She needs to talk to Mr. Wolcott." Ida moved to the side of the sofa so that Pearl could sit beside Olivia.

"Tell me," Pearl said, her hair damp.

Olivia glanced over her twin's head to look at Ida. "Well, as I was saying, I asked him to marry me and he said no."

"But he loves you, I know he does. Tell me exactly what happened," Pearl commanded.

Olivia took a deep breath. Pearl was going to—correctly—assess that Olivia had said all the wrong things at the wrong time. As Ida had, only Pearl was less blunt than their sister.

"You can't say something to him now, at least not before you both have calmed down," Pearl said after Olivia repeated the story, condescending words and all.

Olivia wrinkled her brow in thought. "But what if he thinks my not speaking to him means I don't care? That I actually meant what I said?"

Pearl shrugged. "It's better that he think that for a time than that the two of you never have a productive conversation and you end up alone and miserable."

Olivia's eyes widened. "Well, since you put it that way."

"And here I thought I was the blunt one," Ida said, a note of pride in her voice. "I agree with what Pearl says, you have to wait until you have figured out what you want to say. Perhaps try practicing it a few times so you don't end up making it worse."

"Well, that's hardly comforting," Olivia replied, thinking about how horribly the village encounter went.

Although it did show her that she was not infallible. That sometimes it would be best to ask rather than to assume.

She wished she had learned that lesson when talking to Edward, actually. If she had asked him how he felt about her, and asked him to consider marriage rather than just assuming, she wouldn't be in this position at the moment.

She'd be engaged or she'd know the truth. Or both.

She took a deep breath. "Thank you both. I love you both so much, and I am so glad you are my sisters."

She drew Pearl into a hug and stretched her hand out to grasp Ida on the arm, squeezing her gently.

Ida looked startled, then her face eased into a smile.

It would be fine. She would be fine, even if it ended up he wasn't in love with her. She had her sisters' love, and she had her newfound awareness that she wasn't always right, and she could work on improving herself and the world with that knowledge in her pocket.

Chapter 24

Be bold. Do what needs to be done.
                    LADY OLIVIA'S PARTICULAR GUIDE
                                    TO BEING RECKLESS

*D*inner the following evening had been excruciating. Edward had been able to occupy himself during the day, taking Chrysanthemum out for a long ride and then going through some papers he'd been avoiding, but now he was seated at dinner with all of the guests, including her.

He wanted to get up and just leave, but it would hurt his father and ensure the duchess thought he was even less of a gentleman than she probably already thought.

He'd almost gone to Olivia at least a dozen times that day, but he'd said a few cutting things, and she'd just left—he didn't know what else she might have to say. He would find out, eventually, but at the moment he needed to calm himself down before he approached her.

She and Bennett were seated together at the far end of the table, and he couldn't avoid hearing the very pointed comments the duchess was making.

"You two look so wonderful together. Almost as though you were a married couple!"

Things like that.

He'd seen the pained expressions on everybody else's faces, including Bennett's and Olivia's, to indicate they too were having an excruciating experience. So at least there was camaraderie in their misery.

"Mother," Lady Ida said in a reproving voice. "Olivia and Lord Carson are friends." And then she'd looked over at him and he could have sworn she winked.

It must have been a trick of the light.

"Such dear friends, yes," the duchess said in a pleased voice. Missing Lady Ida's point entirely.

"Mr. Beechcroft, I was wondering if you would allow me to go for a ride tomorrow?" Lady Pearl said in a hurried tone, clearly trying to steer the conversation in another direction. "I have not had much opportunity for exercise, and I believe it will be a lovely day."

Mr. Beechcroft nodded at Edward. "You'll have to ask my son—he is the horse expert in the family. I like them for my carriages, but I gave up riding long ago."

"Of course, Lady Pearl," Edward said. "I would be happy to."

He caught Olivia looking at him, and his chest tightened. He would have to find a chance to speak with her sooner rather than later. He might not like what she would have to say, but he needed to hear her say it.

There was no opportunity that evening, however, which was why Edward found himself in his bedroom, alone except for Scamp, the kitten who'd taken to him, hiding out in his bedroom during the day and sleeping with him at night.

"What do you think, Scamp?" Edward said, leaning back on his bed and allowing the kitten to jump onto his chest. "When should I speak with her? They'll only be here for another week or so." The thought of spending more days in the same house with her without knowing how she felt, or what she felt, was an agonizing thought.

Scamp, however, had no reply.

Instead, the kitten began to knead Edward's chest, tiny claws going through the fabric of his banyan.

He was chuckling when he heard the knock on the door.

It was after ten o'clock—everyone should be in bed by now. So of course it had to be her.

He removed Scamp from his chest, placing the

kitten on the bed and swinging his legs over to the ground, striding to the door in a few quick steps.

"Hello," she said as he opened the door.

He took her arm to bring her inside, shutting the door softly behind her. She wore a night rail and a robe, her bare feet peeking out from under the bottom edge, and her hair was undone.

"What are you doing here?" he asked, tucking the edges of his banyan together. He was nude underneath the robe. "Not that I'm not pleased to see you," he added hastily.

"Are you?" she asked, sounding hesitant. So unlike the usual Olivia he froze for a moment.

"I am. I think." And he paused, sweeping his hair off his face in an effort to gather his thoughts. "I think we should sit down." Of course the only place for both of them to sit was on his bed.

"Yes, we should," she replied, walking over to get onto the covers. Apparently not hesitant at all when it came to that.

"I wanted to say something," he said, but she reached forward and put her hand to his mouth.

Her fingers were warm.

Scamp brushed past him to leap onto the floor and tuck into his slipper, gnawing on the edge.

"I have something to say first." She licked her lips and took a deep breath. "I wanted to say that what I said yesterday was all wrong." She shook her head, and several strands of hair fell forward. He resisted the urge to smooth them back. If he touched her, he didn't know what might happen. Or he did, and he didn't know if that was what should happen. He needed to wait for her to talk, for them to have a conversation, before either one of them did anything they would regret.

"What would you have said if you could say it all over again?" he asked.

She raised her chin and looked directly into his face. The candlelight caught the gold glints in her eyes and the curve of her lips.

"I should have started out with the most important thing." She hesitated, and he caught his breath, wondering what she was about to say.

"Which is—?" he prompted.

"Which is I love you." He opened his mouth in shock as she continued speaking. "And I know you don't love me, and I know that you might believe that I am lowering myself to want to be with you, but if anything, I want to rise to your level." She swallowed, and Edward's throat tightened. She loved him? And she thought he didn't love her?

"I admire your resilience and your determination to be in this world on your terms, not to cow to anyone because of your birth." Her eyes sparkled with the force of her emotions. "You know who you are, you know what you can do, and you don't let anyone stop you. Not Society, not people like my parents." A pause. "Not me."

He leaned forward and swept her up in his arms, placing her on his lap. She was warm and soft, and he couldn't get distracted by that, not when he had to make sure they understood one another.

"I love you too." Her eyes widened, and he heard her draw her breath in sharply. "I was angry because I thought you just wanted me for what you thought you could accomplish with my wealth. Like you wanted to with Bennett, back when you first proposed." He pressed a kiss on her brow. "Plus your timing was terrible, given what had just happened between us."

She grimaced. "Yes, I don't always think before I speak," she said.

"I would say you never think before you speak." He laughed as her embarrassed expression turned outraged. "Not that I want you to ever stop. I love you, I love how you rush into things without wondering how you'll look, and I love your determination, your forcefulness when you see inequality. Whether it's for ducks or bastards," he finished, grinning.

She swatted him on the arm, but she was still here, still very much in his lap, a smile on her mouth.

"You love me?" she said, looking up at him.

"I do," he replied.

"Then let's do something about that," she replied, a wicked look on her face.

OLIVIA STRADDLED HIM, catching his jaw in her hands, lowering her mouth to his.

He loved her. She loved him.

She kissed him, and he wrapped his arms around her body, holding her close against his chest. She ran her hand through his curls, down his neck and underneath the fabric of his dressing gown.

She made a noise in her throat as she realized he wasn't wearing anything underneath.

"What?" he said, moving his mouth to her neck. He sucked her skin into his mouth, then licked the tender spot, making her shiver.

"You're not wearing any clothing," she said, sliding the fabric off his shoulders.

"Well, I was, but then you took it off me," he said, smiling as he shrugged out of the garment.

She leaned back to take the view in. His chest was golden in the candlelight, whorls of hair lightly covering his muscles. She placed her palm on his nipple, making his stomach muscles contract.

That was fun. She drew her fingernails over the nipple, and he hissed, encircling her wrist with his fingers.

"You don't want me to touch you there?" she asked.

"I do," he replied, his voice low and growly, making her shiver all over again. "But there are other places I want you to touch me." And he brought her hand down, skating it over his skin, to his—

"What do you call it?" she asked as she curled her fingers around him.

"My cock," he replied, his eyes shut. "Stroke my cock, Olivia." She began to move her hand up and down, and he made a groan deep in his throat. "Yes, just like that."

She felt so powerful—sitting astride him, feeling how he twitched and throbbed under her fingers. Watching his intense expression as she stroked him, feeling how there, where he'd touched her, was feeling sensitive.

"What do you call what I have?" she asked, shifting off him and lying down on the bed, her hand still on his cock.

He lay down beside her, facing her, his hand going to her neck, her collarbone, curling over her breast, and then yanking the fabric of her night rail up and putting his fingers on her bare skin.

Moving them up . . . and she caught her lip in her teeth, his gaze on her mouth, his hand moving up and up until—

"It's your quim," he said as his fingers caressed her there. Right at her quim. "Or cunny, or if you're being fanciful, your daisy."

"Oh, my daisy. I like that one."

"I like your daisy very much." And then his fingers slid inside her, and she forgot all about words, or where she was, or anything but what he was doing to her. How he was making her feel.

And then he was kissing her again, his cock—*his cock!*—nudging at her belly, his tongue thrust deep in her mouth.

She had one hand still on him, on his cock, while the other was tangled in his curls, holding his face close to hers.

"Need to see you," he said hoarsely, reaching down to her night rail and pulling it up, up over her head.

Which would have been fine except that she still wore something on top of it, so all the fabric was a mad tangle between them.

"Hold on," she said, tugging at the sleeves. And then starting to laugh at the absurdity of it—him naked beside her, her with her clothing entirely disarranged, them doing this.

He helped her with the removal, then tossed everything toward the end of the bed.

And then they heard a noise, and both looked down, and Scamp was leaping up, a piece of Olivia's night rail in her mouth, and they watched as she dragged it down off the bed.

She heard him chuckle, and she began to laugh again too. How was it possible that this—which she had heard was very serious and possibly unpleasant—could be so much fun?

It must be because it was he. Entirely due to him.

"Now that you are naked to my satisfaction," he said, "let us resume."

"I want you to ruin me," she said. "If I am totally and completely ruined, I won't have to marry anybody but you."

"So it's my duty to ruin you?" he said, raising his eyebrow.

"Absolutely," she said, taking his cock in her hand again.

"Well, I suppose this proposal is more enticing than the last one," he replied, his eyes traveling lazily down her body, making her acutely conscious of how exposed she was.

"You're lovely," he said in a low voice, his fingers caressing her breast. He rubbed her nipple, then leaned forward and took it in his mouth, making her gasp.

His other hand had returned to her daisy, and was stroking her, building a heat within that was making her squirm.

His tongue swirled on her skin, and she felt

the familiar tension—familiar because he'd done whatever magic he'd done only the previous day—rise, the feeling building and building until she—

"Don't come yet," he muttered, raising his head from her breast. He edged down her body, kissing her belly, lower. She held her breath, wondering if . . .

"Oh my God," she said as he buried his mouth on her there. Licking her with his tongue as his fingers continued to move, the sensation as intense and fierce as anything she'd ever felt before.

It was decadent, and so erotic, and she gripped her hands in his hair, moving her head on his pillow, biting her lip as the tension increased.

Until—"Aah," she cried out, arching her back as the feeling washed over her.

"That's what I wanted to see again. Your orgasm." He drew up beside her to kiss her. She could taste herself on his mouth.

"That was—that was," she said, not able to finish.

He chuckled, then took her hand and put it back on his cock. It was hard and throbbing, and she swallowed nervously as she thought about what was next.

"Relax," he said, shifting so she could feel him there, right at her entrance. Her daisy. "You're all ready for me, and I'll stop if it hurts."

"I love you," she said, twisting so she was lying back on the bed.

"I love you too," he said, starting to guide himself into her.

EDWARD HADN'T EXPECTED to end the evening with this—a naked Olivia in his bed asking him to ruin her—but he wasn't going to deny it was the best evening of his life.

Tomorrow they'd deal with the messy repercussions, but for right now it was just them.

She was wet, but still tight, and he went slowly, gritting his teeth as he moved.

"Are you all right?" he asked, hearing how strained his voice was.

"Mmm," she said, her eyes wide. "I want this. I want you."

And then he slid all the way inside, grunting as his hips pressed against hers.

"Oh my." She sounded breathless, and intrigued. Her hands went to his arse and gripped him as he started to move.

He pushed up on his elbows so he could look down at her face as he thrust, his rhythm increasing as the orgasm built.

She kept her eyes open, her gaze steady on him, and he felt the swell of his heart as he watched her expression.

He was so close, so close, and he kept increasing his speed, pushing in and out of her, hearing the slap of their flesh with each thrust.

Until he felt the moment peak, and he climaxed with a roar as he stiffened, the rush of it flooding his body with sharp satisfaction.

He collapsed on top of her, and he felt her laugh as he buried his nose in her neck.

"You have most definitely ruined me, Mr. Wolcott," she said in an amused tone. "I should leave, though. I don't want to—" And then she began to laugh again.

"Cause a scandal?" he finished. "Because that is the whole point of this, isn't it?"

She nodded, bumping his head with her chin, and he laughed, feeling as relaxed and comfortable as he'd ever felt.

He didn't feel as though he didn't belong. He definitely belonged here, with her, and it didn't matter who he was or what people thought of him. It only mattered what she thought of him, and she loved him.

That was more than enough.

He rolled off her, startling Scamp who'd climbed up on the bed. She leapt back down with a yowl, and Edward drew the covers up, urging Olivia to get underneath, then scooting beside her and tucking the covers around both of them.

"You can leave early in the morning," he said. "Nobody will be up to see you, and then we can both be presentable when you announce your intention of marrying me."

"Sounds wonderful," she replied in a sleepy voice. She curled against his side, and he wrapped his arm around her, feeling her warm, soft curves pressed into his body.

Chapter 25

Stand up for yourself and what you want.
LADY OLIVIA'S PARTICULAR GUIDE
TO BEING RECKLESS

Olivia."

Olivia scrunched her nose and swatted at the person saying her name.

Only—"Oh!" she said, scrambling quickly to sit up, meaning that she ended up bashing Edward in the nose with her head.

"Ouch, woman," he growled, grinning at her as he touched his nose.

"Sorry, I just—"

"You're not accustomed to waking up beside anybody," he said, pushing her hair away from her face. He leaned forward and kissed her, a warm, soft kiss that made her feel as though she were melting from the deliciousness of it.

"But you should get back to your room—your maid will be in to wake you soon."

Olivia glanced around the room, finally spotting a clock set on the table on the other side of the bed.

She hadn't taken a good look at the room the previous night; she'd been too focused on him, but now she could see it was a large, comfortable room, with only a few items placed on the bureau and tabletops. It was a room designed for relaxation, not work. Designed for other things, also, as she could tell from the size of the bed, which was huge.

It was a room she could see herself being in, living in, being comfortable in.

But only if she were able to fix all the mess she was currently in.

She scooted over to the side of the bed and dropped her feet down onto the plush carpet, blushing as she glanced down at her nakedness.

"Uh," she began, looking over her shoulder at him. He had lain back down, the sheets tangled around his waist, his chest on delicious display, making her want to dive back into bed with him and do more exploring.

"What is it?" he asked, arching a brow. As though he knew just what she was thinking and he was thinking the same thing.

"I need my clothes," she replied, closing her eyes so she wouldn't get distracted. Wondering how the stubble on his cheeks would feel on her skin.

Well, so much for not being distracted. With her eyes closed, she could picture just what it would look like if she stretched her hand out and put her palm on his abdomen, rubbing his chest with her fingers, sliding down until she—

"Here," he said, and she felt a plop of fabric land on her lap. Her eyes flew open, and she saw her night rail, which was twisted inside out. She put it the right way again and put it on, standing up to let the fabric shimmy down her legs.

"If I had my way," he said in a low, smoky voice that made her shiver, "I'd just keep you here and pleasure you until your screams woke the house. Then we wouldn't have to announce anything at all."

She felt a shiver run through her. It was a tempting idea.

"I think we should do the proper thing first," she said in a prim tone. Keenly aware of all his bare skin behind her.

"Fine. We'll try your tactic," he said, and she heard him shift on the bed. "But if that doesn't work, I'm tossing you over my shoulder and taking you back here to ravish you."

"It's a bargain," she said in a laughing tone.

She'd never expected all of this to be so much fun.

Chapter 26

Oh my goodness, that was fun. I cannot wait to do it again.

LADY OLIVIA'S PARTICULAR GUIDE

TO BEING RECKLESS

*H*e didn't have a ring. He should get a ring, to make certain she would marry him.

She'd said she would, but there was something enticing about having a physical claim on her, making sure everyone who saw her knew.

If he told her that's why he wanted her to wear one, he knew she would upbraid him for his old-fashioned notions. Which was why he needed to make certain he bought such a lovely ring that she didn't think too hard about it.

"Doughty?" Edward said, leaning back in his chair. The butler moved forward, inclining his head.

"What may I help you with, sir?"

Edward looked up. "Where would I buy a piece

of jewelry? Is there somewhere nearby?" He'd been to the town—the one that had not wanted Olivia's help—often enough, and he knew there wasn't a jeweler there. Hopefully it wouldn't be too far.

"There is one in Ackleworth, about ten miles from here."

Ackleworth. That was where his father had first met his mother. He generally avoided going there, since his grandfather's house was on the town's outskirts. But if he could just go in, find the jeweler and then get right out, it would be fine. He needed a ring more than he needed to avoid a town with bad memories.

He took another sip of coffee, pleased to find it had cooled enough. Hopefully that was a sign that he would be able to wait. Wait for the coffee to cool. Buy the ring.

Marry the woman he loved. Who loved him.

EDWARD SETTLED CHRYSANTHEMUM at the stables, and then walked quickly into the center of town.

It was far larger than what he was used to, at least out in the country. There were signs of bustling commerce everywhere, from pubs and inns to a milliner's shop, a fabric store, and no fewer than three haberdasheries.

The jeweler was next to the fabric shop, one of the ones his father's mills sold to. He was pleased to see a steady stream of customers going in and out, which he could report back to his father. The mill had been one of his father's first successes, and Mr. Beechcroft still viewed it as one of his favorite business transactions.

Edward stepped into the jeweler's, hoping the shop would have what he wanted—a ring that was as brilliant and sparkling as Olivia, but not too opulent. She wouldn't want a crass display like other ladies in Society. He wasn't certain whether or not such a ring existed, but he was going to try.

"Good morning, sir, welcome to Fotheringay's," an older man with grey hair said as Edward advanced. There were three sections of jewelry on display, one to either side of him and one in front. Sconces were above each, lighting the cases and making the stones within gleam.

Edward blinked against the sudden brightness, taking his hat off and walking up to the counter. "I am looking for a ring," he said, beginning to peruse the case in front of him.

Rings of all sorts were exhibited in the case, as were bracelets, necklaces, and tiaras.

What would it look like if she were to wear only a tiara?

He couldn't get distracted. He was here for a ring, not for something to fuel his fantasies. Perhaps after she said yes they could go tiara shopping.

"What type of ring?" the man said, beginning to remove trays from the case and laying them on the counter.

"A betrothal ring." Edward lowered his head to look at the rings—there were many, ranging from simple love knots to rings with a variety of stones.

He picked up one of the simplest ones; would she like this? Would it speak to her need for equality?

He put it down, picking up another in the case, this one more elaborate, with five stones placed in a line.

"That is the ADORE ring," the man said.

"Adore?"

The man nodded. "Yes, the five stones," he said, pointing to the ring, "each indicate a letter. So we have an amethyst, a diamond, an opal, a ruby, and an emerald. Adore."

"Ah." It was unfortunate that there wasn't a ring spelling out *Equality* or *Righteousness* or even *Equality for All Ducks*.

But anything like that would require a special order, and he didn't want to waste time. Plus he had to admit all his ideas sounded silly.

"I'll take it," he said, drawing his wallet out from his jacket.

The man nodded, writing up a receipt and placing the ring in a box.

Edward heard the door open as he was tucking the box into his pocket.

"Welcome, Mr. Wolcott," the jeweler said, making Edward stiffen.

"Morning, Fotheringay," a brusque voice replied. Edward turned around slowly, feeling his chest tighten as his eyes came to rest on the man who'd spoken.

An older man with curly white hair, who was tall and still fit, despite his age, a sharply inquisitive expression on his face.

He looked as Edward would look in about thirty years.

"You're my grandfather," Edward blurted out, almost before he knew what he was going to do.

The man merely raised an eyebrow at him, a look of haughty disdain on his face.

"You must be mistaken," he said, but his expression flickered, as though he knew the truth but wouldn't admit it.

"I'm not." Edward glanced back to see the jeweler's avidly curious face. "We could continue this conversation here, or we could step outside for a moment."

Mr. Wolcott tilted his head to look over Edward's shoulder, his mouth tightening as he saw the merchant. "Mmm," he grunted, turning back around and walking out.

Edward followed, fury warring with sorrow

in his chest. He hadn't realized how much it still hurt, knowing what he did about his past. Knowing that this man had refused to support him, that he had preferred to put a child into an orphanage rather than acknowledge that his daughter had fallen in love.

"You're Beechcroft's son?" Mr. Wolcott said, looking him up and down. "You seem to have turned out well. Quite the gentleman."

"No thanks to you," Edward replied, the fury winning out over whatever sadness he held. "My father took me when you wouldn't after my mother died. Have you never wondered about me?"

Mr. Wolcott shrugged. "I heard that you were being taken care of. I saw no need to interfere."

His grandfather's utter lack of interest, even now, infuriated him.

"No need to interfere?" Edward said, hearing the growl in his voice. "If it had been left to you, I would have been raised without any love, no support, nothing." He shouldn't have been surprised to feel himself shaking.

"You're a bastard," Mr. Wolcott said in a cold tone. "You have no claim on me."

Edward felt the man's words like a punch in the throat. And then something else eased his anger, making the clarity of the truth stand out as if it were written on his grandfather's forehead.

"I don't want to have a claim on you," he said in

a clear, calm voice. Even though there was a part of him that wanted to rail at the other man for denying them the opportunity to have a relationship because of the lack of a piece of paper. "But I do want you to know what you've missed." It felt as though she were there, behind him, urging him on with her words and her fierce passion and her love.

"Growing up, I knew that I was different from other children. But I wondered sometimes if that was because my father loved me so much. I felt sorry for other children I met, because their fathers weren't mine. My father is the most honorable and strongest man I know, and I am the man I am today because of him. I never knew my mother, but I knew of her because my father spoke of her, told me how much she loved me."

"You caused her death." Mr. Wolcott spoke through a clenched jaw.

Edward shook his head slowly. "I know that her passing must have caused you great sorrow. But that is no reason to abandon a child of your blood who needed you. You are the one who has lost. I am fortunate that I have a father who cares for me and friends who appreciate who I am, not what I am. I wish you could have been the same, but I know you can't."

Mr. Wolcott didn't reply, just stared at Edward, his expression set and angry. Fine. Edward didn't feel angry toward his grandfather anymore; he knew who he was, and he knew he was loved. By his father, by Bennett, and now by her.

He was legitimately—and he nearly chuckled aloud at the thought—rich with love.

"That is all I wanted to say to you." Edward turned on his heel and walked to the stable, aware of the ring in his pocket and the lightness in his heart.

He was wealthy in all the things that mattered. And now he knew it and valued himself as well.

Chapter 27

Explain yourself.

*O*livia, feeling pleasantly sore, smiled to herself as her maid got her dressed.

As Edward had predicted, nobody had seen her leave his room and return to her own, and she'd been able to lie in bed for a while, recalling everything that had happened the night before.

Making her blush, but mostly making her happy.

He loved her.

But there were a few things she had to do before she achieved her unexpected Happily Ever After.

"That will be all," she said to her maid, who nodded and left the room.

Olivia stood in front of the mirror, noting that she didn't look any different from the day before. She was properly attired for one of the duke's daughters—she was wearing a modest gown that likely cost as much as feeding the society's entire community for a month, and she did not look like a woman who'd boldly gone into a man's room and told him she loved him.

Appearances could be deceiving.

She smiled and left the room, descending the staircase quickly.

"Pardon me," she said to one of the footmen standing in the hallway, "do you know where Lord Carson is?"

The footman nodded, pointing to the room she'd been in with Ida and Pearl yesterday. Apparently everyone congregated there.

"Thank you," she replied, moving to the door and knocking on it, waiting for his call to come in.

"Lady Olivia!" He looked wary, as though she were going to propose again. The poor man.

"Hello, Lord Carson. I was hoping we could speak."

He exhaled sharply, gesturing for her to sit on the sofa in front of the fire.

"What is it?"

He stood to the side of her, his arms folded over his chest. Naturally suspicious she might fling herself at him again.

She looked up at his face and smiled. And waited as his expression eased until he was smiling back at her.

He really was a nice person; he just wasn't the man for her.

"The last time we spoke in private, I said some things that I should not have. I apologize for my assumptions."

The thought hit her that she had assumed just as many things about him as she had about those villagers—that he needed her help, that he wanted her, that he loved her.

There was a moment of silence, and then he spoke. "Well, thank you, Olivia. I am glad I've gotten to know a woman such as yourself, and I admire your persistence."

The last was said with a faint tinge of humor.

"My persistence in asking someone to marry me who most definitely did not wish to marry me?" she asked.

He laughed, and she joined him. It felt good to tell someone she was sorry, to truly admit her headstrong foolhardiness.

"What do you feel about Edward?" he asked.

"I love him," she answered simply. "And he loves me."

"That is just what I'd hoped would happen," he replied in a smug tone. "That is why I asked you to help him find a bride. I knew the two of you would be a perfect match, and I knew that neither one of you would realize it unless you were forced to."

Olivia's mouth opened wide and she stared at him. "You planned all that?"

He grinned, and then he was kneeling on the rug in front of her, taking her hand in his. "I did. Edward has been my friend forever, and he is so prickly and defensive about what he is. I knew that it would take a strong woman to push through his reserves, and you are the strongest woman I know." He squeezed her hand, and she felt the tears come again.

She was not a person who cried, and yet here she was, crying again. But this time with happiness.

"Thank you," she said, only to freeze when the other door was flung open wide, revealing her mother, her father, her sisters, and Mr. Beechcroft.

"Oh wonderful!" the duchess exclaimed as they all poured into the room.

Oh God, Olivia thought, realizing what they all must think right now. Bennett kneeling in front of her, holding her hand, while she cried—it couldn't have looked more like a proposal than if Bennett had been holding a placard with "Will You Marry Me, Olivia?" written on it.

Her father immediately went to Bennett, shaking his hand vigorously, a rare smile on his face.

"I knew that if we just got the two of you together that everything would work out perfectly." The duchess paused, and Olivia opened her mouth to tell the truth of the situation, but then her mother started speaking again. "You'll get married, and we won't have to worry about finding a bride for Lord Carson, and the rest of the girls will find equally good matches. See, Duke?" she said, whirling to regard her husband. "I told you that we would get one of the girls married to a future viscount."

"But," Olivia began, her eyes darting between her mother and Bennett. Why wasn't he saying anything?

Well, perhaps because Mr. Beechcroft had swept him up into a great bear hug, clapping him on the back and saying, "My boy!" several times.

It was up to her. It was always up to her.

"Mother."

She spoke loudly, but not loudly enough to drown out her mother, who was currently wondering if St. Paul's could build a wing for the additional guests.

"Mother!" she said again, this time going up to place her hand on her mother's arm.

"What is it, dear?" the duchess said.

Olivia glanced around the room, too small for all of its inhabitants. "Can we go somewhere where we can sit down?"

"Everyone is in the sitting room," the butler told Edward as he returned to the house.

He burned with the urge to go find her, carry her off on his shoulders as he'd threatened, but since they were all there he probably couldn't.

Not that he wasn't tempted.

He strode into the room, his gaze finding her. She sat at the center of the group, her eyes meeting his and smiling.

His goddess. His warrior. His love.

"I wanted us all to be here before things got carried away," she began. "I want to clear up the confusion that might have resulted from before. I am not betrothed to Lord Carson," she said, and Edward looked at Bennett, who grinned back.

What had happened while he was away?

"Instead," she continued, holding her hand out to silence the duchess, "it appears that I have fallen in love with Mr. Wolcott, and I have asked him to marry me."

"You have—?" the duchess sputtered.

"I have."

Edward advanced toward her as he drew the ring out from his pocket. Her eyes widened as she saw the box in his hand, and then her face lit up.

"It is true that Lady Olivia has done me the great honor of proposing," he said. "And I have accepted. I would also, in the spirit of true equality, want to propose to her as well." He lowered

Megan Frampton

one knee onto the carpet in front of her, holding the box in his hand. "Lady Olivia—Olivia, my love—will you marry me?"

He flipped the box open and showed her the ring, watching as her eyes widened and her cheeks flushed.

Not quite as welcome a sight as seeing her in his bed, but this was far more respectable.

"Yes," she replied, her eyes getting bright. "I will marry you."

He stood and took the ring out, placing it on her left hand before looking over at his father, who was beaming. "I found a proper Society lady to marry me, Father," he said.

"But Lord Carson is to marry my daughter!" the duke said. Edward turned to look, seeing the duke's face had gotten flushed, his mouth set into an unhappy line. "I will not have her marry a—" And then he stopped. Edward watched as the duke resolved to say it.

"A bastard!"

Olivia pushed past Edward to stand in front of her parents, and he could see the self-righteous anger in the set of her shoulders.

He loved how she was finally going to be able to stand up for herself as she'd stood up for so many others in need.

"It doesn't matter if Mr. Wolcott was not fortunate enough to be born with the benefits of our

Society," she began. "What does matter is that I am in love with him. He is in love with me. He understands who I am, and what I want to do, more than anybody. He supports me, he fights with me, and he respects me."

She turned to look at him, and he was reminded of that first time they'd met at the ball. She'd practically reverberated with emotion, but it was nothing compared to what she looked like now. Or at least how he saw her now. She sparkled, she blazed, she glittered with all of who she was and who they were together.

"But you will not go against my wishes!" the duke said.

Olivia straightened even further. "I will. I am not yours to be married off to someone who doesn't love me. Who I don't love. Apologies, Lord Carson."

"No apology necessary," Bennett replied in an amused voice.

"I am not Della, running away from an impossible situation. I hope one day we can get her back," she said, her tone somber. "I am running toward something instead. Toward someone. Mr. Wolcott, who is the best man I have ever known and who says he wants me as well."

The duke looked at Olivia for a long moment, and Edward's chest tightened. He knew Olivia wouldn't change her mind, but he also didn't want her to lose contact with her sisters, if the duke stood firm.

"Fine," the duke said in a snarl. "If this is what you want."

"It is," she said, raising her chin.

"YOU WERE TREMENDOUS."

It was later that evening, and Olivia had once again snuck over to his bedroom. This time he'd been waiting for her, and he'd folded her in his arms and made short work of her clothing before losing himself in her softness, her skin, her cries of joy.

Now they lay in his bed, Scamp settled at the bottom, Olivia's head on his chest, her fingers in his hair.

"I was," she said in a smug tone. "I have a lot of practice speaking out for what is right." She propped herself up on her elbow and smiled down at him. "I know how to speak up, but I didn't know how important it was to listen and ask questions until I met you."

"And what questions do you want to ask?" he asked, sliding his hand on her naked back down to her arse.

She tugged on his hair, lowering her face in preparation to kiss him. "Will you kiss me for the rest of our lives?" And then she did kiss him, and it felt right. Perfect.

He deepened the kiss, and he felt her smile against his mouth, her body shifting so she was lying on top of him.

"I'll answer that if you answer this. When can we get married?" he asked as his hands caressed her skin, feeling the heat of her.

"As soon as you let me out of your bed," she replied, sliding her hand from his hair down his body to find his erect cock.

He closed his eyes as she slid her hands up and down the shaft, raking her nails lightly on him.

"We're going to have to wait a bit longer then," he said, grasping her thighs and positioning her so she was able to slide onto him.

"Oh," she said in a delighted voice. "I had no idea this was possible."

"Everything is possible, my love. Now that we've found one another."

"I love you," she said as she placed her palms flat on his chest and began to move.

"I love you too."

Epilogue

How are you feeling, wife?"

Edward bent down to kiss the back of her neck, and she shivered.

They had returned to the London town house after getting married in the village—the same village where Olivia had felt so humbled—and Mr. Beechcroft had joined them, although he was always alert to making excuses so he could leave them alone.

"I am fine, husband." Olivia patted her stomach, which was just beginning to get round. The child would be born in another six months or so, and Edward was already fussing over her all the time, even though she told him she felt fine, if prone to taking more naps.

Her sister Eleanor had had a child a few months ago, and Olivia was looking forward to their children growing up with one another.

Everything was settled, and wonderful, and she was finding she got remarkable results when she asked people what they wanted, not just telling them what they should want.

In the evenings she and Edward spent as much time as possible in bed—much to Scamp's delight—while arguing about names for the child.

"I love you," she said suddenly. She never got tired of telling him, and she never got tired of hearing it back from him.

"I love you too," he said, drawing her up into his arms and kissing her until her knees wobbled and she forgot about everything but him.

Keep reading for the first chapter of

LADY BE BAD,

the first in Megan Frampton's dazzling
The Duke's Daughters series.

And don't miss the next book,

**THE DUKE'S DAUGHTERS:
THE LADY IS DARING**

Coming October 2018

Chapter 1

$\mathcal{N}$ot there, my lady," the bookseller said, unhelpfully. Because obviously what Eleanor was looking for wasn't there since she didn't have it in her immaculately gloved hand.

She turned to regard him, raising her nose and her eyebrow simultaneously. It was a talent she'd learned from her father, the Duke of Marymount, who had taught her little else. Not that she needed to know much from a gentleman such as her father. All that was required of the duke's eldest daughter was to behave properly, marry well, and then give birth to more little children whose only talents might also be in the raising of facial attributes. *They take after their mother*, her husband might say, fondly.

At the moment, her imagined husband looked like Lord Carson, eldest son and heir to the Marquis of Wheatley. At least according to her parents.

It wasn't a future Lady Eleanor Howlett was

necessarily looking forward to, but then again, it was what was expected of her. What was, since the unfortunate elopement of her younger sister Della (with the dancing instructor hired to teach the Howlett girls), *required* of her so her remaining three sisters could escape the scandalous stigma Della had brought on the family.

She just wished she had more time before having to go ahead with repairing the family's reputation on the basis of two words—*I will*—spoken to a gentleman she hadn't chosen for herself. Just time to do some things that were not entirely expected. She'd even begun making a list—though the things she wished to do were hardly shocking, it was unlikely she would be able to do any of them. A sad statement on her life, if she were being honest with herself.

But none of these thoughts had anything to do with the book she did want. As opposed to the husband she did not.

"Where is it, then?" she asked. Her maid, Cotswold, glanced in her direction, clearly keen to raise a ruckus should the bookseller not oblige her mistress. Cotswold didn't share her interest in ancient mythology, but Cotswold was always determined that her lady get whatever it was she wanted.

Unfortunately her maid did not have a say in

what husband she got. Or the things she would never get to do.

The man pointed past her shoulder. "Over in that second room. It's where I keep the rarer books, you see."

"No, I do not see," Eleanor murmured, making her way through the narrow aisles toward where the man had pointed. She did not see because her mother would not allow her to wear her spectacles in public, and this bookshop—even though it was not a place anyone of her acquaintance would patronize—was a public place.

"My lady?" Cotswold said in a clearly questioning tone.

"Just stay there. I will be out in a moment," Eleanor replied in a terse tone. A young lady was never allowed to be alone except when sleeping, and Eleanor seldom got to truly relish those times. Being asleep and all. It was on her list, in fact.

But now, for just a few moments, she was alone. Granted, she was in a dusty bookshop heading toward what was likely an even-dustier room, but she was almost technically alone.

Until she wasn't.

The room she was heading for was even darker than the rest of the shop, and her gaze was transfixed by the shelves crammed with books, the titles just blurry enough for her not to be able to make out.

She reached into her reticule and withdrew her spectacles when she felt something smash into her side, making her fall against one of the bookshelves, which began to teeter alarmingly.

She yelped and thrust her hand out, the one holding the spectacles, and then began to fall, feeling as though her movements were arrested in time, each moment—*I can't right myself, I'm halfway down, I hope the floor isn't too hard, I hope my spectacles don't crack*—seeming as though it lasted an eternity until she came to rest. Not on a hard floor as she'd anticipated, but on a human body, one with an arm that had reached around her waist to do . . . something. Steady her fall? Make her crash harder? She had no idea.

"What—what?" she sputtered, trying to wriggle off the person, torn between wanting to yell for making her fall or be grateful for making sure she hadn't fallen on the hard ground. Though the body she was on was certainly firm enough.

"Get off me, woman," a voice growled. A man's voice. Definitely a man. A rude man, for that matter. No "Are you all right? Here, let me help you rise." Just a curt command spoken in a low male voice.

Why did it have to be a man? Eleanor thought to herself.

She did manage to get onto her hands and knees, her face low to the ground, low enough that, even without her spectacles, which she was still clutching in her hand, she could see the picture engraved on the book that the man had presumably dropped when he'd also felled her.

And then she forgot about everything, about falling, about the man, about the book she had come in the room for in the first place—everything but the picture she was close enough to see, practically brushing her nose against the paper. It was of a man and a woman doing something that Eleanor knew about only vaguely, but was now emblazoned forever in her memory.

"See something of interest?" the man said, his tone much less abrupt than before. Eleanor was vaguely aware of him moving beside her, a long, elegant finger pointing to one of the places where the man and the woman were joined. "I have to admire the man's strength, to hold his lady up like that," he continued, his finger sliding down the page in excruciating slowness.

Eleanor swallowed. She didn't dare look over at him, for fear he would see everything she was feeling reflected on her face. She wasn't certain she could identify everything she was feeling herself, but she knew that young, unmarried ladies did not usually feel this way. Especially not the eldest daughter of the Duke of Marymount, who was only supposed to be making a respectable, non-eyebrow-raising match. She couldn't imagine an eyebrow would remain static if anyone were to see her. Him. *Them*.

"It's Hercules," she said, pointing underneath the picture to where the words were written. There were other words too, in Italian, but she couldn't concentrate enough to read them. "Hercules and Dejanire. He's Hercules—of course he can hold her up." Hold her up while also connecting with her in a very carnal way, Eleanor couldn't help but notice. And wonder what those other words might possibly say, given what was happening above.

"Dejanire," he said slowly, stumbling over the name. "I know who Hercules is, but I don't know who she is." A pause, then a chuckle. "Then again, it looks as though he does, and that's all that is important."

Eleanor cleared her throat. "She is Hercules's wife, only she accidentally kills him even though she was only trying to help."

"This was them in happier times, then," he said in a wry tone of voice.

She dared to glance over at him. Curious to see this man upon whom she'd fallen and was now, inexplicably, exchanging comments over a particularly salacious picture. And then immediately regretted that decision. He was close, so close she could see him clearly, and what she saw was just—

well, *overwhelming* would be one word. Another word would be *gorgeous*. Overwhelmingly gorgeous would be how she could best sum him up.

He sprawled on the floor beside her, leaning casually on one elbow, a lock of long, tawny-gold hair falling forward onto the clean, strong lines of his face. He traced the lines of the engraving with his other hand. *I should get up*, Eleanor thought, not moving.

"You know a lot about these two. Though probably not as much about what they're doing, judging by the color of your face," he said matter-of-factly.

She felt herself blush even harder at his words. At the knowing expression on his face. At the knowledge he'd just pronounced she did not have. But that he, presumably, did. How did he do that? Look so casually at home, so assuredly confident even when sprawled out on the floor of a dusty bookshop?

"How did she kill him?" he continued. He didn't make a move to get up, and neither did she. She knew she should, likely Cotswold was about to burst in and start exclaiming, but she found she couldn't move. Like moments before when she'd fallen, it felt as though this movement was encased in honey, a sweet, languorous feeling imbuing her whole self. Her whole self that could not move.

"It's complicated," she said, giving in to this moment, whatever this moment was. She tilted her head back and looked at him straight on. Yes, definitely overwhelmingly gorgeous. It was too dark to discern what color his eyes were, but she'd have to imagine they were some sort of beguiling color. If colors beguiled.

She could say with certainty that they did. If they belonged to him.

"I believe Hercules was supposed to marry someone who was in love with someone else, and his wife tried to win him back, only he wasn't in love with her, so she decided to make the best of it and gave the new wife something to ensure constancy, only it had poison on it and he died." And that was why she was not trusted with explaining anything. She just made it sound like a muddle.

He shrugged. "Remind me never to get married."

Married. What was she still doing on the floor?

She did scramble up then, grasping his shoulder without realizing she had to help her upright. He made a noise of protest, but then leaned back, long, long legs—how tall was he, anyway?—stretched out on the floor in front of him.

"I must go," she said in a hurried voice, pushing her hair away from her face, tucking her spectacles back in her bag, then rubbing her hands together to rid her palms of the dust. Or perhaps wipe off how it felt to touch the paper, put her finger on that picture, that scene that was so— well, so whatever it was, just that it wasn't proper for her to have seen, nor was he proper for her to have seen, what with her feeling breathless and tight in her clothing and awkward and melting and hot all at the same time.

Because of him. Or the fall, more likely, she assured herself. Even though he had braced the impact with his body so she'd felt not much more than a sharp bounce. It had to be the fall. It couldn't be him and that picture and the way he'd asked if she'd seen anything of interest, as though she were selecting a piece of cake or something.

It couldn't. Even though it absolutely was.

"But we were just getting acquainted," he said, his tone faintly amused.

"Yours is not an acquaintance I wish to pursue," Eleanor replied. She felt uncomfortable with how cold she sounded. At least until he laughed. Then she just felt embarrassed.

"Unfortunate. It seems we share a passion"— and he paused, letting the impact of the word roll through her—"for Greek mythology."

That couldn't be why he was looking at that picture. Nor could she accuse him of being interested for any other reason, because she had already done what no young lady in her position—whether literally on the floor or as a duke's daughter—would do, given that she hadn't immediately raised herself up and given him a haughty set-down.

Instead she'd stayed because she was intrigued.

By him, by the picture, by being alone in a dark room with a man who was overwhelmingly gorgeous.

And she definitely hadn't even thought to put *that* on the list.

She was Lady Eleanor Howlett, she wasn't supposed to be intrigued by anything. She was supposed to be proper, correct, respectable, and every other word that meant she was supposed to do precisely what she was supposed to and rescue her family's reputation at the same time.

Not be intrigued by anything. Or anyone.

LORD ALEXANDER RAYBOURN stayed on the floor for a few moments after the lady had left, his gaze idling on the spot where she'd been. Feeling the impact of her body on his as they fell, hearing the curiosity in her voice, even though he doubted she'd recognize it herself. But she'd been interested, despite what she'd presumably been told her entire life. He could recognize she was a lady, not just because of her appearance, which was exceedingly ladylike, but also because she spoke in the cultured tones of only the best females in society. He wished it weren't his society, but it was.

He'd come to frequent Avery and Sons Booksellers because he'd discovered the shop sold items of a less respectable nature than most booksellers. The collection in the back room had books from a variety of traditions, from texts created by frustrated monks in ancient times to more recent books detailing just what types of positions people could get themselves into in pursuit of the height of ecstasy. He and the owner of the shop (not named Avery, oddly enough, but Woodson) had come to an agreement where Mr. Woodson would set aside any books that might hold particular interest to Alex.

Alex glanced down at the picture that had made the lady's breath quicken and her words emerge equally breathlessly. It really was quite impressive how Hercules was holding his lady—his wife, she'd said—up pinioned on his cock, his arms her only support.

His mind immediately went, of course, to what it would look like if he were to try such a thing. With the lady who'd just been here. Unlike Hercules's wife, the lady was wearing a voluminous amount of clothing, so the fabric would drape over the inappropriate parts. If anyone were to chance across them, it might appear that they were just standing together. Awfully close, to be sure, but just standing.

Of course when they started moving—or rather,

when *he* started moving, thrusting into her—well, then everybody would be able to tell.

She had landed forcefully on him, but most of her parts were soft. Warm. And very womanly.

It was unfortunate she was a lady; if she had been a woman not of his class, perhaps he could have pursued the conversation into even more intriguing depths. Inquired as to her desire to attempt Hercules's pose.

He shook his head regretfully, knowing he was already late to meet his brother and the rest of his far-too-respectable family. The family that barely tolerated him, but had to because if they didn't, the scandal would be far worse than anything he had done. And he had done some scandalous things.

Some of which were pictured in this book.

He closed the book with a smile. He'd buy it to join the rest of his collection, a hidden part of him and his interests that made him chuckle whenever he thought of it—the Raybourn family unknowingly having a collection of erotic literature at their town house. His tiny rebellion against all that he was and was supposed to be.

He strode out to the main area of the bookshop, noting that the lady had already made her escape. No doubt too horrified by what she'd seen to linger where she might encounter him again.

"Wrap this up, please, and send it to my address." He reached into his pocket and withdrew some coins, more than enough to pay for the book. He tossed them onto the counter, and they were swiftly picked up by Mr. Woodson. "No need to write up a bill of sale, and please ensure the book is properly covered up. I don't want to shock anyone with its contents," he said with a wink, which Mr. Woodson returned.

At least, not shock anyone more than he just had. What the lady had seen was just one of the pictures in the book, but it would doubtless be more than enough to keep her awake at night, either in prurient interest or shock. Or both, Alex didn't doubt.

"This is quite rare, my lord," Mr. Woodson said in a low voice, touching the book's cover. "I have had many gentlemen inquire about a possible translation for it. I don't suppose you?"—and he glanced up at Alex, a questioning look in his eyes.

"I can't speak Italian," Alex said.

Mr. Woodson began wrapping the book. "That is unfortunate. I am not in the position myself, you understand, of locating a suitable translator. It would be altogether too precarious a position for me to be in." He looked up again with a hopeful glance. "I don't suppose you know anybody who speaks Italian?"

Alex shook his head. "Not anybody who could

translate this for me with any kind of discretion." His brother Bennett didn't speak the language, and Bennett was the only person with whom Alex felt close enough to ask such a thing.

Although he would have enjoyed the conversation, his brother being the height of discretion while Alex was—was not.

"Well, thank you, my lord," Mr. Woodson said, placing the book underneath the counter. "And I will send word 'round if I come across anything else. As you will, I assume?"

He and Mr. Woodson had a mutual agreement to let one another know about certain books that might have crossed their paths. Alex kept very few of them for his own collection, while Mr. Woodson relied on the sales of the books to keep the rest of his shop afloat.

It was Alex's own peculiar brand of philanthropy, albeit of an obscene nature.

And he'd found he enjoyed having that purpose, odd and clandestine though it might be. Mr. Woodson was inordinately grateful, as well, which made Alexander feel . . . useful.

Alex left the shop and leapt into his brother's curricle, feeling immediately stifled at the constraints. Of his position, of the curricle itself, of why he was here, and being tolerated by the rest of his family. Wishing he could just escape his responsibilities, but knowing he couldn't leave Bennett on his own.

"YOU LOOK UNEXCEPTIONABLE," Cotswold said, adjusting one of the ringlets that hung around Eleanor's face.

I am sure I do, Eleanor thought. And that was the problem. She stared back at herself in the mirror. She was not overwhelmingly gorgeous. Not even whelmingly gorgeous. She was of average looks, heightened only because she was the eldest of the Duke of Marymount's five daughters.

Four that were spoken of.

"I know that look," her maid said. "It's the look that means that you are grumbling about something in your head. You might as well share it. You know you can't say anything in public, not without possibly causing a scandal."

"If only I could cause a scandal," Eleanor retorted. "Nobody expects me to do anything but what I am supposed to." Even her list was remarkably staid.

Cotswold shrugged as she tugged on one of Eleanor's sleeves. "I think you might want to consider causing a scandal. If only to get people's minds off your sister."

"You mean swap one scandalous daughter for another?" Eleanor chuckled. "Can you imagine

Mother's face if I did something like that? And what would I do anyway?" She grinned at Cotswold. "What if I decided to write lurid poetry and somehow people figured out it was me? Or if I stepped out onto the terrace with a handsome gentleman and kissed him?" She should definitely put some of those on her list. She smiled more broadly at the thought.

"Maybe you could run off with someone even more scandalous than a dancing instructor," Cotswold said, her eyes twinkling. "Like your father's second groom, the one with the"—and then she gestured to the sides of her head to indicate the man's very large ears, giving him the distinctive nickname of "Pitcher."

"Do you think Shakespeare's *Julius Caesar* is his favorite play?" Cotswold shook her head to indicate she didn't understand. "'Friends, Romans, countrymen, lend me your ears.'" She emphasized the last part with a waggle of her eyebrows. Her father would not approve of this use of eyebrow movement, certainly.

Cotswold groaned at the joke.

"Do you suppose I could *have a word in someone's ear* about this whole scandal thing?" Eleanor said with a wink.

Cotswold snorted and shook her head. "I can't keep up with you, my lady." She gestured at Eleanor. "You're done for now."

Eleanor rose, her mood growing somber again. "Curse Della," she muttered. Cotswold didn't reply; there was nothing more to say on the subject. If her sister hadn't been so foolish as to run off with someone so unsuitable, she wouldn't have had to be shoring up the family's reputation on her own seemingly average shoulders.

And even before Della had run off, the girls had all known they would have to be settled in marriage, since they were all only girls. When their father died, the title and all the holdings would go to their cousin Reginald, who was pleasant enough, but already had a wife and a brood of children. The only thing the Howlett ladies had in their favor were their substantial dowries.

It had been a distant prospect, back when they were all together. They'd each talked about finding a gentleman to marry, one who was kind, and handsome, and cared for them.

Not that Lord Carson was not a pleasant enough gentleman; he was very courteous, and had a respectable fortune, and was of moderate good looks.

It was only—well, he was *average*, like she. And she wasn't being given a choice, not now when Della had made their reputations so precarious.

They would marry, and likely they would not argue. But neither would they spark together in passion, all outsized emotions, and she'd never feel what it would be like to practically vibrate with feelings, and wants, and pleasure.

For a moment, her mind drifted back to the gentleman from the bookshop. He certainly seemed outsized—literally, he'd been quite tall, as far as she could tell from his lounging position on the floor. And he had been passionate enough to find that book with those pictures and be looking at it in a bookshop. He was a gentleman—she'd been able to tell that from his clothing and manner of speaking. But he was an overwhelming gentleman. The kind that unmarried young ladies were not supposed to pay attention to, but did nonetheless. The kind that would ignite all sorts of feelings in a young woman's breast.

The kind that was not even close to average.

If only she could have a few moments of sparking passion and outsizedness and overwhelmingness—then, perhaps, she could enter this average marriage with more than average expectations.